DEAD TO ME

ARCANE SOULS WORLD

GRAVE TALKER SERIES BOOK ONE

ANNIE ANDERSON

DEAD TO ME

ARCANE SOULS WORLD

Grave Talker Book 1

International Bestselling Author
Annie Anderson

Edited by Angela Sanders
Cover Design by Tattered Quill Designs

www.annieande.com

For all my little weirdos. I see you.

Woman of Blood & Bone

Daughter of Souls & Silence

Lady of Madness & Moonlight

Sister of Embers & Echoes

Priestess of Storms & Stone

Queen of Fate & Fire

PHOENIX RISING SERIES

(Formerly the Ashes to Ashes Series)

Flame Kissed

Death Kissed

Fate Kissed

Shade Kissed

Sight Kissed

"I have never yet heard of a murderer who was not afraid of a ghost."

— JOHN PHILPOT CURRAN

My life would be a lot easier if the dead in this town would just cooperate. Maybe it was the living. They never seemed to cooperate, either.

I hefted one eyelid by sheer force of will and spied the time on my alarm clock. That alarm clock was just for show. No one—not even me—used them much anymore. Lately, it was there so I didn't have to look at the time on my phone. Said alarm clock was blinking 12:00 at me.

The power had gone out sometime since I'd fallen into bed. *Figures.* It didn't matter that I lived in a nice neighborhood. Mother Nature was a testy woman on the best of days, but in the spring in this part of the country? She was downright spiteful.

The knock—well, more like pounding—on my front door rattled through my house again, which was what had woken me up from a very deep, much-needed sleep in the first damn place. I knew that insistent cop-knock. J was pounding on my door like the badge-wielding tool he was. Granted, I, too, had a badge, but I wasn't the jerk accosting *his* door at oh-butt-thirty in the morning.

Groaning, I peeled myself from my oh-so-soft mattress and stomped to my door, yanking it open before J could splinter the wood.

"What?" Yeah, it came out more like a bark, but it wasn't even dawn, and I was in no mood.

Instead of saying anything at all, J waved a to-go cup of coffee in my face as a peace offering. I fell on the caffeine-laden cup like a junkie, sucking down the brew like my life—or more accurately, J's life—depended on it.

Only after the cup was half-drained did I let him pass the threshold into my living room. Shuffling past me, he plopped onto my overstuffed sofa like he owned it. He didn't, but Jeremiah Cooper, AKA, J, was my best friend —hell, my only friend—and he'd spent many a morning, evening, and afternoon on that couch.

J wasn't the only person sitting there, but he paid exactly zero attention to the slightly see-through dead man perched right next to him, lounging on the cushions like the Queen of Sheba. J—and everyone else in my life—couldn't see him.

No one could.

No one but me.

Dead guy was Hildenbrand O'Shea, and he'd died sometime in the 1840s. Hildy couldn't tell me the exact year he'd passed, and records were scant, so it was anyone's guess when he'd actually kicked the bucket. Hildy was adamant about the decade at least, even if the story of his demise changed every time he told it.

Hildy had a lot of fun messing with the living. At present, he was making grotesquely funny faces about two inches from J's nose which was at odds with his posh knee-length jacket, waistcoat, and slacks—the markings of high society in the decade he'd passed. I wasn't positive on the coloring of his clothes because Hildy wasn't exactly solid, but I could tell he had light hair and eyes, wore a cravat with a paisley pattern, and sometimes held a walking stick and a top hat, even though he didn't have either right now. He appeared to be in his late thirties, with a sharp knife blade of a nose and square jaw.

Typically, I'd be trying not to laugh, but half a cup of coffee was a losing battle against my tired body. I was in no mood. I was all in favor of crawling right back into my bed and waking up at the super-reasonable hour of seven.

Maybe even eight.

I'd spent the last three weeks solving a trio of homicides and was just about done with the people in this town killing each other for a good long while. Those three weeks should have been one, but like I'd said, the dead never wanted to cooperate.

"We've got a case, D. You're going to have to get dressed."

My gaze reluctantly moved from Hildy to J. J was dressed in a suit like every other time we'd been called in at the ass crack of dawn. He, too, was sipping coffee, but he didn't look happy about it. No. J's gray face said that coffee would be coming back up sometime in the near future.

Dammit. If people could stop killing each other for about three days, that would be gravy.

Heaving a sigh, I shuffled back to my bedroom and called over my shoulder for him to make me some more coffee. It was a fifty-fifty shot whether or not he'd do it. J could be a contrary bitch sometimes.

It didn't take me too long to handle my business, brush my teeth, and put on my suit pants and tank. The only real trouble was what to do with my hair. Thick, wavy, and a middle-of-the-road blonde, it defied the laws of physics, gravity, and nature. Doing the best I could, I shoved it into a haphazard bun and called it good.

I didn't bother with makeup, even though I probably needed it. I knew without looking in the mirror that I had bags under my eyes big enough to drive a truck through. But I also knew without a doubt at some point in the day I was going to start crying, almost vomit, actually vomit, or all of the above.

Makeup was a waste of time.

By rote, I strapped on my vest, slid my service weapon into the Kydex spine holster, and slipped a blessed rosary around my neck. My rosary wasn't there for religious purposes—at least not on my part. I wasn't particularly religious, to be honest.

Did I think there was an afterlife? Yes.

Did I subscribe to any one way to get there? Not so much, no.

But the prayer beads had been blessed by a priest and had stopped particularly nasty specters from causing bodily harm on more than one occasion. Pissed-off ghosts were not my favorite, and poltergeists were the freaking worst.

Tucking the rosary under my vest, I shrugged on my blouse and jacket, stuffed my feet into low-heeled leather boots, and hit the road. And by road, I meant my living room, following the smell of freshly brewed coffee.

J was the *bestest* friend a girl could have. If I were even a little interested—or if his preference swung anywhere near my gender—we'd have been the perfect couple. Sadly, neither of those things were ever going to happen, much to his mother's dismay.

I slugged down a healthy gulp of steaming coffee and sighed with blissful glee as the caffeine hit my system. Only then did I really focus on J. He was pale-faced and pinched. Neither of those were his norm. Jeremiah Cooper was a golden boy if Haunted Peak, Tennessee ever had one. Dark-haired and tan-skinned, with the palest of blue eyes, J was a football star and straight-A student in high school. Graduated with honors right next to me at the University of Tennessee and was a well-respected member of the community—even if he was BFFs with the town weirdo.

J hadn't been pale-faced and pinched a day in his life.

"I've consumed enough caffeine to not rip your head off. Spill it." My delivery could have used a little work, but I'd checked the time on my phone. It was barely after three in the morning on a Tuesday. I had a good reason to be cranky—especially since I'd done the lion's share of the legwork on our last case.

"We know her, Darby. And..." He didn't finish his sentence, but Hildy did.

"It's another weird one," Hildy chirped from J's shoulder, busy poking his spectral finger into J's ear.

This was Hildy's way of trying to cheer me up, and like every other time he'd done it, it not only did *not* work, it creeped me out. If I'd told him once, I'd told him a thousand times: Don't mess with the living, and they won't mess with the dead. Like always, Hildy didn't listen to my warnings. And as was the norm, Hildy kept right on talking.

"Ya went to school with her, lass. Brenda, Barbara, Blanca, somebody. Cut up like a Thanksgiving turkey, too." The burr of Hildy's Irish accent raked against my nerves. Hildy was up on all the gossip, and he knew when just about anyone died in this town. Even though he was an excellent source to have in my hip pocket, no one wanted guessing games at the ass crack of dawn—especially with his flair for the dramatic.

"Blair?" I blurted, too tired and too irritated to bite my tongue. *Shit.*

Rule number one was never converse with the dead in front of living people. That said, I broke rule one so often, it was a miracle I was still a cop—even with a damn near perfect close rate.

As expected, J's eyes went round, his face paling like I'd tapped his jugular and cranked it wide. I'd guessed right.

"I swear to god, it freaks me the fuck out when you do that."

Playing it cool, I asked, "Do what? Extrapolate data based on your mood and make a hypothesis? It's literally my job."

J smacked his mug down on the counter so hard I was surprised it didn't break, crossing his arms as he sized me up. "You know damn well that's not what you were doing. You were talking to a ghost just now, weren't you?"

He was way too with it this early in the morning.

J was the only person in my life that knew I saw the dead long after they'd gone off to their final rest. He wasn't cool with it by any stretch of the imagination, but he still hadn't carted me off to a psychiatric hospital to have me committed, so at least there was that. Granted, it had taken me talking to his deceased grandma Marcy to get the goods on him, but it was nice not to worry that my best friend thought I was crazy.

Well, J thought I was crazy, he just didn't think I needed medication.

"It's too early to hide it, man. Cut me some slack. Do you know how hard it is to try and keep a straight face every minute of every day while the dead just chatter on like I'm in their freaking knitting circle?" I stopped my rant to slug back more nectar of the gods, drained the cup dry, and smacked it back down onto the counter. "It's fucking exhausting, and I'm tapped out. So quit being a bitch about it."

J's face got that irritated, squinty quality I hated before it fell away. I got the "big sigh" that said he would forgive my weirdness, and he pulled me into a huge bear hug. "I'm sorry I was a dick, D. But do me a favor, don't talk to any ghosts while we're out there."

His warning gave me a niggle of unease. He knew I never planned to, but that didn't stop me from slipping up on occasion.

"You got a reason?" Did I accidentally use my cop voice on my BFF? Maybe. But even though J was my partner and had heard that tone about a zillion times in the last fifteen years, he still answered me like a perp.

He sighed, pouted at his empty mug, and answered, "We aren't the only ones investigating this one. Word is there's a Fed there."

A Fed was stomping all over my crime scene? I cursed loud enough and inventive enough that both J and Hildy were threatening to wash my mouth out with soap. I ignored them both, snagging my badge and clipping it to my belt before I tossed my messenger bag over my shoulder and tagged my keys.

"What the hell are you doing just standing there?" I

growled, my hand already on the doorknob, my key in the lock.

It took three ages and half a millennium for J to get his ass in gear, but when I made for my Jeep, J snagged my sleeve and redirected me.

"We don't need to drive," he muttered, nodding toward the end of our block that was just past the apex of a hill.

Only then did I see the faint flash of lights from a black-and-white at the end of my street.

It was not a good feeling to have a homicide less than a block from my house. The last thing I needed in my general vicinity was more ghosts.

And only J would think we didn't need to drive the half-mile up the steep incline. Haunted Peak was at the base of a mountain, and J and I lived in a newer development in one of the foothills. As fit as I was, I still wasn't hiking up that hill if I didn't have to.

"You want to be sweaty and slow, be my guest. I'm driving."

I needed to get there before whatever idiot the FBI sent tramped all over my crime scene or scared off my source. And by source, I meant the deceased. It was always tough when they were new. Their deaths were so fresh, they were still reeling from the transition. Hell, most of them didn't even know they were dead.

I didn't blame them for being out of sorts. If I'd been killed in a super-weird way, I'd probably be a little messed up, too. But explaining that no one could see them but me, *and* they were dead? Ugh. Not my favorite way to spend a morning.

Plus, if J and I were being called in, the case was not just weird. It was *weird*.

Those were the only cases we got nowadays. Add in Hildy's description of being carved up and well... I already knew I was about to have a rough one.

Climbing into my Jeep, I waited the three-point-five seconds for J to get his ass in gear before cranking the engine. He slid into the seat beside me just as I threw it in reverse, barely managing to close his door before I peeled out of the driveway. The trip took less than a minute, but that was still far too long for me. Had J told me there was a Fed on my scene before I wasted time getting dressed, we'd have been there already—bad breath, pajamas, and all.

"What do you know? What am I walking into?"

J ran a hand down his face as he let loose the mother of all sighs. "It's bad, D. It makes those fake Satanists we busted last year look like fluffy bunnies and rainbows."

Those "Satanists" we'd busted last October weren't Satanists at all. They were a bunch of fledgling witches with an ax to grind against their coven leader. I'd seen many a witch and warlock in my day that weren't even the least bit homicidal. Those chicks were straight-up lethal and aching to get into the dark stuff. It'd taken a boatload of legwork, a promise to the new coven leader that I wouldn't be dragging the whole coven into it, and a binding spell the size of Texas to get those girls cornered.

Not that J knew that.

He'd lost his mind when he'd learned my secret. I couldn't blow up his narrow world view any more than I already had. What was I gonna say? *I know you don't like to think about the ghosts that are crawling all over the planet, but you might want to start worrying about the shit that's actually alive. AKA, the shit that can kill you.*

Yeah, I didn't see that going too well. It would make his fool brain explode, and then I'd be out a best friend.

"Super," I muttered, wishing I had about a pot and a half of coffee under my belt and roughly four days of sleep.

I threw the Jeep into park behind a black-and-white and got out. The whole damn park was taped off, which was not a good sign. The ME's van wasn't here yet, which, at least for me, was a good thing. Sure, it meant that I wouldn't have an approximate time of death, but I also wouldn't have to deal with the way-too-perceptive eyes of the county medical examiner.

The park was littered with the fallen blossoms of the dogwoods—the pretty white petals mounding like snow-drifts against the playground equipment and the bases of trees. The rains last night must have been rough if there was this much on the ground. Add in the blinking clock this morning, and we'd be lucky if there was any phys-ical evidence left.

There were a good bit of people milling around a second taped-off area—both living and dead—the majority of them on the outside of it clustered around the floodlights that illuminated the scene. My lips curled up into a smile all on their own. I'd finally trained my colleagues not to step into one of my crime scenes. My retribution was swift and painful. I was the reigning queen of pranking, and I wasn't going to lose that title anytime soon after the sardines in the desk drawer prank I'd played on Sal Whitestone last year. That taught him and all his buddies not to stomp all over one of my scenes.

The ghosts, however, I couldn't do much about.

Sal and his partner Tommy gave us both a grave sort of nod as we approached the taped-off area, moving out of my way as I strode closer. The body that lay beyond wasn't covered, even though modesty and respect dictated otherwise. Still, they had their backs to the woman since it was the best they could do.

I'd had a small niggle of hope left when I'd answered Hildy's ramblings, but looking at the scene, I knew without a doubt I'd guessed right.

Blair Callier was dead, and it was a weird one, all right. But it wasn't Callier anymore. Her last name was Simpkins now—or at least had been before Blair was brutally murdered in a public park sometime during the previous twelve hours.

Careful of my steps, I ducked under the tape, making sure I didn't walk on any evidence. There didn't seem to be much to be had. No blood drips away from the scene, no muddy footprints, nada.

"Jimmy took pictures, right?" I called behind me. Sal would know.

I could practically hear Sal hitching up his pants over his potbelly and smoothing a hand over his bald head before he answered. "Sure did, Darby. Didn't get too close but used his tele-whatsis lens to get what he needed. He'll get the rest when you're done."

Jimmy would rather smash one of his super-expensive lenses than walk onto one of my scenes. He knew better.

I pointedly ignored the silent man at the northernmost point of the taped-off square. The living one, anyway. He stood to the side, not facing me, but not with his back turned, either. At his back, peering over his shoulder, was a specter I'd seen plenty of times around town. I couldn't tell which era the ghostly man came from—the dark slacks and jacket nondescript enough to be any decade from here to the turn of the twentieth century. In all the times I'd seen him, he hadn't so much as said a peep to me but did spare me a glance, though, tilting his chin up at me in acknowledgment before turning back to see what the Fed was typing out on his phone.

I also ignored the pissed-off female ghost hovering close to her now-defunct body. Her hip cocked, her foot out just so. It was a sore reminder of how she'd stood in life—like she was owed attention, and she was real put out she wasn't getting it. It was as if she knew she was dead, knew I could see her, and was solidly displeased I wasn't fawning all over her because she was now a member of the dearly departed.

It figured that my old high school nemesis would be the first with-it freshly transitioned ghost I'd ever come across. Typically, when I encountered a fresh one, I had to pretend I couldn't see them so they would leave me alone. Not Blair. Oh, no. She just wordlessly stood there and stared at me, her ghostly eyes boring a hole in my face.

Her incorporeal form held little resemblance to the corpse on the ground. Luckily, her spectral self lacked the method of her death—not always the case with the fresh or violently departed ones. If she wasn't see-through, I wouldn't be able to tell that the expensive sundress and heels weren't the faint memory of what she believed she should look like—her hair in carefully constructed waves, makeup on point. I studied her for a moment, noting that while she had earrings in her ears and a necklace around her neck, she lacked the massive rock masquerading as a wedding ring she'd lorded over all us single ladies since the moment she'd gotten engaged.

Interesting.

But Blair's fuming silence wasn't going to last forever, and I had a job to do.

I opened my messenger bag, pulling out booties and slipping them on my feet, one by one. Next came my phone and earbuds—a necessary evil in my line of work. If I wasn't paying attention, I'd start answering questions to people who weren't visible to the masses, and then it would be padded-room city. The buds went in my ears, I queued up some hard rock, and hit play. Once I was positive no other sound could reach my ears over the singer's screaming, I slipped on a pair of nitrile gloves, passed off my bag to J, and got to work.

It was a well-known fact that I had a process—one that used to earn me untold amounts of shit. Well, until I had the highest close rate of any other detective in three years. I was fastidious, methodical, and thorough. It helped that I had insider knowledge that only the recently deceased could provide.

That said, the dead didn't know everything, and often enough, their information was unreliable.

Mentally gridding the space, I scanned my surroundings for obvious clues before I took a few cautious steps to get a better look. Blair's body was laid out on the spongy spring grass like a sacrifice—which with the way her chest had been carved up, she likely had been. They weren't stab wounds, exactly. No, some lunatic had carved sigils into her skin—not ones I was familiar with, either.

I'd have to remember to look them up in my occult texts.

Blair was in a white nightgown I could never have pictured her owning. It was a white granny-style one that laced at the throat—or at least it had been before the fabric was cut wide to display the carvings. Carvings that were likely made by the slender dagger in Blair's cold hand.

I moved closer to inspect her, vigilant of where I stepped. Just because I couldn't see any evidence, didn't mean there wasn't any. The knife was slender—less than two finger-widths wide with a golden filigreed handle that I knew we weren't going to be able to pull a print from. Etched at the top of the tang was an upside-down pentagram. The etching had been done by hand and poorly. The sides of the star were irregular, ill-fitting on such a pretty knife.

The tip of the blade was stained red, but not enough that the work had been done while Blair was still breathing. There was little to no blood staining the gown either, which meant Blair hadn't been killed here. No, her body was arranged just so, the evidence nearby nil. She'd been killed somewhere else and dumped here. Based on the swollen tongue and purple coloring around her mouth, my guess was that she'd been poisoned, but without a tox screen or an autopsy, I wouldn't know for sure.

A breeze fluttered through the trees, ruffling the wisps of my hair that had already escaped my haphazard bun. I caught sight of a little bit of movement at Blair's other hand. I walked even closer, pointedly ignoring ghostly Blair's glare. The movement was a business card flapping in the wind, the white cardstock bearing the familiar seal of the Haunted Peak Police Department.

And underneath that seal was a familiar name: Detective Darby Adler.

Blair Callier, my high school nemesis, had been dumped less than a block away from my house and arranged like a ritual sacrifice with my business card in her hand. And there was her pissed-off ghost not two feet from me and a Fed watching my every move.

This day was just getting better and better.

I had two options—two shitty options, if I was being honest. I could pretend I hadn't seen my business card in the hand of a dead woman and try and steal it out of evidence later, or I could do the right thing.

I had—on occasion—taken things from evidence. But the objects I stole were either a danger to humans, likely to blow up the entire building, or pointed at me busting supernaturals. I wasn't proud of it, but I'd done what I had to. But this wasn't something I could steal. Well, I *could*, but I wouldn't. Still, my "fuck" was audible over the hard rock music as I mentally chose door number two.

Popping out an earbud, I called for J, "Is Jimmy still

here? I need him and an evidence bag. We've got something."

I didn't look at J when I said this, but after a decade and a half of being friends, I could feel his eyes boring a tiny hole into my skull as I retraced my steps to the police tape, keeping my eyes trained on that fluttering bit of cardstock that was about to ruin my whole week.

I knew without seeing when Jimmy walked up. He had a mousey energy to him that made me want to tuck him under one of my arms—even if he wouldn't fit there anymore. I'd defended Jimmy Hanson from more bullies than I could count. From the time we were kids all the way to now, he exuded something that made someone either want to protect him or shove his head in a toilet. Even at the ripe age of twenty-seven, he was still bullied by lesser men and women and it pissed me off to no end. He was a good man, humble and braver than anyone would ever expect. Whip smart and so kind it hurt my heart. Jimmy wasn't that puny kid anymore, and I had a feeling if J would get his head out of his ass, he'd see the six-foot-five-inch Viking dreamboat that gave him smexy eyes at least thirty times a day.

I stared up at Jimmy, craning my head to meet his eyes. I had a feeling he forgot on a regular basis that he was so damn tall. "I need you to take a picture of the card in her hand. Step where I step, cool?"

Jimmy nodded but didn't bother ducking under the tape. No, he could just lift a leg right over the waist-high police line like the giant he was. He handed me an evidence bag, and together we made the short trek to Blair's body. Jimmy fired off about a dozen shots before I felt it was time to take the card out of her hand.

Oh, so gently, I removed the cardstock, careful not to cut into her palm or disturb the paper. Jimmy took about five more shots of the card once it was free of the dead woman's clutches, and I gently put it in the bag, sealing it tight.

"I don't like this. Someone wants your attention, D." Jimmy spoke low, but his voice was so deep it carried like nobody's business.

"I'm aware, and I don't like it either. Pass this off to J, will you?" I handed him the evidence bag.

Jimmy held the bag for all of five seconds before he passed it back. "I'm not dumb enough to deal with that bomb on my own. You're just going to have to deal with J's wrath yourself."

Jimmy was too smart for his own good. "Fine, jerk. Be that way. Tell him to come here, then."

He didn't bother to nod before he got the hell out of there. Smart man.

"You're just going to stand there and pretend you don't see me, aren't you?"

I knew Blair's silence was too good to be true. Instead of meeting her gaze, I looked over her corpse and nodded slightly. I pitched my voice low, barely moving my mouth. "Not being labeled insane is kind of a job requirement. I'll talk to you when there aren't people around."

"Oh, my god. You really can see me. All this time I thought you were crazy, but you're not, are you? I knew it." Blair paced all over the place, and I was lucky her feet couldn't destroy evidence because she was stomping all over her body, her incorporeal heels landing somewhere in the vicinity of her corpse's face. "I knew you were a freak in high school, always talking to yourself, always staring off into space, but it's real. You really can see ghosts."

It wasn't the first time I'd been called a freak by a ghost. One would think that they'd be grateful someone could hear them, but ungratefulness didn't quit when their bodies did. That shit was eternal.

I was almost relieved to hear J coming because it meant I could focus on literally anything but the bitchy specter still ranting about my freakiness. But when I turned to look at him—with his face like thunder and his eyes flashing—I rethought my relief.

"She had your business card in her hand," he hissed,

the accusation pitched low in light of the nosy Fed in our vicinity.

I didn't bother answering and passed him the evidence bag. "Yeah, Jimmy seems to think someone wants my attention, and I have to agree. Log that for me, will you? I need to process the rest of the scene."

"Oh, no, you don't," J growled as he yanked his phone from his pocket, brandishing the tiny bit of technology like a weapon. "I'm not having a repeat of the Dunleavy case. I'm calling your dad."

If we weren't in the middle of a crime scene, I would have lunged for the phone. Alas, I did have a tiny inkling of decorum, and let J retrace his steps back to safety. My dad was going to lose his shit. Since he lost his shit on a regular basis, I should be used to it, but his shit-losing was not typically directed at me.

Fabulous.

I was too busy watching J rat me out that I didn't sense when the Fed decided to mosey on up to the plate until he spoke.

"I was wondering whether or not you'd turn in that evidence," the Fed drawled, his voice a burr of a rumble. He was three strides from me—way too close for my personal comfort—which seemed to be his goal.

He was in a dark-blue suit, the color so deep it could

pass for black in the right light. The suit was the only thing that pegged him as a Fed. The rest of him, not so much. It was like he'd been shoved into that suit rather than choosing it for himself. His hair was rumpled, the black strands swept up and away from his face like he'd been shoving his hands in it. His eyes were a fathomless brown, the color so dark it might as well have been black. Maybe it was the low light, or maybe not. His beard wasn't quite a beard at all. More like the scruff men got while on vacation, too lazy to grow out their facial hair and without the patience for a razor. It would be rough to the touch, I'd bet.

His nose was slightly crooked, like someone had taken a fist to it a time or two. His lips were full under the scruff, and somehow all of those things added up to him being one of the most attractive men I'd ever seen. I couldn't help thinking it was a shame that someone with such a large air of assholery was so pretty.

"Why wouldn't I?" My hands ached to notch themselves on my hips, but I wouldn't give this guy the satisfaction of seeing me defensive. Also, how in the hell had he seen the card? I'd barely seen it when I was right on top of her.

Unless…

"Did you walk the scene before I got here? Did you follow proper protocol? You're not wearing booties now, so I really freaking doubt it. You realize I'm going to have to take your shoes, right?"

The man had the gall to smirk at me like I was a tantrum-throwing toddler, and I fought the urge to sock him right in his smug nose.

"I took all the protocols necessary for this case, Detective Adler. Why don't you finish processing the scene, and then we'll talk about why the victim had your card in her hand. Looks like you've got a secret admirer."

"Yeah, I've gathered as much. I assure you, they won't like it too much when they're sitting in a cell right along with all the other killers I've put behind bars."

I wanted to ask him if I was a suspect, but that was stupid. If he thought I was a suspect, he wouldn't let me process the scene. Instead, I turned my back to him, ignoring him the best I could for a man smack-dab in the middle of my bubble.

Focusing on the scene in front of me, I methodically catalogued the symbols drawn into Blair's chest, before moving on to the knife in her hand, and on and on until I had everything I needed before the ME took over. In the middle of all this, J came back, passing me evidence bags as he helped me collect everything we needed.

I might not have liked Blair—hell, I couldn't stand

her even if she was dead—but no one deserved this. Not even her.

By the time I was done, the sun was up, the birds were chirping, and my coffee had worn off the hour before. Somehow, the medical examiner still wasn't here, so we played the waiting game until she showed up. It wasn't like we could just leave the body there.

The Fed was MIA, so I took this little bit of time to wrangle the pissed-off ghost aching to yammer my ear off about her current situation. Moving away from the scene, I parked my ass on the bumper of a black-and-white and stuffed an earbud in my ear, pretending to make a call. Only then did I look Blair in the eye.

This wasn't my first rodeo. I knew better than to just talk to ghosts out in the open without a solid explanation. I'd learned long ago that holding a full-court conversation with a person no one could see was a horrible plan unless I wanted a padded cell.

"Okay, I'm listening. Tell me what happened to you."

"Oh, so now you're going to talk to me? You ignore me forever while you fiddle with my body—which is beyond yuck, by the way, and *now* when it's convenient for *you*, you want to talk?"

Oh, goodie. She was one of those ghosts. I'd dealt with many in my time. The ones that thought their shit was the only thing going on in my life and wanted me to be at their ghostly beck and call.

"Yes. Just because I can see you doesn't mean I have to drop everything I'm doing—which in case you forgot, is solving your murder—to ask you questions. While I would love to do that because you likely know pertinent info, I have to at least look like a non-crazy person. So again, what happened to you?"

Blair crossed her incorporeal arms and huffed.

"Unless you don't know anything," I taunted. There was more than one way to skin this cat.

She whipped her head back to me. "Oh, I know plenty."

Sure she did. "Then where were you last night?"

Blair's spectral mouth opened to answer right before she snapped her lips shut again, her brow wrinkling in frustration. It was pretty common for the recently departed to forget their last moments. It was also common for them to get defensive about it.

"Okay, if we need to wait on that, where were you yesterday?"

"Oooh! I know that one. I was getting a mani and pedi with Suzette. We went to the new spa place on Concord. The fancy one that has a three-week waiting list." Blair stomped her foot as she struggled to remember the name of the place. "Serenity something. Ugh. Why can't I remember anything?"

I wanted to pity her a little bit. Even if I loathed her in life, it wasn't her fault she got dead and splayed out like a sacrifice in a public park. The transition was hard on people who knew it was coming, so I didn't expect her to be much different.

"It's okay to be missing some pieces, you know. It's common in the newly transitioned. You'll get it back soon enough."

Blair's face screwed up into a sneer. "The newly transitioned? Way to slap some lipstick on that pig. I'm dead, Darby. Not transitioned, not downsized, not previously alive. Dead."

It wasn't the first time I'd heard that rant from a ghost. "True, but eventually you'll go somewhere else, and that's a life all on its own. So, you're moving on somewhere, which is a transition. Which is a much nicer way to put it since the majority of your kind are a teensy step away from batshit crazy, so excuse the fucking euphemism, okay?"

Blair glared at me for about three more seconds before she lost the fight with her anger.

"Fine. Transitioned isn't so bad, I guess." She sighed before she started clapping her hands. "Serene Waters Day Spa. That's where I was. Well, that's the last place I remember being until…" She trailed off, worry passing over her features before the hard shell of a mask was back.

"That's very good. I'll start there. And Suzette? Do you mean Suzette Duvall? The sitting mayor's wife?"

Guessing Blair was hanging out with the mayor's wife wasn't too big of a leap. Blair and Suzette had been wreaking havoc and destroying lives together since they were in middle school. They were the kind of girls who looked so pretty but were nothing but ugly on the inside.

Interrogating Blair's BFF was going to be super fun, too—assuming she didn't lawyer up first. Those types always called their attorney even when they didn't do anything. They wasted my time because they watched *Law and Order* one too many times and thought I gave a shit that they had a mistress or smoked a little weed.

In this day and age? *No, sweet pea. I give a shit if you fucking killed someone.*

Didn't they understand that I only cared about the dead bodies on my docket and the cases in my inbox?

Idiots.

I opened my mouth to ask another question when a familiar blue van pulled up with the words "County Medical Examiner" emblazoned on all sides. A small woman hopped out the front seat, her dark ringlets bouncing as she did. Why the county medical examiner wanted to go out to see the cases instead of sending her assistant, I had no idea, but Tabitha was a peculiar entity all on her own and entirely too perceptive.

"Hey, Darby," she called as she went to the back of the van to get her supplies. "You talk to your father yet?"

I pulled the earbud from my ear as I searched the cloudy sky for answers. Tabitha had been dating my father for four years. They didn't live together, weren't married, and as far as I knew, had no plans for that to change. They didn't go on dates. They didn't kiss in public. Nothing. Honestly, if I hadn't caught them cavorting in the front freaking room of my childhood home, I likely wouldn't know their relationship was anything more than platonic. That had taken a whole bottle of gin to scrub from my brain, and even now I shuddered a little every time I saw her and my father in the same room.

"No." Not that she needed an answer to the question. It wasn't a question at all. It was a thinly veiled directive disguised as an innocent inquiry, which grated on my nerves in the most epic of ways. I couldn't say for sure why I didn't like Tabitha. She was polite enough, she did a stellar job, and she wasn't a complete asshole. But something about her rubbed me the wrong way, and I didn't know if it was because she was diddling my dad or if it was something else.

Either way, I kept my distance as much as I could. Tough, considering our jobs, but it was how it needed to be until I figured out why she irked me. My gut said I couldn't trust her, and I liked my gut far more than I liked her.

"Jeremiah called him a few hours ago, talking about your business card in the deceased's hand. Your father is mighty riled up about it. You might want to give him a ring, dear."

Dear. Ugh.

Yeah, we were in the South and people called each other honey and sugar and sweetheart all the time. It was common vernacular. Still. *Dear*. I struggled against the urge to tell her to kiss my ass.

First off, this whole conversation was unprofessional as fuck. There was no reason why I should call my father about any case until I was ready to submit evidence to the DA. I was a grown woman, a highly venerated detective handling a case, not a twelve-year-old schoolgirl telling my daddy about a bully. Second—and probably the most damning of all—she was acting like a stepmom. I did not need a go-between with my dad. I did not require motherly chiding or her advice on how to deal with him, either.

Overstep, thy name is Tabitha.

Still, I forced myself to be polite when I responded. "I'll call him after I make the notification to the family. I'd like to establish time of death first and get her loaded up. Dad can wait."

Even though I couldn't see her, I knew Tabitha was giving me a stern expression. I could feel it through the van's steel doors. Too bad. In all honesty, I wanted to flip her off, but I knew somehow, some way, she'd know it.

"If you think that's best," she returned, the warning clear. *Your father isn't going to like it.*

Yeah, yeah. Fuck off.

I followed Tabitha to the crime scene and let her work, watching as she took the liver temp and checked the body over.

"Based on liver temp, I'd say she's been dead about twelve-to-eighteen hours, but I won't know for sure until I get her back to the office. Her lividity doesn't support that and the swelling and discoloration to her mouth. Do you see it?"

If she meant the broken blood vessels all around her lips and the purpling, swollen tongue that protruded from her mouth? Yeah, I saw it. I'd have to be blind not to see it.

"I'm throwing this out there, but I'm pretty sure she's been poisoned. But it's odd. Usually it takes days for this kind of swelling to show up. Not hours."

Days? Blair could have died days ago, and she was just turning up now? This was not good.

"What the hell happened to you, Blair?" I murmured, staring at the ghost not the body. Blair's spectral form crouched next to her corpse, sadness and fear etched into her expression.

She didn't know what had happened to her any more than we did.

But I was going to find out.

Notifying someone that their spouse was gone was not my favorite part of the job. The process was two-fold, and both parts sucked. First, I'd have to inform someone that they'd lost a loved one. The second was to watch their reaction. Because even if I didn't have a ghost in my ear telling me that they'd been killed by their spouse, or brother, or great-aunt Mildred, I usually knew based on their face.

Reading people was a skill, and to be a good cop, one needed to hone this particular skill as sharp as they could. Granted, I had a leg up on most other detectives, but still. Since Blair had potentially died two days ago, and precisely zero missing-persons cases had been filed, that was usually a massive red flag. Especially for an unseparated couple who touted the illusion of a happy family. Add in Blair's nonexistent ring—both on her corpse and spectral form—and it smelled fishy.

The Simpkins' house was a big white monstrosity in the Hollows gated community. Two stories with a double wraparound veranda, it looked like something out of *Gone with the Wind*. Sure, we were in Tennessee, but a plantation-style house built in this century was just wrong on *all* the levels.

By the time we'd made it to the door, I was irritated, coffee-starved, actually starved since I hadn't had break-fast, and more than a little put out that I'd had to call in a favor to get the homeowner's association code to the gate. And I'd had to do that, because no matter how many times I'd called Hank Simpkins, he was not answering the blasted gate. That and his wife had decided to follow her corpse instead of helping me dig for clues.

I supposed if there wasn't '80s hair-band heavy metal rattling the windows, I'd be a little more worried about the state of Mr. Simpkins, given his wife's demise. By the giggles and squealing that I somehow heard over the screeching of *Guns and Roses*, I was pretty sure he was doing just fine.

Since I'd had about enough of literally every being I'd come across today, I pounded on the door with a cop-knock, leaving even J's in the dust. When that didn't work, I glanced over to J. "You hear screaming? I think I hear someone in distress."

J, like the good man he was, smiled before putting his size thirteens to work, busting the door wide open.

"Haunted Peak Police. We are entering the premises," J barked, his gun drawn and raised like he was actually worried about the occupant, ready to eliminate a threat.

I said nothing, drawing my weapon and leaving it at my side. Based on the noises coming from the house, there was no assailant or dastardly villain. There was just an idiot. A fact that was no more apparent after I got a good look at Hank Simpkins snorting a white powder off a woman's ass cheek. Well, "woman" was a stretch. The girl couldn't be more than twenty. Dressed in an honest-to-god French maid uniform complete with fishnets and hooker heels, I had a feeling she was of the working girl variety.

Hank himself was in a stained singlet, droopy boxer shorts, and black crew socks, his pudgy fingers holding onto the girl's thong-clad backside as he used her as a shield against us.

Classy. Real fucking classy. I was glad Blair hadn't followed me to her house—a fact I was cursing her for just earlier, was now a boon. No way would I be able to concentrate with her screeching once she saw this shit.

J had the good sense to stomp over to the frighteningly loud sound system and shut it off. It was either that, or I was going to shoot it. Well, not really. That would be too much paperwork.

"We're with the HPPD." I showed him my badge as I stowed my weapon. "Are you Hank Simpkins?"

Hank finally seemed to grasp that we were authority figures by the way his gaze darted to the drug paraphernalia strewn all over the likely antique coffee table. By the lines and the hundred-dollar bills rolled into straws, he was having a good old time. Add in the hooker, and well, Hank was living his best life.

Too bad his wife had lost hers.

"That depends, officers."

I had a feeling Hank was trying to be smooth, but he

lacked the grace or wherewithal. "You do realize that we can arrest you for possession, what appears to be soliciting a prostitute, and disturbing the peace, right? I could probably think up a few more charges, but honestly, I'm too tired to do the paperwork. Are you Hank Simpkins or not?"

I may have implied that I didn't want to arrest him for those things, but that couldn't be farther from the truth. I wanted to, and I was gonna. Just after he told me what I wanted to know.

"Sure, I'm Hank—Henry to my mama. What can I do for you fine officers of the law?"

Pedantic prick.

J took over for me then, because this was our routine. He would be the comfort, and I would be the bad guy. He would smooth them over and offer a shoulder to cry on, and I would analyze their every move. We made a good team, and I only felt *marginally* bad about him always having to do the dirty work.

J moved closer, clapping a hand on Hank's shoulder as he asked the scantily clad girl to scooch over. Despite the cops busting in the door, she seemed almost bored with the goings-on.

"It's my sad duty to inform you that your wife, Blair, was found dead this morning."

J used his soothing cop voice and everything, but

Hank appeared confused. "Found dead? That makes no sense. She was just here."

"Interesting, Mr. Simpkins. Because the ME thinks she died two days ago. Care to elaborate on what 'just' means?" Oooh, J was using his cop voice, which meant he'd had about enough of old Hank.

"Well, sure. She said she was going to get her nails done with Suzette, and we had a little tiff about her spending money because the company was goin' under. Then she told me to stuff it, and she was taking care of herself while she could. Then I called Tiffany, because if Blair was gonna blow all our cash at the spa, I was gonna have a bit of fun. And here we are."

So, he'd had an argument with the deceased likely the day she died, his company was going under, and they were strapped for cash. Jesus, it was like he was begging to be a suspect.

"And what day do you think it is?" I asked because I honestly wanted to know if the blow he'd been snorting fried all his brain cells or just a few.

"Sunday of course."

I snorted (pun kind of intended because laughing outright would be rude). "Mr. Simpkins, it's Tuesday. My guess is you've snorted enough blow to keep you up for two straight days."

Hookers and blow. What a freaking cliché.

I was unaware I'd said that aloud until Tiffany corrected me. "I'm not a hooker. I'm his girlfriend. We'll be official once..." She trailed off, letting the reality of her situation catch up to her mouth. "Well, I guess there's nothing stopping us, is there, Pookie? With Blair out of the picture, we can run away together like we planned."

She pushed past J and snuggled up in Hank's dumbstruck arms. He was just now grasping that he was more fucked than he'd been before, and now he had the added hundred pounds of bimbo to contend with. I really did want to laugh at them both, but I managed not to. Barely. They weren't running anywhere. Especially with no money.

"Where were you this whole time, Tiffany?" I asked, giving J a reprieve when he needed to get the hell away from the couple. Tiffany was trying to kiss Hank, but he was struck dumb—or dumber than he had been before—and she was oblivious.

A match made in hell.

She paused her assault on Hank's mouth for a second to answer me, "Here, of course. I could never leave my Hanky-Panky when he needed me. That silly Blair wouldn't know a good thing if it hit her with a bat." She gasped and put a hand to her mouth like she was giving a sad Marylin Monroe impression. "That's not how she was killed, was it?"

Hanky-Panky? What the fuck? And just...What. The. Fuck?

I had to will my eyes not to narrow at her, but I did study her closer. She seemed familiar, and if I squinted and mentally scrubbed her face and put her in a twin set, I could place her. "We are unable to discuss the particulars in this case, only to inform you that your wife was murdered. We will need the both of you to get dressed and come down to the station."

"I'll do no such thing," Hank blustered as he rose.

Uh, yeah, he was. He just didn't know he was going to be doing it under duress. "Well, let's see. Tiffany here is Judge Payton's youngest daughter. I wonder how he'd feel about you snorting coke off her left ass cheek? Or about her thinking about running away with a man twice her age who would be more likely to embezzle their family's money than provide for her?"

I couldn't say why I was married to the thought of Hank Simkins being a liar and cheat. Really. I had no idea.

"Also, you don't get a choice." J pulled the cuffs from his belt and latched one onto Hank's wrist. "Hank Simkins, you are under arrest for the possession of narcotics with the intent to distribute. You have the right to remain silent."

J continued reading Hank his rights as I frog-marched Tiffany to a full-to-bursting bag and let her pick out something that covered both of her ass cheeks. Then, I read her her rights, too. There was half a kilo of coke on the coffee table, and I had no idea whose it was. I was real broken up about following the letter of the law and all that.

Before I called in for a patrol car to pick them up, I stepped out and made a call to Judge Payton.

"Well, hello, Detective Adler, to what do I owe the pleasure?" Judge Payton was a buddy—if a sixty-something robe-wearing guy could be anyone's buddy, so this call was a courtesy of epic proportions.

"Hey, Judge. Umm. I have Tiffany here, and I'm about to book her on possession." I knew I'd recognized

Tiffany from somewhere, and that somewhere was a family photo displayed on Donald Payton's desk in his judge's chambers.

"What?" he barked before sighing low and long. He'd been here before, I'd bet.

"She was at the home of Hank Simpkins and well..." I trailed off, not wanting to get into the particulars.

"Well what?"

I pinched my brow and prayed he didn't shoot the messenger. "She is his girlfriend? And we found his wife dead this morning? And there was half a kilo of coke on the coffee table?"

I said them all like questions, but they were anything but.

Judge Payton cussed a blue streak. It sounded like he was ready to spit nails, and I didn't blame the man. This wasn't Tiffany's first brush with the law. "Lock her little ass up. Put her with the really mean ones if you can. I swear that girl is gonna be the death of her mother. Cavorting and carrying on like she is. She can pay for her own damn attorney this time, too."

Judge Payton had had just about enough. "Will do, sir. And I'm sorry."

"Nothing to be sorry about, Darby. You're just doing your job. Maybe she'll get scared straight this time."

Politically, I couldn't say if having a delinquent for a

daughter hurt his position or not. But Judge Payton was a good man, an honest and fair judge, and according to scuttlebutt, was an absolute shark at rummy.

"I hope so."

After we said our goodbyes and the patrol cops picked up our partying couple, my cell phone rang in my back pocket. Without looking, I answered it, "Adler."

"She had your card in her hand?" My father's voice was dialed to boom levels. It was only slightly different than his closing-argument voice. My dad was the Assistant District Attorney for Haunted Peak, and he'd sealed the fate of many a bad guy using that tone.

"That's the rumor." Well, it wasn't a rumor, but being cute had gotten me out of many a scrape. I'd use it if I had to.

"Don't get cute with me, Darby. This is serious. I don't want you involved in this case."

I narrowed my eyes, sure he could feel the sear of it through the phone. "That's not up to you."

Technically, it was up to his boss and mine, but if he wanted to, he could convince them to see things his way.

"We'll see about that," he hissed and hung up. Two seconds later, I got a ding of a text.

Dad: I love you.

Thirty seconds after that, I got another call. This time I checked my phone. "Hi, Captain. How can I help you on this fine Tuesday morning?"

Was I really this chipper? Absolutely not. Did I want him to side in my favor after my father threw down? *You're damn right I did.*

"You can come see me in my office. Apparently, you and I have a meeting with a Fed and the ADA. This about the Simpkins case? J made the rounds this morning."

Fucking J. Did he call everyone in the state of Tennessee or what?

"Which Simpkins case? The murder or the soon-to-be possession charge?"

Cap whistled, and I heard his chair creak down the line as he tilted it back. "The murder most likely. I hope you got enough coffee in ya. Your dad is about to cause a ruckus."

Joy.

"J and I will be there in thirty. I have to supervise the booking."

Cap chuckled. "You still do that?"

Yes, I still made sure every single one of my collars was processed correctly. And, no, I did not trust the two rookies to process them properly. According to my father, it only took one mistake to tank a case. "You know I do."

"Fine, fine. Just don't make the rookies cry this time. We want them to learn, not cower in fear every time they hear your boots in the hall. That's my job."

"I make no promises. Jefferson bungled up one collar so bad, if I hadn't reprocessed the guy, the whole damn case would have been thrown out. I'm not in the habit of letting murderers off."

The captain chuckled before disconnecting, and I trudged back to the Jeep, praising whatever deity thought up air-conditioning.

"I called in an order at Carmine's. It should be ready by the time we have to go into the meeting." J was smart enough to say this without looking me in the eye. I just found out about the meeting a second ago, and he'd already had time to queue up guilt food and get the AC going?

Cap had most definitely called him first.

I narrowed my eyes at him, wishing they were made of lasers or acid or something. "What did you order me?"

As long as J had known me, as many times as he'd sat next to me and eaten meals, he always managed to get something wrong on my order. When I took care of it, his was exactly the way he wanted it. When he ordered, he always left the pickles on a sandwich—*I'm allergic*—forgot the extra cheese on a meatball sub—*rude*—or let them put lettuce on a perfectly good hamburger—*gross*.

J wriggled in his seat like he was under the gun. "A turkey club, no pickles, extra tomatoes, spicy mustard, mayo, red onion, and parm. I also got the triple-fudge chunk cookies and a still water." He paused, thinking hard. "And jalapeño kettle chips."

Holy shit on a stick, he got one right. He must really be feeling shitty about tattling. Either that, or he had some more shit to shovel my way. I waited, letting him squirm and spill. It was a tried and true interrogation tactic. People naturally wanted to fill the silence. All you had to do was wait them out, and they'd eventually say something that incriminated them. When it came to finding shit out, I was the most patient woman on the planet. Mostly.

"Okay, fine. I was the one who called the Fed into the meeting with your dad and the cap."

I fucking knew it. Rearing back, I knuckle-punched him right above his elbow, deadening his whole arm with one carefully placed strike. It was an art perfected in childhood since J had been bigger than me since forever.

"Ow! Jesus, fuck, Darby. I'm sorry, okay?"

Instead of answering, I growled at him and put the Jeep in drive, refusing to look at him until we got to the station.

Haunted Peak Police Station was a larger building in the center of town. Well, at a hundred-thousand people, we were solidly city territory. A small city, but still. There were five other stations, but I worked at the main one that was attached to the municipal building and courthouse. I left J to procure our lunch and inspected the booking of Hank and Tiffany.

Hank's information was so bad, I was sure a ten-year-old could have done better. In fact, I was sure one of our kids from the junior officer's program probably could have ran circles around Jefferson.

The paperwork was a hot mess, the wrong finger-prints were in his file, and he'd been booked for jaywalking?

Don't yell. Don't yell. Don't...

"Jefferson!"

A quivering man—six foot one or not, the man was shivering like a wet chihuahua—peeked around a corner. He was hiding from me like a child which only pissed me off more. "How can I help you, Detective Adler?"

"Did you process Hank Simpkins and Tiffany Payton? Don't answer that. I know you did. I just have one ques-tion. Do you hate me for some reason? Have I done something to you to earn this level of fuckery? Or do you just enjoy potentially tanking literally every single case that comes across your desk?"

"Wh-what do you mean?" He might be tall, but he was a skinny little thing, probably only outweighing me by twenty pounds. Maybe he was shivering because he was cold. Still. This was a hassle.

"Well, you have a female's prints in with Hank's file, you put in that he was arrested for jaywalking, and you're missing two angles of his mugshots. Again, do you hate me? Is that it?"

Jefferson rubbed his buzzed hair for what I hoped was luck and squinted at the booking file. Bigger cities had a fully integrated system, but we were still getting it up and running. My gaze drifted from his face to his uniform, the shirt probably the smallest male size they made, and still, it swam on him.

That's when I noticed the black-rimmed glasses peeking out of his uniform pocket. I sighed and prayed this would fix the issue.

"Jefferson, please, for the love of all that is holy—do me a favor?"

He blushed and stood taller, puffing out his chest. "Anything." I'd swear, romance-novel heroines every-where wished they could get their voice as breathy as his was just then.

"Put on your glasses. Please? I'm begging you."

He screwed up his mouth but plucked the frames from his pocket and shoved them on his face. They weren't too bad and actually made his blue eyes pop. I nodded in approval and showed him the file. "Please fix this now that you can see. I'm coming back here after I meet with the cap, and it better be right or so help me, I'll sic Cooper on you."

Jefferson's eyes widened at J's last name and nodded. I was an evil bitch on wheels who pranked with abandon and damn the consequences. J was a well-respected man and built like a Greek god. And he held the singular ability to guilt someone to death. I could ruin your day. J could torch someone's whole psyche. It was his gift.

Only after I was sure Jefferson understood the seriousness of the situation, did I leave him to search out my lunch. Oh, and I guessed, talk to the captain, and my dad, and the stupid Fed who made me uneasy on a bevy of levels.

I spotted J with a brown paper bag with the green Carmine's logo on it and snatched it out of his hands as we trudged into the cap's office. My dad, Cap, and the Fed were all sitting, waiting for us, and I didn't pay any of them any mind except the captain. I shook his hand before perching on one of the conference tables positioned at the back of the room and started digging in my paper bag. I could feel three of the four men in the room staring at me. To his credit, J wasn't, too busy digging in his own bag.

Unearthing my sandwich, I peeked at the innards before taking a bite. All I needed today was to eat a damn pickle. Once I was sure the sandwich was pickle-free, I bit into it with abandon. Most people wouldn't dare eat in their captain's office or park their asses on a table instead of at one. Truth be told, if Cap, AKA, Captain Stevens, AKA, Uncle Dave, AKA, my dad's best friend since they were in the womb, weren't who he was, I probably wouldn't. But he was, I hadn't eaten since yesterday, and I had a psycho aching for my attention.

Yeah, Mama needed her some food.

Once I'd inhaled about three bites, the Fed piped up. "You have no decorum at all, do you?"

I snorted, popped open my chip bag, and munched one. Loudly.

Cap sat forward in his chair, his slender fingers steepled as if he were trying desperately not to clench them into fists. Uncle Dave did not like it when people acted like assholes in my presence. He hadn't tolerated that shit in grade school when I'd dealt with bullies the old-fashioned way, and he for damn sure didn't like it now.

"Special Agent La Roux, let me formally introduce you to Detectives Darby Adler and Jeremiah Cooper. Not only are they the best detectives I have, but they also have the highest close rate in three counties. Maybe even the state," Cap scolded, his voice a deep burr of no-nonsense chastisement. "Not only that, but they also closed a triple homicide last night, didn't get home until the wee hours, and woke up to another dead body this morning. Moreover, if I don't have a problem with my detectives grabbing sustenance in my office as we conduct this bullshit meeting, you shouldn't, either."

Cap hadn't taken any shit from the asinine racists who didn't want a black man to hold his position, and he wasn't going to take any from the Fed, either.

"Apologies, Captain. I didn't realize." It was a bull-shit way of saying he was sorry, but I didn't really fault him for it. I was acting this way on purpose to keep him off-kilter. The Fed was paying far too much attention to me for a reason I couldn't decipher, and I wanted to know why. Keeping him guessing was the best way to get him to slip up.

I met the captain's dark-brown gaze, munching another chip. Within a second, I knew he'd figured out why I didn't want to give up the case—because that was the only reason the Fed would be here. Uncle Dave just wanted to see it for himself.

La Roux was an asshole. I so very rarely gave assholes anything they wanted.

"Okay, you've consumed enough calories to stave off your ire. Let's get down to business," my father piped up from his seat at the cap's desk. "I want you off this case."

Here we go.

"There is no way the DA is going to go along with this. The victim had your card in her hand. Do you remember the last time you had a perp desperate for your attention?"

Righteous anger was my father's bread and butter. It convinced juries to see his side; it lured judges to think of maximum penalties for capital crimes; it persuaded angry sixteen-year-old girls not to sneak out and frolic with the other underage drinkers.

It would not, however, work on me today.

Especially since he was the second person in as many hours to remind me of the Dunleavy case.

Ezra Dunleavy had been convinced I was a witch and needed to be cleansed. He was a bigot, a zealot, and out of his fucking mind. He'd stalked me for almost six weeks before I caught the bastard. Well, I made J do the actual catching because I was the victim, but I was the one who found him, thanks to my odd little ability.

I was the one who'd talked to the string of ghosts that clung to him like a staticky sweater. I wasn't the first woman he'd stalked. If the photos and manifesto we —*officially J*—found in his house were anything to go by, he'd "cleansed" eight women. I was meant to be the ninth.

Each one of us had ties to the arcane world. I was just the only one who had the means to stop him.

Normally, I was the first one to listen to my father. He was smart, level-headed, and a legal marvel. He knew where every single loophole in the law was and tightened the noose on all the ones he could. He was also a really good dad. After he married my mother and adopted me, I never thought of him as anything other than my father. I didn't even do the shitty things teenagers did to stepparents by telling him he wasn't my real dad. Even after my mother died, he was just Dad.

But I didn't want to listen to him right then.

Especially when I'd caught what he likely hadn't meant to say.

"What you really mean is, you haven't brought this to the DA, and you have no idea which way he'd side, so you're trying to get me off the case now before he backs my side instead of yours. See, I can read between the lines, too." I took another bite of my sandwich and munched as I stared him down.

My father stood from his seat, planting his fists on his hips as if he weren't telegraphing his every thought with his body language. *Rookie mistake, Dad.* "You're involved, Darby. You can't be on the case."

I really hated it when people spoke in absolutes. It was a major pet peeve of mine.

"I don't think that's your call, but even if it was, it would be the wrong one. I have a perp who murdered a woman less than a block away from my house. She had my card in her hand. Her body was arranged, well, left like a sacrifice of some sort. Carved up like a turkey. These are all facts. What you might not know is that she had my desk card in her hand. I don't give those out. They're sitting in a drawer at the bottom of my desk under about twenty case files. I had other cards made without the police emblem or my title. I give those out to people because not everyone wants the HPPD logo on something they need to keep secret."

I paused, eating a chip while all four men digested that little nugget of information. Only the Fed fidgeted in his seat.

"So, whoever killed that woman had access to my desk. Has walked through the bullpen like it was nothing. And you think keeping me off the case is going to accomplish what, exactly? It's not going to make me safe at work. My home is already close to a dumping ground —what would you like me to do instead? Join a nunnery and pray this sick bastard doesn't follow me?"

J snorted. "They'd kick you out in a day—tops. You cuss too much."

"True, but it'd be entertaining to see all the nuns blush," I shot back. "Since there have been no overt signs that I'm a target, you legally have no call to pull me off the case. Plus, I'm likely going to investigate this thing anyway, so can't we just cut out the middleman, and let me be? If it looks like it's going sideways, you know J will tattle on me again."

Yes, that was a low blow, but J deserved it. He called my damn daddy, the dick.

"She has a point, Killian. Cooper will be on her like glue," Cap said, backing me up. "Plus, if the Fed here had any call to steal the case out from under us, he would have by now."

La Roux sat forward in his seat. "I still might. Blair Simpkins was tied to another case I've been pursuing. We believe her husband mishandled government funds."

I snorted—*yeah, I'm a lady*—and responded around my food, "Hate to break it to ya, Bubba, but murder trumps embezzlement any day of the week and twice on

Sunday." And if there was mustard on the side of my cheek, well, then so be it.

"Damn right it does," J chimed in. It was one thing to be up my ass about being a murderer's fixation and quite another to let a Fed walk all over our shit.

I don't think so.

"Yeah, *it does.* And if Blair Simpkins had information on my case and got killed because of it, it makes it my jurisdiction. No offense to your Podunk town and the wonderkid detective, Captain, but I don't much care what you think about it. I'm here to make sure things are run the way the federal government needs them to be run, and that's it." At that, La Roux stood, buttoned his suit jacket, and slammed out of the room.

He seemed so nice, that guy.

"I'm not off the case, am I?" I asked the cap more than my dad who was probably trying to figure out how to tank La Roux's career with the least amount of fuss. I didn't blame him if he was. That Fed was an asshole.

"Of course not. *Podunk* town. Pfft. Who the hell does that guy think he is?"

I shrugged and took another bite. I wouldn't speculate too much about the Fed. He had too many variables to him—too many ways for him to be something different than what I thought.

"Where are you on the murder?" Cap said, still

staring at his door like it would tell him why the Fed threw a hissy fit.

"Not far. No conclusive time of death, and I won't have that until tomorrow at the earliest. The preliminary is anywhere from two days to twelve hours. If we go by the two-day model, then we have a person to question, but until I dig into her life, I won't know for sure. I need to question the best friend but that might get dicey."

J snorted and then coughed, slightly choking on his pop. "I'll say. She's the mayor's wife."

Cap's eyebrows did a little dance that said he was trying to hold in a laugh. And he was holding in a laugh because my father's face just turned purple. My father *hated* the mayor with a passion. Always had—not that I knew why.

"Tread easy," Cap warned. "You know she's going to lawyer up as soon as you spook her."

That was what I was afraid of.

After checking up on Jefferson's progress, I trudged through the bullpen. I always wondered why it was called that. At best it was a sea of desks paired off two by two, the cheap metal workstations nearly as old as I was. Honestly, I was surprised the higher-ups decided to spring for the upgraded computers, and truth be told, I'd take a shitty desk over a shitty computer any day.

There were more than a few ghosts hanging around the joint, too. A few at the watercooler, pretending to gab with the few officers hanging out there. A former perp or two who liked to try to move things on Sal's desk.

And then there was Margaret.

Margaret Harris had been a secretary who worked the reception desk in the 1980s. She'd passed before I was born—in a freak gas explosion that was the talk of the town back then—and was the nosiest entity I'd ever come across. Hildy was a gossip, but Margaret made Hildy look like the patron saint of silence. There were several reasons why I didn't hang out in the office, but Margaret was one of them. For some reason—known only to beings much more powerful than I—Margaret couldn't leave the precinct. A fact that likely saved what little sanity I had left.

Margaret hopped from one foot to the other, desperately trying to flag me down—even though she knew I couldn't answer her—and in less than a second, I knew why. The Fed was waiting for me at my desk.

No. Not *at* my desk.

He was sitting in my chair, twirling my *Mont Blanc* in his fingers like he had the right to be there. I might have held in my ire at the crime scene, but this was just fucking rude.

Margaret parked her shapely behind on the edge of my desk, getting her front-row seat. I shot her a quick glare before turning my ire to the shmuck sitting in my chair.

"I don't know you. You don't know me. I get it. We play in two different sandboxes and that's fine. But if you don't stop touching my shit and sitting in my chair, things are going to get real, pal." I tried and failed to unclench my teeth.

My mother had given me that pen when I was nine. Sure, it was a semi-fancy pen, probably the lower end of the brand and still too expensive to give to a child, but that didn't matter. She'd said if I wanted to take fancy notes in my notebook, I should have the right equipment. Yes, *Nancy Drew* was my hero even before I could see ghosts.

"You tell him, honey," Margaret chimed in, and it was all I could do not to roll my eyes. "This little upstart didn't even hesitate. He walked in here like he owned the place, went right to your desk, and sat down. You don't even have a nameplate on your desk, so how he knew where to sit is a mystery."

That little nugget of info did not give me the warm fuzzies. Not. At. All.

Still, La Roux heeded my warning and gently returned the tortoise-shell pen to its cradle. What he did *not* do was get up.

"I want you to give me this case," he began, probably ready to go into some spiel about jurisdiction and some such other bullshit.

Whatever.

"No." Succinct, to the point, and a complete fucking answer. And what else could I say that hadn't already been said? Plus, he put his mitts all over my shit. I'd say no until my dying breath.

This would be the hill I died on.

Margaret agreed with me because she added her commentary to the mix. "Mm-hmm. Do you hear that, you federal stooge? N-O."

I had the urge to tell her to shut up but refrained. This was likely the juiciest shit she'd seen since Thatcher McCrary broke up with his girlfriend in the lobby last year. I'd heard her go on and on about that one for a month.

La Roux sat up in my chair, leaning toward me like he was posturing, even though he was at a height disadvantage. "You don't know what you're doing. You think you do, but you don't. No matter what your sources tell you, no matter what little woo-woo bullshit you think you know, you have no fucking clue. You're going to get yourself hurt."

As much as I didn't want to telegraph anything to this man, my eyes narrowed of their own accord.

"Oh, no, he did not just say that to you. Who in the Sam Hill does this fool think he is?" Margaret was getting worked up, and if she didn't cool it, I'd punt her ghostly ass to the lobby. I speared her with another glare hot enough to curl paint, and she mimed buttoning her lip.

As for the Fed? He had no idea what I did or didn't know and couldn't possibly comprehend what woo-woo bullshit I had under my belt. "I'll take your concerns under advisement. Get the fuck out of my chair, La Roux."

At my growled command, he reluctantly stood from my chair—his body in my space now that he was upright. Dammit. I did not like him there, using his size and menace against me. Like a dick.

But I'd put bigger men than him on their knees, and I was pretty sure my face said as much when he took two steps back. "I know you're probably new to social norms, but crowd me like that again, and you'll regret it. Not only is it considered sexual harassment, you'll also be choking on your own balls until the end of time. We clear?"

"Crystal." He seemed almost impressed that I would tell him where to go and what to do when he got there.

"I'm not dropping the case. Someone made sure my business card was left at the crime scene. Said *someone's* got my attention. Now, get out of my way."

He gave me a truncated sort of nod, like a head bow, but not. "As you wish. When you get into something you can't get out of, call me."

He passed me an all-black square business card with a gold emblem I'd never seen before. It sure as shit didn't look like the usual FBI logo. He waited until I accepted the card before turning away, and I made sure he was really gone before I flipped it over.

"Ooh, what's it say? Let me see," Margaret complained, and it was all I could do not to scream at her right there in the crowded bullpen. Nosy-ass ghosts.

Still, I did as told, letting her get a good look at the card before I read it. His first name was Bishop. And like the business cards I'd had made, it didn't list his title. Just a phone number. I flipped the card over and inspected the emblem etched into the cardstock. I'd seen it somewhere before, but I couldn't place it.

Unsettled, I slipped it into my back pocket before gathering my things. As much as Margaret annoyed the ever-loving shit out of me, I did appreciate her backup— even if she couldn't exactly do anything if things went sideways. I whispered a little "thank you" to her as I left, feeling the full beam of her smile as it crested on her face.

But as nice as it was to make Margaret smile, I still couldn't shake the pit of dread in my belly. La Roux knew something I didn't. I was sure of it.

Meeting J at my Jeep, I passed my keys over to him, letting him drive us to what was likely going to be a fruitless interview.

"What was that all about?" he asked once I belted in and closed my eyes.

"What was what?" Already half-asleep, I didn't even bother cracking my lids. This day was far too long for my liking.

"This posturing with the Fed. Why was he waiting for you? And what was with touching your shit? That was a dick move."

How much of that had J seen? Who was I kidding? Probably all of it. J had a way of standing out when he wanted to and blending in when he didn't. It was a creepy-as-hell trait for a human to have, and as much as I didn't like it, it had served us well so far.

"He was warning me off the case. Again." I yawned, shimmying in my seat to get comfortable. "Wake me up when we get there, will ya?"

All too soon the Jeep rolled to a stop, and I instantly opened my eyes. It took forty-five minutes to drive up the mountain to the bougie fake cabins that surrounded Whisper Lake. I called them fake cabins because anything bigger than two-stories tall and had more than three rooms, had no right calling itself a freaking cabin. They were log mansions, no two ways about it.

Whisper Lake was a tiny, crystal-clear man-made lake dug out of Haunted Peak. There were only twelve houses surrounding it with no public access. It was a rather big sticking point for the locals since not many of us wanted to tarnish the mountain in the first place—especially because it dicked around with the ecosystem.

But the mayor—or rather his first wife—wanted a lake house, so there was now a lake. Or at least that was how the rumor mill spun it. I didn't put all of my eggs in the rumor-mill basket, though. That same gossip had me and J in a secret relationship. I was pretty sure since I didn't have a penis and would never get one, that was never going to happen. Plus, it took years to get state and federal permission to change the landscape like that with enough red tape to paint the whole damn town. If an entire lake could be constructed on the whim of one lone mayor's wife, I was Tommy Lee Jones.

I rummaged through my bag for breath mints and my rose-water sprayer. Okay, so I knew spraying myself with rose water was prissy as all get out, but I needed a little something. Suzette was Blair's BFF, partner in crime, and second in command of the bitch squad. I didn't have a stitch of makeup on, I'd been up since the ass crack of dawn, and I was running on a serious sleep deficiency.

Basically, I looked like a bag of smashed ass, and there wasn't much I could do about it.

"You about done primping?" J grumbled. Whatever. He didn't look like ass. He looked perfectly rumpled as always, and it didn't matter if he had smeared himself with dirt and hadn't showered in a week, Suzette would likely try to climb all over him.

"Maybe. Or maybe I'll let you do all the questioning without backup," I threatened. And it was a legitimate threat, too. If I weren't there to run interference, J would likely be eaten alive by fake Southern charm and avarice.

"You wouldn't dare."

"Keep fucking around and find out."

"Fine. Spray away. Just don't leave me to that

woman. I swear, she was a mercenary bitch in high school and that shit has only matured with age." J shuddered in his seat but managed to shut off the Jeep. "We have to play this the right way. One accusatory question and she'll lawyer up so fast…"

"I know. Jesus. What is it with you guys today? It's like you've never seen me question people before."

J opened his door and climbed out, and I did the same. Over the hood, he leveled me with an expression he'd patented in tenth grade. "Have you heard yourself today? No offense, D, but you're a one-woman wrecking ball. Just go easy?"

"Fine. I'll be sweetness and light. A fucking lady, even. Let's go. The sooner this is done, the sooner I can go home and sleep. Remember sleep? It's that awesome thing we do when we lay down and rest our eyes. I need that before I rip someone apart with my bare hands."

"Sure thing, Cranky Pants," he muttered under his breath, using the giant eagle knocker at the front door.

We didn't have to wait too long before someone answered. A tall man in a no-shit butler outfit opened the door. Now, I had nothing against rich people. Nothing against people hiring domestic help. But a butler? In Haunted Peak? The fuck?

I managed to keep the judgment off my face by sheer force of will. But I couldn't quite manage the surprise when the butler announced us, even though we hadn't introduced ourselves.

"Madam, Detectives Darby Adler and Jeremiah Cooper of the HPPD. Would you like to visit in the parlor or the den?"

My Jeep was unmarked, and I knew I'd never met this man before. Plus, I was very good at situational awareness—*being a cop and all*—and at no time could I ever recall seeing this man around town.

And yet, he knew us.

This did not give me warm and fuzzies. No, that straight-up creeped me the fuck out.

"The parlor, Kingston. The den is for guests." Suzette's snooty voice drifted out the open door.

Ooh, burn. I struggled not to roll my eyes. *So, it's going to be like that, is it?*

J managed to keep me calm with a gentle squeeze to my forearm, but even that was furtive and fleeting. The both of us hated Suzette, and that had been the case since childhood. Even at our age, whatever grievance we had should have been squashed by now.

Alas, it was not.

The Duvall cabin was just as opulent as one would expect, just as ostentatious. I tried to see it without the lens of utter distaste, but I just couldn't. But I had a poker face to rival the best of them, and I succeeded in making my expression a blank mask.

Resting bitch face was my friend.

The butler led us to the parlor, a place that could be classified as a sitting room only, with spindly furniture that might be expensive but in no way comfortable. Nor did it match the outside of the cabin. The exterior was all giant logs and eagle-head knockers. The inside was as if a first lady threw up chintz and florals. The both of us waited until Suzette sat before sitting ourselves, and I resisted the urge to plop down and smash the dainty sofa to bits.

Barely. But that was only because of the rather irritated ghost lounging on an ornate fainting couch. She appeared eighty if she was a day, a ghostly afghan thrown over her legs as she stared at the doorway. She seemed to be waiting for Suzette, and she was not pleased. When Suzette swept into the room, the ghost's frown only deepened.

I liked Granny already.

Suzette was just as blonde and just as beautiful as she had been in high school. Granted, she hadn't had the expert hand of a plastic surgeon then. Her skin had the appearance of zero pores (which was impossible) with the plasticized quality of the surgically refreshed. What she could have believed was a flaw at the ripe old age of twenty-eight, I had no idea, but to each their own. Dressed in a pale-yellow skirt suit, she resembled a banana a little bit, but in a put-together classy way. Her blue eyes were just as sharp as they'd always been, assessing and calculating every movement and word like a well-dressed snake.

I struggled to start, but J had no such issues. He began by using his patented old-lady voice. That voice could get him out of almost anything, and I had a feeling he'd need it now. "Mrs. Duvall, it is my sad duty to inform you that Blair Simpkins has passed away. We recovered her body this morning. I do realize ya'll were close, and you might have seen her on the day she died. I'm sorry to trouble you, ma'am, but I would like to ask about the last time you saw Blair."

Mrs. Duvall. Pfft. She graduated the same damn year as we did, and he was calling her *Mrs. Duvall?* J was giving her a mighty amount of leeway on those questions—not that any of them were even in the form of a question. I didn't like it one bit. If she were anyone else, I would have started squeezing them by now. Suzette wasn't acting like she was just hearing the news, nor did she seem to be altogether broken up about her best friend dying. She did, however, give a delicate little sniff, retrieved a handkerchief from who knew where, and gently dabbed the side of her eyes.

Granted, there wasn't even a hint of tears, but maybe she'd had so much Botox, her face couldn't produce them anymore.

"Yes, I heard about her passing. Such an awful thing. I'll do whatever I can to help you." Suzette's voice was emphatic, even if her face wasn't, a dramatic shift from her parlor-den instructions. "I saw Blair two days ago. We went to the spa together, then went to dinner at Caprisi. We parted ways at the restaurant, and I haven't seen her since. I've called her phone maybe a dozen times, and she never answered. I thought..." Suzette gave a delicate little shrug. "I thought maybe she was mad at me because I was chosen to chair the Haunted Peak Restoration Society, but that seems silly now."

She dabbed her dry eyes again, patted her nose with her handkerchief, and leveled J with an expression so innocent angels would weep. "I got home at about nine-thirty and stayed in for the rest of the night. Kingston can attest to that."

It wasn't lost on me that Suzette hadn't met my gaze once. Nor had she spoken a single word to me since we'd gotten here. Pretending I wasn't there had been a staple in her bitch arsenal since we were kids. The slight was noted.

Kingston stepped forward from whatever dark corner

he'd been hiding in and chimed in. "Madam did indeed arrive at nine-thirty Sunday evening."

Suzette had a solid alibi—corroborated and everything.

That didn't mean I believed it. Especially when Granny met my gaze and shook her head. Yeah, I didn't think so, either.

Exiting Suzette's house was the biggest breath of fresh air on the planet. As soon as I crossed the threshold, the weight of her home fell away as I let the sun warm my face. If ever there were a person on this plane of existence that was shrouded in bad energy, it was that woman.

Yeah, I sounded woo-woo as shit—even in my own head—but Suzette had always given me the creeps. And I dealt with murderers for a living.

"You want to call the spa?" J's question broke me out of my sun-warming reverie. Rude.

I cracked an eyelid, sending him an irritated glare. Couldn't he tell I was trying to slough off Suzette's icy demeanor? Sheesh.

"You'll take the restaurant then?"

J nodded. "I don't put too much stock in her alibi, but if we can hammer out the times with the wait staff and get a good picture of her last day, then we'll have a better snare for when she trips up. She's involved. I don't know how, but she is."

There was the partner I knew and loved. I might get the most information—given my ghostly informants—but J was no slouch in the investigating department, either. J's gut had saved our bacon more times than I could count.

"Sounds good, but I'm making those calls from my house. It's already five, and without a solid time of death, we're dead in the water. I'm calling the spa, and then it's naptime until tomorrow." I punctuated my statement with a yawn so huge it popped my jaw. Which in turn, made J yawn just as big. He hadn't gotten any more sleep than I had.

Without a word, J put the Jeep in gear, and we headed back down the mountain. Cell service was spotty up here, and it wasn't until we got closer to town did it pick back up. By the time I'd finally gotten through to the spa, they had closed for the night. There was nothing else for me to do but put on my jammies and lay in the warm cocoon of my covers. I couldn't wait.

J pulled into my driveway and we said our goodbyes, each heading to our houses with all due haste. J had lived next door since we'd gotten our places, so his trek home was a short one. My covers were calling me by the time I slipped my key in the lock. I'd have to tell Hildy to scram for a while so I could get some sleep.

But when I opened my door, there wasn't just one ghost to greet me.

There were two.

8

Blair sat in my peacock-blue velvet accent chair like she owned it, her hips to the side and her ghostly feet tucked under her ass. Her elbow was planted on the armrest, her head resting on her hand like she'd been waiting for me this whole time and was not amused I'd kept her.

This was going to go well. Sure.

What I wanted to know was how she knew where I lived. Ghosts in transition didn't just know all the secrets to the universe when they popped over to the deathly plane. Until they headed where they were supposed to go—unlike Hildy who was a snoop and gossip of the highest order—they were just like us: floundering away with only the knowledge they perceived. Unless Blair already knew where I lived in life

—or she followed me without my noticing—she shouldn't know where I lived.

"What are you doing here?" I hissed, not at all happy my house had another ghost in it. Hildy was usually good about keeping specters out. That's why I didn't banish the gossiping bastard. Plus, he was a good room-mate, didn't drink my coffee, and had superb intel.

Blair's eyes narrowed, her face screwing up into a bitchy frown. I did not have the patience to deal with this shit. Not. At. All.

"You've been gone doing whatever it is you do all day, and I needed to talk to you. Jeez, it's like you're avoiding me or something."

Whatever it is I do all day? Was she delusional or just stupid? Oh, wait. She was both.

"I'm a detective, Blair. And just in case you weren't aware, I'm in the process of trying to solve your murder."

Blair had the actual nerve to roll her eyes at me. Ghost or not, I was seriously contemplating punching her in the face. I'd never punched a ghost before, but I was positive if I put my mind to it, I could accomplish the task.

"Fat lot of progress you've made. I don't see anyone but my husband in handcuffs, and I know that fat shmuck didn't do it."

"Oh, come off it, you bitter tart," Hildy barked, the burr of his accent thicker than usual. "You come in here like you've got a right and insult the one person who actually gives a ripe shite about your death. It makes me wonder what kind of blistering she-beast raised you."

I couldn't help it, I snorted. Blair's mother made Suzette seem like an angel. If the Wicked Witch of the West and Satan had a baby, that would be Blair's mother. And yet, I hadn't heard word one from her or her father all day. With the rumor mill likely going full-tilt, I highly doubted they didn't know. Or maybe with Hank Simpkins' recent money troubles, they'd cut them off.

Still, those were questions for tomorrow after I'd gotten actual sleep.

"I have exactly zilch to go on, and I'm tired. I'll start fresh tomorrow. Unless you have more information for me?" I raised my eyebrows, waiting for her to answer.

Instead, she screwed up her mouth, venom ready to spew from her spectral lips. I'd seen that look many a time in my youth. When she'd made fun of my hair, my semi-nerd nature, my clothes, or my dead mother. *Yeah, she went there.* The revenge for that one was sweet and untraceable. Let's just say there was a very good reason why her parents had to get her a new prom dress three hours before the big event, and there wasn't a single shred of evidence pointing to who ruined her old one.

"Save it. Unless you have a blinking neon sign that points directly to your killer, shut your fucking mouth and get out of my house. You are not welcome here." My voice was commanding, a teensy bit of power threaded in my tone. She wasn't the first ghost I'd had to give the boot, and as long as this power stayed with me, she wouldn't be the last.

Blair abruptly stood from her lounged perch on my favorite chair, shock stamped all over her face as she involuntarily floated to the door. More like zoomed, but whatever.

"But wait!" she screeched. "Are you still going to solve my murder? You aren't going to just leave me like this?"

I didn't answer. I just gave her a finger wave as she dematerialized through the door. Of course I was going to solve her case. I just wasn't going to be able to use her as a source. Not that she'd been helpful so far.

There had been a time when I couldn't banish ghosts. As a teen it had been all I could do to stay sane —especially in the first few years. It wasn't until I met Hildy, did the bulk of the spirits leave me alone. He'd scared most of them off for me. He also taught me how to banish them, how to keep them out of my sleeping space, and how to prevent them from dicking around with my sleep. Apparently, that was a ghostly pastime: noodling around in people's subconscious. Talk about rude.

I wondered a lot about how Hildy knew all the shit he knew. Did he spy on people? Did he know someone like me in the centuries past? I'd even asked him a time or two, but all he would do was give me a sly smile and change the subject, the cagey prick.

"You could have kicked her out at any time, Hild. Why didn't you?" I asked the brooding specter. He seemed affronted that Blair had been in "his" space, sitting in his—okay, *our*—favorite seat. Well, that and the fact that she'd insulted me. Hildy hadn't ever been a fan of that.

"I knew you needed information from her, but that lass is two pickles shy of a picnic. Coming in here like that." Hildy huffed and plopped onto the seat I'd just made Blair vacate. Well, plopped was a very generous term. More like he flounced to the chair and dramatically "fell" onto the cushion—as much as one could do that while floating three inches off the floor. "Plus, I figured if I kept an eye on her, she wouldn't go digging where she wasn't wanted. I had to stop her three times from snooping in your room."

"Shocker," I deadpanned. Blair was the gossip hub

when we were in school. It made sense that she hadn't changed even in death. "But you and I both know she can't get into my room. I dislike the beating around the bush, Hild."

Hildy seemed troubled, his lips pressing together in a grimace. "She's different, that one. Something was done to her. Something unnatural. She's not like the other specters." His brow pulled into a deep frown as he studied his hands, refusing to look at me.

Not. Good.

"You need to show me the sigils carved into her body. There might be something to them."

Show him? What was I, his secretary? "You and I both know you can zoom over to the morgue anytime you want. Go look at them yourself. I'm going to bed."

It was like the universe was just dicking with me at that point, because no sooner had those wonderful words left my lips, they were instantly dashed by the damn doorbell ringing. I seriously contemplated not answering it. I mean, I didn't get many visitors other than J and my dad, so whoever it was on the other side of the door was probably trying to sell me something.

Apparently, I'd waited too long because the damn thing rang again.

"You'd better answer it, lass," Hildy advised, a smug little smirk on his face. "No sleep for you."

I promptly flipped Hildy off, muttering under my breath, "See if I do anything for you ever again, you miserable old goat."

By rote, I unholstered my sidearm as I peered through the peephole. If it looked like a salesperson, I'd just ignore them. But when I took a gander at my visitor, I quickly realized I wasn't that lucky.

I threw open my door, making a show of slamming my service weapon into the Kydex holster. As long as he knew I was prepared to shoot him if necessary, we'd likely get along just fine. Maybe. Well, probably not.

No longer in the stuffy blue suit, the Fed stood on my doorstep in jeans and a T-shirt, holding a white paper bag with the *"Sí Señor's"* logo emblazoned on the side. How he knew to go to *Sí Señor* instead of *Plaza Mexical* or *Marco's* was anyone's guess. *Sí Señor* was the best Mexican food in town. Problem was, it was a family owned place with no website, no phone, no tables, and a menu written solely in Spanish. They only served take-out, and you had to order in Spanish because Martine and Blanca didn't speak one lick of English. *Sí Señor* also wasn't on a main strip of any kind. No, it was located on the outskirts of town, damn near in the woods, in a tiny two-room shack, and you wouldn't know how to get there without a guide because there were no signs.

It was a well-kept local secret. Everyone knew

Martine and Blanca Bernal and held them in the highest regard. Unwashed plebeians went to *Plaza Mexical* or *Marco's*. If you wanted authentic, blessed by the grace of god Mexican food, you went to *Sí Señor's*.

The fact that he had that bag in his hand meant someone had talked. Traitors, all of them.

At my quiet assessment, the Fed seemed almost uneasy, bringing the white paper bag up in between us like he was fending off a lion.

"Peace offering?" he rumbled, his eyebrows raised. It was as if his face was trying to show an approximation of niceness while the asshole lurked in the shadows. I wasn't falling for it for a second.

"What do you want?" It came out a tad bit harsher than I'd intended, but he was holding tacos hostage in the form of a bullshit bribe for the Simpkins case.

The Fed rubbed at the back of his neck in a nervous gesture I did *not* expect from someone like him. Unkempt hair and overgrown stubble notwithstanding, he seemed a little too self-contained to let that slip. And I decided to focus on that little bit of information instead of goggling at how his bicep stretched his T-shirt in a truly delicious way.

Do not ogle the terminally hot dickhead out for your case, Darby.

"Look, we got off on the wrong foot today," he

began, and I had to hold in my snort by the skin of my teeth.

Way to state the freaking obvious. I raised my eyebrows in an "And?" sort of way, my silence compelling him to continue.

"I know that's my fault, and to bribe myself into your good graces, I did a little sleuthing to find your favorite place to eat. I offer tacos in exchange for a polite conversation about the Simpkins case. Please." The "please" was tacked onto the end nervously, since I hadn't made a move to let him into my house or said a single thing.

"Gimme the tacos and I'll think about it." I snatched the bag from his fingertips before he could stop me. I left him on the doorstep, not inviting him into my home on purpose. There were a few supernatural creatures that couldn't enter a person's domain without invitation. Demons, the Fae, and a few others. If he were any of the above, I had no intention of letting him into my house.

Ever.

I dropped the bag onto the coffee table and planted my ass on the couch, waiting for him to either get with the program or vamoose.

"Smart girl, not inviting a stranger into your home. But I wouldn't be eating the morsels, lass. Trusting men like that won't get you very far," Hildy advised and I snorted.

I was eating the tacos. Poison be damned.

La Roux sighed before proving he wasn't a nasty sort of entity by following me into the living room, closing the door behind him. I was busy digging into the bag for my prize, but I kept an eye out for where he sat. He didn't bother.

Just as I was about to take my first bite, he started talking, and I lost whatever appetite I may have had.

"How many people in this town know you can see ghosts?"

9

I didn't even get to taste the yummy goodness of my wonderfully crispy taco—which was what I was focusing on so I could keep my face a blank mask.

How many people in this town know you can see ghosts?

I wanted to quip back with something like, "Living or dead?" but I knew better. Instead, I gently set my taco down, got up, and went back to the door. "It's time for you to leave. Less than a minute and you've already worn out your welcome. You must be popular with all the girls."

In less time than it took him to toss a verbal bomb into my living room, I had my door open and had gestured for him to walk through it.

Despite my clear invitation for him to get the fuck

out of my house, La Roux sat down in Hildy's favorite chair and settled in. "Oh, I do okay. Come on, Adler. Don't you want to know how I know you can see ghosts? Don't you want to know if I think you're crazy?" He leaned forward in the chair. "Don't you want to know who I really work for? 'Cause it's not the FBI, that's for damn sure."

La Roux reached behind his back, and my service weapon was out of my holster and drawing down on him without so much as a thought on my part. His hands shot up in surrender. "Whoa, there. I'm reaching for my badge, Adler. Don't shoot me."

Most people got amped up when a weapon was in their hand. They'd get skittish and jumpy. Not me. The weight of my service weapon in my hand slowed everything down, put the world around me in clear focus. My senses went on high alert, even though my heart rate slowed.

"How about you reach real slow, and I'll think about it," I warned, watching as his hand moved to his back pocket again.

Hildy took that moment to begin cackling like a loon. "I'm not helping ya bury him in the backyard if ya kill him, lass. Plus, I have a feeling this one might have friends who'll come looking."

I wanted to tell Hildy to shut up, but I was certain La

Roux was either dicking with me or trying to take me in on a psych hold to get me off the case. Something. He brought his hand back around with the promised badge resting on his palm. Only when he handed it to me did I holster my weapon again.

The black leather holder was unremarkable, but the badge inside was decidedly not. The main emblem matched La Roux's business card, only slightly different. Now that I got a good look at it, I recognized the two triangles positioned on top of each other, crowned with two crescent moons—one larger, one smaller—nestled, facing one another. At the center was an open eye.

And around the symbol were the words: Arcane Bureau of Investigation.

My whole body went cold, but I did my best not to let it show. The absolute last thing in the world I needed in my life was to have the Arcane Bureau of Investigation up my ass. At least with the actual FBI, I could play dumb to the workings of the arcane. With the ABI on the case, all bets were off. I could feel cold sweat break out all over my skin as fear literally leaked out of my pores.

Don't panic, don't panic, don't panic.

I was likely failing miserably at the "no panic" edict if La Roux's chuckle was anything to go by. It was low and mocking, like I was a cute fluffy bunny and he was about to gobble me up.

I'd been trying my entire adult life to keep the ABI out of Haunted Peak. I'd helped covens stay under the radar. I'd cleaned up messes that weren't mine to clean up. Relocated ghoul and vampire nests, and generally tried to keep the peace as best I could. I'd done things I never thought I'd do just to keep them from looking too closely at our small corner of Tennessee.

Don't panic, Darby. He has no idea what you are, right? The ghost thing could be a fishing expedition.

But I wasn't fooling myself. I knew without a shadow of a doubt in my mind that he not only knew what I was, he was here to collect me. I'd be carted off to some black site somewhere and studied. I'd be tortured for information. I'd be dead and gone, that's what I'd be. For a brief —albeit solid—moment, I contemplated drawing my service weapon and shooting La Roux in the head. I could bury him in the woods, and no one would be the wiser.

I must have telegraphed that somehow, because La Roux was up and out of his seat in an instant, his eyes changing color as he did so. The Fed's once-brown peepers were now a glowing green, as black-and-purple swirls of magic bloomed over his palms.

I couldn't help it; I drew my weapon. Only, my gun

didn't stay in my hand. Before I could even think of firing, the cool metal was out of my hand and across the room, the muzzle embedded into the drywall. *Shit.* Without my gun, I was about as good as dead. I didn't have power over the living, and even my abilities when it came to the dead were about as strong as wet newspaper.

I could only talk to the dead—and on occasion keep them out of my house—it wasn't like I could raise an army of corpses to do my bidding.

La Roux took a menacing step toward me, his face a mask of fury. "You were going to kill me, Adler? That's not very 'serve and protect' of you. I wonder what your mother would think."

That caught me off guard. "My mother's dead, asshole. And what the fuck are you? You're no warlock I've ever seen."

La Roux's frown deepened as his magic grew larger, the swirls of it spinning faster as he gathered power. *Shit. Definitely not a warlock.*

"That's because I'm not one." His smile was all teeth as he advanced, his slow, sure movements calculated as he navigated my furniture like he'd been there before. It was all I could do to keep my couch between us.

"You need to run, lass. This mage is not your friend. He'd just as soon kill you, as you him," Hildy advised, but I was still stuck on the word "mage." I knew the arcane world was bigger than I knew, but *mages*? What the hell was that?

"I've had about enough of this shite," Hildy muttered, and then I felt a freezing cold deep down in my bones as he zoomed toward me.

"Don't you fucking dare!" I screamed, but Hildy didn't stop. Oh, no. He shot toward me like a bullet, the impact of his ghostly form hitting me straight-on made me stumble back, nearly losing my feet.

And then I no longer had control over my body.

"What the hell was that?" La Roux asked, but I was too busy fighting for purchase over my own brain to answer him.

"That was me taking over for the lass for a minute. You aren't welcome in this house, death mage. You aren't welcome in this town. It's time for you to leave before I make you." Hildy threatened from my lips, his accent spilling from my mouth in *my* voice. "And don't be thinking you can just wave your sparkly fingers at us and put me out. She is my blood, and I'll be doing what I must to protect her. You aren't taking her. I don't care what your bosses say."

I wanted to pay more attention to La Roux and his reaction to Hildy's words, but I was a little too busy trying to shove his spectral ass out of my brain.

"Get. Out," I growled, shoving at him with all my mental strength. "I swear to all the deities I know of, Hildy. I will banish you from this house and my life. Get the fuck out!"

A ripping sensation yanked at my middle, making me want to vomit. I took it as a good sign and pushed some more. A feeling similar to my whole body being waxed at once, I shoved Hildy out of me, the effort making me collapse on the unforgiving wood floor. Covered in sweat, I relished the feeling of not being possessed.

"You're grounded, Hild," I croaked, unable to pull myself from the blessed ground as I closed my eyes. La Roux was either going to murder me in my own house, cart me off somewhere to be studied, or Hildy was going to repossess me and then everything would go promptly to shit. I had limited control, so what the fuck *ever*.

La Roux spluttered, "Hildy? As in Hildenbrand O'Shea? One of the most famed grave talkers in known history?"

I cracked an eyelid, canting my head to the left so I could peer past my coffee table to see La Roux's face. It was quite a few shades paler than before, and his magic was long gone. "Is he? He's been a little tight-lipped about his origins."

"You're related to Hildenbrand O'Shea." He said it like a statement of fact rather than a question. Yeah, that was news to me, too, but made a lot of sense. Ghosts tended to watch out for relatives if they failed to move on. Either that, or they started to deteriorate and turned into poltergeists. Hildy being as old as he was, he should have gone coo-coo ages ago.

"It's possible. You planning on killing me, La Roux?"

He grunted like he was thinking about it. "I prefer Bishop. La Roux is my coven name."

I did notice he didn't answer me, so that was fun.

"Coven? *Pfft*. More like a pack of mangy death deal-ers. Don't be cozying up to death mages, Darby. They are a bitter, dangerous lot," Hildy advised, but I'd had about enough of his shit to last *allllll* day.

I met his spectral gaze and glared. "You lost the right to be helpful when you took over my body, you ghostly fuck. I'll talk to you later."

"What's he saying?" Bishop asked, his posture relaxing a bit, my ire at Hildy seemingly a form of protection of some kind. Hildy must have been a badass in his day if Bishop was running scared.

"None of your business. Just because I'm mad at Hildy does not mean I'm on your side. And death mage? That sounds... ominous."

Bishop rolled his eyes, plopping down on my favorite chair. "It's not as bad as it sounds. Death mages. Necro-mancers. Death dealers. It's all the same. I can summon souls to do my bidding or reanimate corpses. Occasionally, I can resurrect the dead, but that has more rules than is really prudent, so I don't bother. I can't talk to the dead like you can, though. That's your kind's deal. Grave talkers. Man, you're rare."

I didn't know what was so good about my kind—and rare or not, my abilities weren't much to write home about. So I could talk to the dead. Big freaking whoop. Unless I was solving a murder, this ability wasn't very useful and a pain in the ass ninety-eight percent of the time.

True, the psychics or mediums who said they could talk to the dead were totally full of shit. I'd come across more than a few in my time, and not even one knew about the spirits that surrounded them or could communicate with a single one. I got it—people were trying to make ends meet—but it was rude. Pretend to predict the future for heaven's sake; don't prey on people's dead relatives.

That was just a dick move.

"And I take it my rareness is why you're here?" I prompted, waiting for the veritable other shoe to drop.

"You'd be right. Listen up, little grave talker, I've got a proposition for you."

Groaning, I managed to peel my upper body from the floor. I wasn't hurt exactly, but the lingering effects of Hildy's possession made my whole body feel like it'd been shoved into a washing machine set to spin. Rather than wait for Bishop's likely pandering speech, I reached across the coffee table, snatched the bag of tacos, and started munching.

A proposition meant he needed something. It meant I'd likely have to do a thing I didn't want to do in exchange for another bullshit thing. More than likely: his silence. I could practically see the upcoming conversation play out in my mind.

Yeah, I needed calories for that malarkey.

As luck would have it, the tacos were still warm and crispy and filled with all the delicious goodness that was a half-steak, half-shredded pork, meat and cheese and veggie-filled concoction built to make my taste buds roll over in delight. I really wanted to know who talked to him about my favorite kind of taco. Whoever they were, they would remain on my shit list for a while.

Bishop opened his mouth to speak, but I shushed him until I'd wolfed down two tacos. There had to be silence to appreciate these goodies, and I wasn't going to focus on anything until my belly was at least pulled from the ledge.

Before I unwrapped my third, I motioned for him to continue.

"So that's a thing? Huh. I wondered if the stories were true, but I've seen it twice now," he muttered vaguely, which was annoying as fuck.

"What?" I griped, my mouth full.

Bishop rolled his eyes, sitting back in the chair before bringing up his foot to rest on his knee. "Grave talkers expend an enormous amount of energy just by being around ghosts. It's why you consume so many calories, and why you're perpetually hangry and tired. I'd be willing to bet there are at least a dozen protein bars and snacks in that monster of a bag of yours."

He had me there. My messenger bag was an organized chaos of snack food, girl supplies, and crime scene PPE. I shrugged as a way of saying "yes" before stuffing half a taco in my mouth, around which I prompted him to continue. "You said you had a proposition? Out with it, Death Boy."

The delivery probably lacked the appropriate venom, but it was the best I could do under the current circumstances.

"You've been on the ABI's radar for a while—long before Ezra Dunleavy painted a bright-red bull's eye on your ass. Your efforts to keep the arcane from humans has not only *not gone* unnoticed, there are whispers around the office that you're amassing an army."

I damn near choked on my food. "Yeah, right." I chuckled. "It's all I can freaking do to keep those assholes from killing each other or anyone else. Sure. Amassing an army."

Rolling my eyes, I chomped crispy goodness. At least tacos made sense because this poor, deluded fool definitely did not. *Amassing an army? More like herding cats.*

"Think about it from their point of view. You have an alliance with the local vampire and ghoul nests, the witches owe you a favor, and this town has more than enough dead for you to syphon from."

"You blithering idiot," Hildy muttered, his gaze locked on Bishop. Hildy seemed ready to rip Bishop's head off, and all I could do was stay stuck on that last bit.

"Syphon from the dead? What? No. Sorry, Death Boy, but someone fed you a line. I can't do that, and moreover, why would I?"

Bishop's perpetual frown deepened. "You have no idea." He let out a bitter-sounding laugh. "And they sent me here to scout you. Proof positive the brass is more interested in covering their asses than actual facts." His gaze broke from mine as his eyes scanned the room. "You should have told her, Hildenbrand. You've done her no favors by keeping the truth from her."

I had no illusions that Hildy had kept things from me, but I didn't trust Bishop to tell me the truth, either. Hildy himself was practically apoplectic, and I could tell he was seriously considering possessing me again so he could shoot Bishop. Bet he was wishing I'd have done that before. That's what he got for not offering to help me bury the asshole.

"Why don't you stop blathering on about Hildy and get to the point. Proposition? Out with it."

Bishop clomped his booted foot back down to the floor, leaning forward in his chair to look me in the eye. "Fine. The ABI is looking into the death of Blair Simpkins—specifically who killed her and why. There was a major energy surge reported from this area around a little before two this morning. The surge of power had a radius reaching all the way to Knoxville. It's what knocked out the power to this neighborhood and a few others. Unfortunately, I cannot pin-point what kind of magic was used, nor can I commune with the dead to find out who did this. All I know is, if I can't bring the culprit to the brass within a very limited amount of time, I won't be the only ABI agent in Haunted Peak, and I seriously doubt you want that."

I sighed, setting down my last bit of taco on the crinkled paper. "I'm still waiting on the proposition part. What do you want from me?"

"I can't do this by myself. Scout you, yes. Solve Blair's murder? No. I just don't have enough to go on, and the ME is being more than cagey with me. If she didn't read human, I would have thought she was in on this, but no such luck. I need your help. In exchange, I will tell the brass that you're a grave talker with limited powers and not much influence over the undead. You know, instead of what you really are."

Whatever the hell that meant. I had a feeling his "proposal" was more threat than actual partnership, and considering the vague details he'd provided and lack of a happy feeling in my gut, I was leaning toward a no. Still, I wanted him out of my house, so pandering was necessary.

I pulled myself up from the floor, and for the second time in as many minutes, opened the door and gestured for him to scoot. Reluctantly, Bishop stood, striding toward the door like he had life all figured out.

"I'll think about it," I offered, and as soon as his feet crossed the threshold, I added, "But I wouldn't hold your breath. No, scratch that. Do. Totally hold your breath until I call." With that little quip, I slammed the door right in his face, relishing his shock right before the door closed. It was as satisfying as shooting him would have been—well, almost—and there wasn't any clean-up. Well, except for my service weapon stuck in the drywall.

That would be future Darby's problem.

I yanked it out of the plaster and inspected the Glock. Other than plaster dust, it seemed to be in working order, but I would have to clean it before firing it again. Grumbling, I got my cleaning kit and made way for the kitchen island. This was going to be a two-birds, one-stone event.

I could feel my eye twitching as I opened the cleaning kit, methodically spread out my towel and instruments, and started disassembling the Glock. My eye was twitching, because even though Bishop was gone, Hildy was just floating there like he didn't have the mother of all explanations on the tip of his tongue. I gave him five more seconds before I lost the very last bit of my shit.

Staring him dead in the eye, I volleyed my threat.

"You have five seconds to start talking or I'm banishing you from this whole fucking planet, Hildenbrand."

Hildy appeared shocked, but he really shouldn't have. I'd banished more than one ghost in my time. Hell, he'd been the one to show me how. He'd been the one to warn me off of giving headspace to liars. *As soon as they start lying to ya, lass, you make 'em move on. Nothing worse than a liar. Livin' or dead.* That's what he'd said when I was thirteen years old, when I was eighteen and getting over my first heartbreak, and *again* at twenty-one when I'd kicked my college boyfriend to the curb, deciding to stay single until the end of fucking time.

Why he expected I'd treat him any different was a freaking mystery.

"Five, four, three..."

"Fine! I'll tell you what I know." He groaned long and loud, doing a full-body hissy fit before composing himself. "You were supposed to stay hidden, lass. They weren't supposed to find out about you. I..." He shook his ghostly head, his eyes sad like he'd let me down. "Hello, my name is Hildenbrand O'Shea, your grandfather. Your mother, Mariana, was my youngest."

That... did not compute. He'd said he died sometime in the 1840s. That would mean my mother would have had to have been born sometime before then. And if she was born during the 1840s, she would have been over a hundred and fifty years old when she died, a feat tough for a woman who looked like she was barely pushing forty.

"We age slower than most, faster than some," he offered, reading the confusion on my face. "The only ones who don't age at all are the undead. If you start syphoning power, you'd regress a few years. You'd have more energy, too, but the side effects are not for the faint of heart."

I blinked, my shock getting the better of me. My mother had known what I'd go through, what I'd see. She knew and she never said a word. Did she just run out of time, or did she want to keep her secrets? And how many secrets could she have kept with me seeing dead people all the damn time?

"What are the side effects?" I croaked, not wanting Hildy to stop talking. At that moment I was so mad at my mother I wanted to scream.

Hildy sighed, his breath nonexistent, but the action was one of habit. "There is a reason we're so rare. The ABI aren't the first group to get a bit twitchy around grave talkers, and they for certain won't be the last. Syphoning amasses power. The more souls the bigger the battery."

"That's great and all, but power for what? I can't do magic. I can't cast. I can't do anything but talk to the dead. What the hell am I going to do with a boatload of power?"

Hildy gave me an expression of bewilderment before he started bleating out a laugh so obnoxious, I had to cover my ears. When he finally calmed down, he wiped spectral tears from his eyes. "The fact that you have to ask..." He trailed off, shaking his head. "You don't syphon, lass, so how would you know what you can and cannot do? How would you know what abilities you do or do not have?"

I wanted to ask him what was possible—what I might be able to do if I could bring myself to suck the energy from a spirit. Would it hurt the spirit? Would it take their afterlife away? Would they move on? I didn't know, and that was information I needed to have before I even considered it.

Because I knew without a doubt in my mind, the ABI was going to come for me whether I did it or not.

11

I thought long and hard about the ABI and what they could really want from me as I cleaned and reassembled my service weapon. If I could amass a shit-ton of power, wouldn't it be a super idea to have me as a potential ally rather than an enemy? Because sending out a scout to antagonize me was a great way to make enemies.

Then again, bureaucrats and logic never seemed to mesh too well together.

"I don't think it matters to them whether I have power or not. They're going to see me as a threat regardless. It would be in my best interest to understand what abilities I do or don't have, along with the consequences of them. I've never needed someone to tell me that,

Hildenbrand, and it pisses me off that you think I'm too stupid to figure it out for myself."

Hildy didn't appear even the slightest bit abashed. "You haven't seen what I have, lass. You aren't the first young one I've taught and knowing what we are—what we can do—is something that can't be undone. I've seen many a fledgling consume too much power and burn themselves up. I've seen some amass so much that whole kingdoms have risen against them. You think I didn't trust you, and you'd be right. But I swore I'd do my best to protect you, so that's what I'm doing."

So amassing power was far more dangerous than I thought. Good to know. But that didn't explain anything —at least not really. It didn't explain how old my mother was, or why she didn't tell me about what I really was. It didn't explain if my father knew about the arcane world, or if he was just as much in the dark as I'd been.

It didn't explain dick.

And that was by design, I'd bet.

As I slipped my weapon back into the Kydex holster, I studied Hildy's face. This wasn't his "I have a secret" face or even his "I'm being coy on purpose" face. This was a healthy dose of fear with a little "fuuuuuuucccccc- ckkkkk" thrown in. It made me simultaneously want to pick his brain and bleach mine all at the same time. If I didn't know that Hildy was my blood, if I didn't know that he was my grandfather, if I didn't know that I was a weakling grave talker with no idea of what I could really do—then maybe I could stop picking at those truths like a scab in my brain.

But those were questions to be answered later. Right now, I had a murderer to catch and an ABI agent to send packing.

"Fine. Moving on from that thorny topic, are we helping the mage or not? I'm thinking yes but also no. You? I mean, we're already on the case, so we should definitely help, but also, the someone who killed her put out a power surge big enough to reach Knoxville. Add that to the business card in Blair's hand, and this whole thing does *not* give me the warm and fuzzies. Not at all."

The last thing I needed was this case getting more sideways than it already was, and I had a feeling that would be the only way it was going. Plus, what the fuck was I going to tell J? He wanted to know less about this world, not more. And I had the distinct impression Bishop was a "arcane only" kind of person.

"What we need to do is interrogate that Blair woman. She has to know more than she's letting on," Hildy offered, and I had to admit, it was a solid suggestion.

"Yeah, but I banished her from the house. I made her leave. It isn't like she can just pop back in."

Hildy snorted. "Ah, lass, there is much I still need to teach you. Your mind is the door, the wall, the whatever. Your will keeps her out. Not a spell, not an incantation. If you want her, call her in your mind."

That seemed overly simple and strangely anticlimactic, but I'd give it a shot.

"Close your eyes, think about her walking through your door. Think about her sitting on your couch."

I did what he asked, but every time I thought of Blair walking through my door, I'd get the mental image of me slugging her right in the jaw.

Shaking myself, I tried again. But all I could see was her sneer—the ungrateful set of her jaw as she asked what I did all day.

Groaning, I threaded my fingers into my hair. At some point in the possessed-unpossessed-death-mage drama, it had come out of the pitiful bun I'd shoved it in this morning. "No dice. I'm pretty sure my brain will set itself on fire before it lets her back into this house."

Hildy speared me with a scathing expression. "You aren't trying hard enough. Stop focusing on what you hate about that blistering harpy and more on what you need from her. You need information. Picture her spilling her ghostly guts to you."

Grumbling like a disgruntled child, I did as told, closing my eyes and picturing her in an interrogation room out of an old black-and-white movie. My imagining even had the spotlight I could shine on her face that always seemed to make the perps talk. But when I opened my eyes, Blair was still nowhere to be found.

Shoving up from my barstool, I started pacing the room. I had to figure this out. We needed Blair. We had to figure out who was with her when she died, and what caused the power surge. Obviously, it was a spell of some kind, but I'd never heard of a spell reaching that far. Granted, what I *didn't* know about the arcane could probably fill a whole damn library. Probably several libraries.

I hated to think that Bishop's earlier words were right on the money. Whatever I thought I knew, it wasn't going to be enough.

"If she can't get in here, maybe I could summon her outside the house. Like in the backyard or in the park or something?" I suggested, exhaustion and hunger nagging at me.

Before I knew it, I was digging in the *Sí Señor's* bag to see if I had any tacos left. By some sort of miracle, there were still two in the bag. Not as warm as I'd like, but they were still yummy morsels that could possibly tide me over until I got more food.

Who was I kidding? I was going to be hungry and tired until I freaking died because being around ghosts was literally sucking the life out of me. Grumpily, I munched on my food until Hildy got with the damn program.

Hildy scratched his chin. "The park would be better than anywhere on the property. She'd likely be tied there even if it wasn't where she died because of the spell."

"There is no *if*. I know the park wasn't where she died. There wasn't so much as a speck of blood anywhere in that damn place. Unless the techs found something I didn't, I'm pretty sure she was killed somewhere else, held, and then used as an offering? Sacrifice? Something." It didn't make any sense. Who the hell was in that park, and what the fuck were they doing with Blair?

Rather than talking it out even more, I grabbed my keys and bag and headed to the park, locking up my house and driving the block down the road. Night had fallen in earnest, the streetlights casting an eerie glow on the broken police tape. I wasn't a fan of being out at night—not that I could avoid it with my job.

For someone like me—someone who felt and saw and heard ghosts—the night made death just that little bit closer. The veil that seemed so far away in the daytime was that much nearer, that much thinner. There was just something about the night that brought death front and center. Nervously, I fished the rosary from beneath my vest that I'd yet to take off, clutching the blessed beads in my hand so hard they hurt.

One would think someone like me couldn't be scared. I saw ghosts all the time. Every single day was a parade of specters. And I was a cop. I saw the worst of the worst of the living every time I caught a killer, every time I watched life get stolen and I had to mop up the pieces. I should be desensitized by now, right?

Well, I wasn't.

On the upside, Hildy didn't stay in the house to do whatever the hell he did most days. He'd been right next to me in the car, and he was right next to me as I stared at the broken crime-scene tape trying to gather the courage to summon a ghost in the middle of the night.

"You all right, lass?" Hildy whispered, and I did my best not to jump a mile in the air.

"Fine. Let's just get this done." I worried what someone would say—me being out here in the middle of the night. Would they think I was trying to figure out what had been done to Blair? Or would they think I was more of a weirdo than they already assumed I was?

There was no way to know how the citizens of this sometimes-backward-ass town would talk about me in the morning. And if I could keep the ABI out of Haunted Peak, I didn't really care. Being the weird one kept me out of a ton of social situations I wanted no part of. Solid win for me.

"Close your eyes and visualize Blair walking toward you. Just Blair. We're out in the open here, so there are more than a few that will hear your call. Think of Blair and only Blair." Hildy's instructions were not at all frightening. Nope. Not even a little.

My fingers clutched the rosary tighter on reflex as I closed my eyes. I pictured Blair as I saw her this morning: white nightgown, sigils carved into her flesh, her purpled tongue hanging from her mouth. The filigreed knife in her hand. I called to her with my mind, asking her to come to me. But I couldn't feel her here, or anywhere for that matter. All I could feel was Hildy's gaze on me as he waited for me to do a thing—*like summoning?*—I didn't think I could do.

Scrubbing my face with my hands, I shuddered out a groan. "Why don't you go do something useful. You need to get a look at the sigils on her chest. You said those markings made her different, right?" I prompted Hildy. "Why don't you go to the morgue and take a look. Maybe I can focus without you staring at me."

Hildy didn't seem too enthused to leave me out on my own. If only I could tell J about this shit. If only he wasn't more of a wimp than I was—at least when it came to the arcane.

"If you think that's best, lass. But don't be doing anything cute. Just imagine Blair. We're too close to the witching hour for you to be doing anything else."

"Comforting, Hildy. Real fucking comforting." It wasn't like I was two seconds from coming out of my skin or anything. Nope. Not me.

"The truth isn't meant to be comforting, lass. When will you learn that?"

Rolling my eyes, I shooed him with my fingers, feigning bravado with the best of them. But with Hildy gone, I knew better than to shut my eyes in this dark corner of the park. Haunted Peak had been the site of four major battles in American history; plus, whatever had happened before history was written down on paper. There were ghosts freaking everywhere. Many of them had moved on, but there were more than a few with bones to pick long after their actual bones had rotted to dust.

Which was why when I'd caught sight of a familiar T-shirt and jeans skulking in the tree line, I couldn't help but be comforted just a little. Bishop was out there watching me, and I couldn't bring myself to care that much about the lack of privacy. As long as he wasn't out there to kill me, I was golden.

With that thought, I parked my ass on top of a nearby picnic table, closing my eyes once again as I tried to call for Blair with my mind. Only this time when I thought of her, I actually saw something. There were shadows lurking in my brain, and when I mentally called for her, they moved faster. I caught a mental glimpse of her white nightgown—the same one she'd been dumped in, her dark hair a mass of waves around her elbows.

She flitted about, moving faster than anyone had a right to. I called to her, louder, stronger this time in my mind, so much the whisper of her name left my lips. And then she was right there in my brain, her poor distorted mouth screaming past her swollen tongue. She slashed at me with her knife—the same one that had been used to carve the marks into her chest.

My eyes flashed open, and I nearly fell off the picnic table as I scrambled for purchase in reality. All I could see in my brain was the corpse of Blair Simpkins, so I barely registered the warm arms around me or the fact that my ass was definitely not parked on the wooden picnic table.

"Shh, Adler. You're okay. Shh…"

All too quickly, I got with the program. Blair wasn't here. She'd refused to come back, to answer my call. No, not refused. She'd flat-out tried to hurt me, tried to stop me from calling her.

Also, Bishop La Roux was cradling me in his lap, rocking me like a child as the pair of us sat in the dirt.

12

"You're bleeding."

Bishop's fingers reached for my face, and I scrambled out of his lap to avoid them, finding my feet, even though they were unsteady. I did *not* want him touching me. I did not want *anyone* touching me. Nor did I want to be in this park, and most certainly did not want his kindness.

My whole body was on red alert as adrenaline surged through my limbs. Blair should *not* have been able to do that. No ghost had ever done that to me—never reached me in my mind and attacked. None of this made any sense whatsoever.

Bishop reached for me, but I shuddered away from him. "Darby, you're bleeding. Let me help you."

"Don't." My voice was a scratchy, ragged mess.

"Don't touch me. Don't…" A loud whine of a buzz filled my head, and I couldn't finish that sentence. I also couldn't stand anymore, the world tilting on its axis, hard. All too soon, I found myself with my knees in the dirt, and my hands gripping tufts of grass just so I could stay on the surface.

This was bad. This was soooo bad.

The shadows that filled my mind earlier were coming back, the streetlights winking out as blackness filled my vision.

An icy-cold hand closed around my forearm, the grip shocking me back to the here and now. My eyes popped wide as a flood of warmth crashed into me, even though the hand on my flesh burned—it was so cold. Somehow, my gaze met Hildy's, his ghostly eyes glowing an unearthly shade of blue.

And then I could breathe again, I could hear. The ground was steady under my knees as the clouds rolled back from my mind. Without really thinking about it, I yanked my arm from his grip, goggling at him when the color in his eyes faded.

"What the fuck was that?" I whispered, fear getting the better of me. Hildy had never scared me—even though many other ghosts had—and I was ill-prepared for the instant mistrust that hit me like a sledgehammer.

"That was me saving your bloody life, that's what. I

told you, just think of her. How in the depths of Lucifer's hell did you get cut?" Hildy railed, his shoulders practically vibrating with rage.

I took that opportune moment to get to my feet again. The few steps back I also took were just a precaution on my part. My fingers found the beads of my rosary—the same damn rosary that failed to protect me from Blair. I had a feeling that if Hildy got well and truly mad, it wasn't going to do much against him, either.

"Knock it off, O'Shea. Can't you see she's scared?" Bishop growled. I didn't know when he'd moved so close to me, or when he'd migrated over to my side of the argument, but there he was, defending me against Hildy of all people.

Hildy seemed to shake himself, anger leaking off his face leaving blind terror in its wake. "She cut you, didn't she?"

"I was just thinking of her, and then it turned weird. She was there screaming in my face, and then she slashed at me with the knife—the one from this morning." My fingers found my cheek, the cooling wetness and coppery tang that could only be blood was present, but the cut was gone. "Did you… heal me?"

"Is that what that was? He healed you?" Bishop muttered more to himself than to me, still scanning the air for Hildy, even though it was impossible to see him.

I nodded and then shrugged, my brain still trying to wrap around what had actually taken place. All I really knew was I wanted to get the hell out of this park. But more? I wanted to know why the hell Blair tried to hurt me.

"Yes, lass, I healed you. Well, I forced energy into you so you could heal yourself, but that's not what's important. Whatever they did to her, she isn't like a regular specter. Don't try to summon her again." He didn't have to tell me twice. "And whatever is going on in this town, something is up with the morgue. No matter how hard I tried, I couldn't get into the building."

The County Medical Examiner's office was separate from the municipal building. As far as I knew, Hildy had never had trouble getting in there before. "That's a problem. And a huge red flag if there ever was one. I want to know what sigils were carved into Blair's chest, and I want to know now." Really, I wanted to know what the fuck was going on in my town, but I had to solve this puzzle first. "We need to go to Jimmy's. He took the crime scene photos today. It's possible he hasn't submitted them into evidence."

I was all set to get over to Jimmy's when Bishop said something that made me freeze. "What sigils?"

My whole body rotated of its own accord as I faced him, bewilderment probably stamped all over me. "What do you mean, 'what sigils'?" The markings that were carved into her chest. The symbols. They might not have looked familiar, but I knew what they were when I saw them this morning."

Bishop's eyes widened as his face paled slightly. "Darby, there were no sigils carved into her skin. Yes, she was cut up, but…"

He didn't have to finish that sentence for me to get it. Bishop couldn't see the markings. My gaze met Hildy's. "Please tell me there is some weird grave-talker juju that makes it so I can see strange spells that he can't, because if not, then we've got some major shit going down."

I totally left off the part about how if this shit was more major than it already seemed, then I was ill-prepared and nowhere near equipped to handle said shit. Not at all.

Hildy didn't say anything, but I knew from the expression on his face that his answer was likely a "no."

"We need to see those crime scene photos. Now-ish. I hope Jimmy doesn't mind us popping in to see him this late."

In fact, Jimmy did mind that we showed up on his doorstep at eleven-thirty at night without so much as a single call announcing our visit. Granted, when it came to Jimmy, many couldn't tell when he was annoyed. His face played an excellent game of being open and honest, but knowing him for as long as I had, I saw the secrets there. I saw emotions he tried his very hardest to keep hidden. And I didn't pry too hard into Jimmy's secrets— not unless I thought he was hurting—because I had plenty of my own.

I didn't like lying to my friends. I did it enough by omission every single day.

"Darby? What are you doing here?" Jimmy asked once he finally opened his door, his long blond hair curling in all directions, likely from sleep. "And what's the Fed doing here? What's going on?"

I was doing my best to stare at Jimmy's face and not at the rippling muscles on full display, his shirt likely forgotten in his haste to get to the door. Yeah, J was an idiot not to see the giant photographer for the hot tamale he was.

Shaking my head, I brought myself back to the task at hand. "I need to see the photos from this morning. It's important. Can we come in?"

Jimmy's eyebrows rose so high on his forehead they practically disappeared under his hair; the shoulder-length strands a halo of frizzy curls. He'd used to catch untold amounts of shit for refusing to cut it as a kid, but it had never been shorter than shoulder-length for as long as I'd known him.

"Of course," he muttered, allowing Bishop and I to pass.

Hildy, however, stayed on the porch. "It seems Mr. Hanson's house is not one I can enter. Watch yourself, lass. I don't particularly like it when I can't follow you right now."

I silently agreed, my apprehension rising when Jimmy shut the door. I wasn't sure why, exactly. I'd known Jimmy since we were kids. But if his property was one Hildy couldn't enter, well, with everything going on, I was not a fan.

Jimmy led us to a desk that could only be described as a command center. Four giant computer screens were mounted to the wall in a square. Another drafting computer was off to the side, along with several other gadgets I wasn't sure the purpose of. He plopped onto his desk chair, rubbing his face as he pulled up the files for the day. "There you go."

In the process of pulling up the files, he had flicked a few wayward strands of his hair behind his ear, and I had to ignore whatever it was on the screen as I stared at him.

Jimmy's ear was not shaped like a human one. Not. At. All. They were rounded, sure, but they came to a very distinct point at the top, the outer shell shimmering slightly in the low light.

Bishop elbowed me lightly in the arm, but I could not peel my eyes from the obviously nonhuman hallmark smacking me in the face from a guy I'd known my entire life. I didn't want to admit it, but the fact that he hadn't told me kind of hurt my feelings a little bit.

Not that I could really judge the man. It wasn't like I was screaming my nonhuman status from the rooftops, either.

"Huh. I didn't know there were elves in this part of Tennessee. Isn't it too populated here?" Bishop asked, and both Jimmy and I turned to stare at him.

Jimmy's eyes widened, and his hands flew to his ears, quickly covering them back up as he shot to his feet. "I don't know what you're talking about."

I couldn't help it; I'd been protecting Jimmy my whole life and wouldn't stop now. I volleyed a glare at the death mage. "For the love of *Krispy Kreme*, Bishop. You can't just out someone's nonhuman status like that. You want me to snag a bullhorn and tell everyone you're a death mage? No. You don't. Jeez." I turned to Jimmy. "It's okay, Jim. We aren't human, either. Or at least not all human, anyway."

I added that last bit because I wasn't exactly sure about what I was. My mother was a grave talker—

evidently—but since I had no idea who my birth father was, I could be anything from half-human to who knew what. Vampires and ghouls tended to stick to their own, but there were plenty of supernaturals who mixed with humans. Well, witches and shifters didn't seem to have any bias on that front, at least.

Jimmy cleared his throat as he blinked at me like I was an alien. "I know you aren't." He gave a quick jerk to his head before clarifying. "Human, I mean. I've always known—even when we were kids."

I took a teensy step back. I didn't start seeing dead people until I hit puberty. The first day of my cycle was bad enough, but add in the ghosts, and I thought I was going crazy. But Jimmy had known before I did. Shit. Did everyone know? "Really? How?"

Jimmy frowned at me, his whole face saying he thought I was pulling his leg. "I'm an elf?"

He said it like I was supposed to understand why that explained anything. "Yes, I gathered, but I have no idea what that means, so... How exactly did you know I wasn't..."

Jimmy seemed to understand my confusion. "Many Fae can see past glamours, some can see auras, and some can see magical potential. Elves—unlike most—can see all three. You have a black aura, amongst other things. Only those with death magic have a black aura."

I would have to file all this away for later because it was way too big to process right now. But Jimmy kept going, jutting his chin at Bishop. "That's how I knew he wasn't a Fed as soon as I saw him. ABI?"

Surprise cut through me for the zillionth time that day as Bishop gave Jimmy a no-shit bow, tipping an imaginary hat at him.

"At your service." Bishop gave him an actual smile, and was... polite? "The spell that Blair was used in this morning sent a shockwave all the way to Knoxville. We need to find out what was done before some idiot opens a portal to the Underworld or something. Darby said there were sigils carved into Blair's chest?"

Jimmy gave him a slow blink and took another step back.

I moved forward to comfort the tall man, putting myself between Bishop and him. "It's okay, Jim. As soon as we solve this, he'll be on his way."

If Jimmy knew what I was, he'd probably heard what I'd done for the others in this not-so-small town. Maybe he knew how hard I'd worked to keep the ABI out of here. Perhaps—given our history—he would trust me. At least I hoped he would.

But that wasn't why he took a step back, I quickly found out. "Darby, there weren't sigils carved into her chest." He lifted his chin at the computer screen. "Look."

Each of the four screens was filled with a different picture of Blair's dead body.

Not a single one showed the sigils I'd seen this morning.

That couldn't be good.

13

"Does Jeremiah know about this?" Jimmy asked under his breath, breaking me out of my computer screen stare-down.

There was nothing on the image that suggested anything remotely close to sigils, and it was pissing me off. Still, I yanked my gaze from the screen. "Does J know about what?"

"About you. About what you're doing." Jimmy had had a crush on J since forever. It made sense why he would ask, but I still didn't like it. I didn't want to examine exactly why I didn't like it, either.

"He knows about me, but things have developed tonight that he's not in the loop on. I'll brief him tomorrow." With Jimmy being an elf, I didn't want to tell him just how out of the loop J was on the arcane front. J had always said he didn't want to know. He freaked when I talked to ghosts. He, at one point, even stuck his fingers in his ears and screamed "lalala" at me when I'd tried to tell him about all of this.

Did I want to break Jimmy's heart? Hell no.

Might he be better off not pining after my idiot best friend? Maybe. Only time would tell on that front.

Jimmy didn't seem at ease with my explanation, but there wasn't much I could do about it. I needed sleep. And food. Only not in that order. And I wasn't getting it here.

"Come on, Bishop. Let's get out of Jimmy's hair." I turned back to Jim. "Keep your eyes peeled for weird shit. Something strange is going on in this town, and the sooner we figure it out, the—"

"Sooner the ABI quits sniffing around you?" he quipped, finishing my sentence. "Yeah, I got that. See you tomorrow, D." Jimmy gave me a little two-fingered salute and then we were out the door.

Hildy was waiting on the porch, rocking in one of Jimmy's chairs. I knew he could move objects if he concentrated, but knowing that Bishop couldn't see him, made the act creepier.

"You find anything, lass?" He floated close to me as I trudged to the Jeep. My limbs felt heavy all of a sudden as exhaustion smacked into me.

Sighing, I rubbed my face, trying to wake myself up enough for the drive home. "Nope. We're going to have to go to the morgue in the morning. But first, sleep." I punctuated this with a yawn wide enough to pop my jaw. "Hey, do you think there are any tacos left in that bag? Unlikely, but I'm starving."

I yawned again as I fished my keys from my bag, but they fell from my fingers, jangling as they hit the pavement.

"Oh, no, you don't," Bishop scolded, snatching my keys before I could grab them. "The last thing I need is you driving us off a mountain because you're so tired you can't see straight. I'm driving. I'll even get you some food on the way back to your place where I will be installing a death-proof ward. I don't trust that Blair won't come find you in your sleep. I need you alive, Adler."

Blearily, I frowned at him. That was about as much as I could come up with in the way of ire, and I let him lead me to the passenger side of my Jeep. I knew he only needed me for the case, but it was hard not to read anything into his actions. J totally took care of me—I wasn't discounting that—but it was nice that Bishop was doing it.

Maybe it was because there was the possibility of a romantic future—not that I'd ever act on it—but the possibility was there. It was like a little hope locked away in a portion of me I didn't even know existed.

The part that looked on the bright side. The part that didn't have to hide all the time. The part that held just a tiny bit of opportunity.

Or maybe I just needed a nap. Yeah. That was probably it.

It was the smell of greasy burgers and fries that woke me. Somehow—and don't ask me how—I knew the second there was food in Bishop's hand, because my eyes flashed open, and I snatched the bag from his fingers in an instant. He hadn't even had the chance to roll up his window from the drive-thru before I'd already unwrapped a burger and stuffed a huge bite in my mouth.

At that point, I did not give that first shit that I was willfully shoveling poison into my mouth. Food was food, and if I wasn't so damn tired and slept the whole way here, my stomach would have been yanking on my chain to get sustenance.

Around another bite, I garbled a "thank you," and dug back in. In less than two minutes, the first burger was gone, and I was unwrapping the second. Like a smart man, Bishop had gotten three burgers, a large fry, two apple turnovers, and a shake. He might have gotten vanilla instead of chocolate, but I'd let it slide. When I was halfway through my second burger, I remembered to check the sandwich for pickles. Luckily, there weren't any, but my eyes narrowed of their own accord as my suspicions rose.

I was too tired, so my mouth ran away without my brain and I blurted out my suspicions. "This burger comes with pickles. You have to request that they leave them off. How did you know to do that?"

Granted, I didn't quit eating, but I did begin an epic staring contest with the side of Bishop's face.

His lips pursed as he navigated toward my house, his eyes going squinty as I watched the internal debate play out on his face. Whatever he was about to tell me was *not* going to be the truth. Or it was going to be a half-truth of some kind.

"Let's just say your dossier is thorough enough to include the fact that you're allergic to pickles and most vinegars, you hate the smell of vanilla candles, and you secretly wish you knew how to knit, and leave it at that."

I couldn't do much but blink at him. How long had the ABI been watching me? And if they knew that much, how in the hell was I going to keep them out of my life? Uncomfortable—but still starving—I munched on the fries silently. What else was I going to say? *Please don't look too deep into my life? You probably won't like what you find.*

Yeah, I didn't see that working out too well.

When Bishop pulled into my driveway, it was all I could do to stay in the car until the vehicle came to a complete stop. Only when he shut off the car did I hop out, my unfinished food in tow. He followed me, face abashed but determined.

"Look, Adler, it isn't like I was the one who dug into your life. And it isn't like the ABI is going through your trash or anything. We just have people on staff who... know things. Truth be told, that was about as much as Sarina could glean on you. She says you're murky."

"Sarina?" Yes. That came out of my mouth, and yes, it sounded as bitter and accusatory as a possessive girlfriend. *Someone, pretty please, shoot me now.*

The tip of Bishop's lips tipped up just slightly, but he answered me. "Our resident psychic. But don't tell her I called her that." He mimed zipping up his lips and throwing away the key. "She says psychic is derogatory, even though it's the scientific term, but whatever. She insists on being called an oracle, even though she isn't a blind eighty-year-old with a hunchback." He shrugged, handing my keys over so I could unlock my house. "I try to stay out of her way."

Hildy zoomed past me, the wash of cold brushing my

arm a stark contrast to the balmy Tennessee spring night. "If you're gonna ward the property, get to it. But whatever he does, you tell him to make sure I can stay. I don't have to sleep, so I can keep an eye out."

A part of me considered what it would be like to have a completely ghost-free house. No Hildy. No Blair. No random specters that seemed drawn to me. No one popping in without permission. But the logical, non-tired part of my brain piped up, reminding me that Hildy was looking out for me.

Reluctantly, I relayed Hildy's message to Bishop. I was already over this whole telephone-game bullshit. "I swear, I'm about to give you a dry-erase board and a marker and let you relay your own damn messages."

Even though I still had half a bag full of food, I was almost too tired to eat it. "I'm going to bed. Let him stay if you want or don't. Whatever. I'll see you in the morning." I crossed the threshold before I remembered that Bishop didn't have to be nice to me and managed to turn around. "Thank you for what you did tonight. For looking out. I appreciate it."

Surprise colored Bishop's face, and he was silent for a beat too long. "You're welcome, Darby. See you tomorrow."

With that, I closed the door, trudged to the kitchen to stow my leftovers, and practically stumbled to bed. I just managed to take off the most uncomfortable clothes in existence, changing into cozy pajamas before I fell onto my bed and cocooned myself in covers, falling asleep damn near as soon as my eyes closed.

I was going to murder whoever was knocking on my door. No one would ever find the body.

Growling, I hefted my tired limbs from the bed and stomped to my front door, ready to tear into whoever it was. I didn't care what time it was or who was on the other side. They were mincemeat. Before I could close my hand around the knob, a key jangled in the lock and the lever turned.

J walked right into my house like he owned it, damn near running into me as I leveled him with a glare that could melt steel. "What the fuck, man? Can't a girl sleep around here?"

J seemed equally relieved I was standing there, and so pissed he couldn't see straight. "You didn't answer your phone, and I've been knocking for ten minutes. You scared the shit out of me." At my air of utter confusion, he continued, "Someone put your card on a dead body, for fuck's sake. You're now required to have your phone surgically attached to your person—do you understand me?"

The mystery business card. With all that had gone on yesterday, I'd completely forgotten about it. I let out a petulant groan, and I may or may not have stomped a foot.

Childish? Yes.

Necessary so I didn't snap at my best friend? Also, yes.

Rather than say sorry—because I sucked as a person —I stomped over to the coffee pot and began the process of cleaning the carafe and dumping yesterday's grounds. Hildy sat at one of my barstools, searing a hole into the side of my face with his judgy glare.

"We both know you can move shit. I don't know why you don't help out more. Would it kill you to make me coffee? No, it wouldn't because you're already dead."

"Well, someone woke up on the wrong side of the bed this morning," Hildy shot back. "Don't take it out on me just because you aren't in tip-top shape."

I flipped him off as I dumped new grounds into the basket.

"Why are you flipping off a barstool?" J asked. "And who are you talking to?"

My eye actually twitched, but I resolved that he'd actually asked for it this time. "J, my house is haunted. Everywhere is haunted. I'm flipping off the ghost of my grandfather because he's a secret-keeping dickhead who refuses to make me coffee in the morning."

J's tan face went white as he took three steps to the

side to avoid Hildy's barstool, and I couldn't help but roll my eyes. What a wimp.

"Any other questions before I get my coffee?"

J settled onto the farthest barstool from Hildy, his fists clenching and unclenching as he aimed a rather irritated glare my way. "Yeah. Why did I get a call from Cap at six this morning, telling me that we agreed to work with the fucking Fed?"

As the elixir of life dribbled into the glass carafe, I seriously debated whether or not vodka was an appropriate substitute for creamer.

14

I wanted to smash something. It was one thing for me to tell Bishop that we were working together. It was quite another for him to act all high-handed and call my captain.

"Please tell me you didn't agree to work with that asshole," J growled. If I wasn't one hundred percent certain he was human, I would have worried he was a wolf about to shift.

Even though I was turned away from him, somehow J knew when I winced. Maybe it was the set of my shoulders. Maybe it was the way I refused to answer him. Maybe he'd just known me the longest and had a mental catalogue of my tells. It didn't matter which way you sliced it—J knew the answer to his question almost immediately.

"Darby..." He elongated the last syllable of my name like a curse. "Why would you do that? What happened from yesterday to today that has this fuck thinking he can horn in on our case?"

Bishop didn't say I couldn't tell J about the case. In fact, there were exactly zero instructions given for how I was to deal with my partner. Which meant I could tell him as much or as little as I needed to.

Turning, I studied J. At a glance, one would think he was mad at me—and he probably was a little—but I could see the lines of worry on his forehead. That added to the press of his lips—which only happened when he was really freaked—and I knew I couldn't exactly lie to the man. Not about this. I would just have to woman up and ask him which version he wanted.

Leaning onto the counter, I leveled my gaze with his. "How do you want it? Unvarnished truth or watered-down human version?"

"What?" J shook his head, confused.

"If you want to know, I'll tell you. But you have to answer my question first. Which way do you want the truth? The real reason, or the watered-down bullshit I'm going to have to tell the captain? You can't un-know this shit, J."

I could see the war play out on J's face. I could see it plain as day as if the thoughts in his head were stamped all over his skin. He wanted to know what was going on, but he wanted plausible deniability. He needed answers, but he feared the world that butted up against his. He'd avoided the real truth for so long, I didn't know which way he would go.

And the longer he debated, the more I could feel the bitter pang of hurt rise in my gut. I'd been hiding in my own town, in my own home, in my own skin for so long. It stung not to be able to tell my best friend the truth— not to let him see what I really was.

Not to have a home at all.

I spun back to the coffee maker, busying my hands with making myself a much-needed cup. And if I happened to let a tear or two fall in the wake of J's silence, well, no one would know but me. I didn't turn back to him. I just doctored my coffee—with creamer not vodka—and left him to his internal debate while I went and got ready for the day.

By the time I'd washed my face and gotten dressed, I'd managed to hide the majority of the redness on my face and dried my tears. As silent of a crier as I was, the results were still not pretty. I was a blotchy, puffy, swollen-nosed crier, and no amount of foundation or concealer was going to cover it all. Still, I did what I could before heading back to my kitchen.

J and Hildy were where I'd left them, but we had a

new addition. Bishop stood on Hildy's side of the island, a cup of coffee in his hand as he and J had a silent stare-down. When I entered the room, the tense silence only ramped up as Bishop studied my face.

"Morning." I said it like an accusation, still faintly irritated Cap knew about Bishop and I working together even before I did.

"That it is. I take it you haven't seen your phone this morning?"

I poured myself another cup of coffee—this time in a stainless-steel to-go mug. "I don't even know where my phone is. I fell into bed last night. It's probably still in my bag and dead as a doornail."

"Surgically attached, D," J growled. "I'm not kidding."

I had just enough hurt left in me that it showed on my face as I turned to him. Enough to make him wince. I'd venture a guess I didn't do too well on the cover-up portion of my makeup.

"So, you care enough to make sure I'm alive, but you'd rather avoid the rest?" I asked, my voice calm but brittle. "Because this isn't a case where you can pretend I'm not a freak, J."

Bishop huffed out a disbelieving laugh. "Wait a minute. You're telling me you do this shit on your own? All this time I actually thought you had backup, and you've been wrangling the supes in this town by your-self?" Bishop started laughing in earnest, tears leaking out of the corners of his eyes as his mirth spilled out all over my kitchen.

J and I were not amused. Hildy was even less so, but he'd been silent since I'd come back into the kitchen.

"No fucking wonder," he mused, his chuckles dying down. "No wonder why they've been keeping an eye on you."

J stood, his bulky body seeming to take up more room in my kitchen than anyone had a right to. "D, what's this guy talking about?"

J wanted to know? Well, I'd tell him. "Jeremiah Cooper, meet Bishop La Roux. Bishop here is an agent, not with the FBI, but the ABI. ABI stands for Arcane Bureau of Investigation, a secret government agency that monitors the arcane. Not only is he here because of what happened to Blair, he's also here to monitor me since I seem to have gotten a little too big for my britches for their liking. In exchange for him going back to his bosses and lying right to their face about what I can do, I'm helping him find Blair's killer. There. You're up to date."

J didn't seem too happy when I started, but by the end, he appeared downright ill. "What... what happens if he tells them what you really are? What you can do, I mean?"

I thought on that for a minute. "They could kill me. Or torture me. Or take me to a black site and dissect me. Or put me in a cell and throw away the key. There isn't a sure-fire way to tell." I turned to Bishop. "That about right?"

For what little I knew about the arcane world, I knew that the ABI didn't suffer rule breakers or wave makers. And I was both.

Bishop winced. "Yes and no? They could also offer you a job. But it would be up to management, and some of them don't take too kindly to grave talkers. Too many of your kind..." He trailed off, shaking his head.

It was Hildy who finished his sentence, and I was glad that no one but me could hear him. "Too many of us killed too many of them. Like I said, lass. Whole kingdoms have risen against us. There's good reason for that. We haven't always been the good guys."

This was what I got for assuming Hildy would tell me things when he was good and ready. I was stuck learning my own freaking history bit by bit instead of all at once. Something I couldn't afford to do when I was now around people who knew more about this world than I did.

"So, we solve this, and everything will go back to the

way it was?" J asked, and that bitter wrench of hurt yanked at me again.

I swallowed down the lump in my throat. "Yeah, J. It'll all go back to the way it was."

Rather than wallow, I crossed to the coffee table and began rummaging in my bag for my phone. The battery wasn't dead, but low, and I'd missed fifteen calls and twenty-three texts. Of the calls, J was responsible for fourteen of them. The fifteenth from a number I didn't recognize. Of the texts, J accounted for twenty of them—each of varying levels of threats. Two were from Bishop, telling me exactly what he was about to do and why—we needed access to the body, and Tabitha was stonewalling him. That was problematic already, and I had a feeling we hadn't even gotten the half of it.

And one text was from my dad.

Dad: Even though he's a bastard, I'm glad you're working with the Fed on this one. Love you, Darby. Keep yourself safe.

It was hard not to be pissed, even though being angry made no sense. Why did he think I couldn't handle this? He was unaware of the arcane angle, and yet, he still thought I couldn't deal with a case that didn't appear much different than all the others I'd solved. Why was he more attentive, more worried about this one? And then I remembered the reason J had practically kicked my door in this morning.

The business card in Blair's hand.

I couldn't help but think that business card was less of an attention-grabber and more of an albatross, making sure all eyes were... on me.

Shit.

That was it, wasn't it? How was I going to move in the shadows undetected if I had a couple of babysitters on my ass at every turn?

Answer: I wasn't.

Because I wasn't the worst daughter on the face of the earth, I texted back an "I love you too" before shoving my phone back into my bag with enough force to crush a cereal bar to pulp. Swallowing the scream brewing in my throat, I checked my service weapon, made sure my keys were good to go, and replenished my snacks, tossing the battered cereal bar in the trash.

When I felt a small semblance of calm, I took stock of my guests. Both seemed to be waiting for me to lose my shit—the pair of them on the edge of their barstools like I was going to explode at any minute, and they'd have to take cover.

Bishop was new, so he had a pass, but J knew better.

"I'm not going to dissolve into a fit or anything. You can both stand down."

"You can't see yourself like they see you, lass. The look on your face spells murder better than if you had a bloody knife in your hand. Better school that mask of yours if you're gonna go where ya need to."

Right. We needed to go to the ME's office to see Blair's body. And Tabitha was far too keen an observer for me to be as ragged as I was.

"Fine. I'll get myself together before we walk into the snake pit." I sighed before rummaging into my bag for a non-pulverized cereal bar.

J stared at me with a confused expression. "Snake pit?"

Bishop didn't say anything but raised his eyebrows at me as if he was asking for permission to explode my best friend's fool mind.

I nodded at him.

"I don't know about Darby, but I don't trust your ME. She's stonewalled me at every turn, and Darby's grandfather can't get into the building. That means someone in that building warded it against ghosts— something only a member of the arcane can do, and it is only done on purpose. There are no members of the arcane registered in that building, and surely no members with that kind of power."

Which meant that if my heebies where Tabitha was concerned meant anything, then she was immersed up to her neck in the arcane world with no one the wiser. Yep, that filled my belly with sunshine and happiness. Totally.

But that also brought up another question I wasn't sure I wanted the answer to, but asked anyway, because I was just too damn tired not to. "Registered? Am I registered, or is there some kind of secret decoder ring I need to get first?"

Bishop let out a low chuckle that sent ice running through my veins. "No, Adler, you're not."

But the ABI still knew about me, anyway.

Fabulous.

15

When I first started seeing ghosts—like any rational person would—I assumed I was going crazy. It didn't matter how many fantasy books I'd read or how many episodes of *Supernatural* I'd watched, I knew normal people did *not* see ghosts just walking around everywhere.

I was a late bloomer, hitting puberty like a battering ram at thirteen, unlike my peers who'd experienced the bullshit of Mother Nature a few years earlier. Mom had been gone for three years by that point, and Dad was doing his best, but he probably wasn't as attentive as he needed to be. Which was why I skated by with little sleep, dipping grades, and a bad attitude until Hildy showed up, cane and top hat in hand explaining what I was.

Between J and Hildy, I managed to stay sane, got my grades back up from their slide into the abyss, and managed to hide what I was. It wasn't that I thought my father would disown me or anything. But Killian Adler was a man who required proof, and it wasn't like my mom's ghost was just hanging around for me to get dirt on the man.

And I supposed that was the rub. I'd always felt abandoned in this life—not really knowing what I was or what I could do. I did my best not to blame her. I mean, wouldn't she want to see me? Especially if she knew I could see her, too? Wouldn't she want to talk to me? It was a difficult thing to be mad at a dead woman, particularly when she wasn't there for me to yell at.

I mean, couldn't she have left an instruction manual or something?

Pursing my lips, I studied the glass double doors leading into the medical examiner's office. Unlike the last time I was here, there were no ghosts lurking near the doors, nor were there any on the concrete stairs leading toward the entrance. That didn't mean I couldn't feel the buzz against my skin that heralded a veritable slew of them lurking nearby. Whatever warding that was done to the doors didn't stop me from feeling the specters that clustered inside the ME building like a hive of bees.

I *hated* coming here. Hated. It.

It was bad enough that the entire building smelled like death rolled in shit, but the people—*er, ghosts*—that hung around the place were not the friendliest of sorts. Not that I blamed them, exactly. Typically, if a specter hung around a place like this, it meant their death was either a shock, or they didn't know they were dead.

I tried to stay away from the ones who didn't know they were dead. It was bad enough to tell a family that they'd lost their loved one. Telling someone that they'd died? No, thank you. I think I'd rather dip my fingers in acid or run through a sticker bush backward.

For one, ghosts who didn't know they were dead, did not believe you when you told them the truth. I supposed it didn't help that I could see them, thus proving me wrong. For another, they usually turned violent—their psyche not equipped to deal with the knowledge, making them lash out.

"You okay, Adler?"

Shaking myself, I glanced up, realizing both J and Bishop were standing in front of me, and I was right in the middle of the walkway, frozen like a statue.

"It's the building. She hates it here," J answered for me. I couldn't tell if he did it because he was saving me from answering, or if he was trying to prove he knew me better. It was sad I couldn't tell something like that from my best friend, but here we were.

"Can't you feel them?" I turned my gaze to Bishop, suppressing a shudder. "It's like they're buzzing against my skin. Even through the ward."

Bishop's brow furrowed as he shook his head. "Not like you can. But then again, I don't perceive the dead like you do. I only see them when I'm using them, but otherwise..."

It was tough not to be annoyed on behalf of ghosts everywhere on principle. I was pretty sure my face said as much because Bishop raised his hands in surrender. "I don't make the rules, Adler."

"And they call us the evil ones," Hildy muttered. "At least we actually speak to the dead. All they do is use us and discard us." He was conveniently forgetting the whole "we haven't always been the good guys" bit of truth he'd spewed earlier.

I had a feeling there were plenty of bad people on all sides for the game to be a murky mess of entanglements, but I wasn't going to look too closely at it right now. The goal was to stay out of it, not dunk my head so far in I couldn't get out. Shaking my head at both Hildy and Bishop, I started forward, figuring the ire in my blood would be enough to keep me afloat.

As soon as I opened the door, I realized I was so

wrong it was comical. Without thought, I let the door fall closed without going through it and backed up about ten paces.

"This is bad. This is sooooo bad." I hadn't meant to say those words out loud, but I was solidly out of fucks to give and this was ramping up to be the biggest shit-storm ever.

"What?" J hissed, his eyes darting around.

The few times I'd been in the building, Hildy and J had been with me. Hildy acted like a ghostly bodyguard, keeping the dead from getting too close. With Hildy not being able to get into the building, not only was I going in there without backup, but the hallway alone was filled to the brim. There would be no way I could just walk in there without help.

Swallowing hard, I did my best not to tear up. It was stupid, I know, but they would swarm me, the tendrils of their fingers touching me. And unlike J and Bishop, I would be able to feel it. It was enough to make a girl want to puke.

"They're everywhere. The hall alone is full, and that's not even the bad part."

J gulped audibly. If I could have swallowed without wanting to gag, I would have, too. "What's the bad part?"

"Hildy can't go in with me. Which means they'll

surround me. And I can't do a damn thing to stop them because Tabitha is a way-too-perceptive nosy bitch on wheels with a direct line to my dad." I started giggling, but it was less from humor and more from hysteria. "Also, the hallway is chump change compared to the holding area. Which means my normal level of fucked just went up about a zillion degrees."

I did not want to go in there, and I most certainly did not want ghostly hands on me. Most ghosts were happy to just give you a nod, but the specters in that building were like a freaking zombie horde.

"Jaysus, Mary, and Joseph, Darby," Hildy chimed in. "I've taught you better than that."

He most certainly had not. At no time in the history of him yakking my ear off had he ever brought up what to do against a horde of ghosts. Not once. I was one hundred percent certain I would have remembered that little tidbit.

"No, Hildy, other than shoving people out of my home, you have taught me exactly fuck all, so how about you dial down the bullshit shame? If you have any insight, now would be the time to share."

Hildy rolled his eyes at me, his fist tightening on the walking cane he so often had on his ghostly person. Only I caught a glimpse of the cane's head for the first time—a silver skull with emerald eyes. It made me want to roll my own. But then the eyes on the cane seemed to glow, like Hildy was drawing power from it.

Why would a ghost need to draw power from anything at all, let alone a relic like that?

He saw my inspection, and waved his opposite hand over the cane, making the thing disappear.

Shady, Hilds. Real shady.

"Never mind that. Yes, I taught you how to banish ghosts from your home and from the land, how to shove them away from your person, too. It's the same principle. You think it and they do it."

Sure. Because that worked out so well before.

"I followed that advice with Blair and ended up bloody and feeling like I was going to fall off the face of the earth. Care to be more specific?"

"Please tell me I'm not the only one a little freaked out that she's having a full-blown conversation with a ghost in public," J said under his breath, talking about me like I wasn't even there.

I leveled him with a glare. "I can hear you." *Prick.*

Bishop moved closer to me, adjusting his body so it appeared like I was talking to him and not Hildy. How exactly he knew where Hildy was in relation to me was anyone's guess.

"There. Now no one can tell, and she gets the information she needs." Bishop said it like a scold, like J should be the one doing this shit and not him. Like J should have been the one to back me up.

He wasn't wrong.

J shot something back, but I paid little attention to their squabbling, making sure Hildy didn't just pop out of here when the conversation turned tough. He was good at that.

"I can't be more specific. You have to do it your own way. You have the power. You are in charge. There isn't another way to teach you," he huffed, exasperated at me like this was day-one shit.

This was not day-one shit. This was day-eleven-million shit, and I was not prepared.

I was beginning to see why all his previous students had blown themselves up.

"You are the worst Obi-Wan, ever," I growled, stomping out of our little huddle and heading back for the entrance.

Before I could run away screaming like the coward I was, I shoved myself through the doors, managing to make it a whole ten paces in the hall before stopping. Vaguely, I felt the guys at my back, a welcome feeling since there was nothing but coldness ahead of me.

You think it, they do it. Easy-peasy, right?

Even with the fear clawing up my throat, I managed to close my eyes. In my head, I pictured the ocean of specters parting, leaving a path for me to walk through, unimpeded. Reluctantly, I cracked a lid before blinking both eyes open in amazement. The twelve-foot wide hallway wasn't exactly clear, but they'd actually done what I pictured: the ghosts leaving a three-foot space in the middle of the corridor for me to walk through.

I couldn't believe it. Other than shoving ghosts out of my house or making them leave the living alone, I'd never exerted this much power on this many specters, ever. Granted, I felt like I'd been run over by a Mack truck, and either J or Bishop was probably going to have to carry me out of there.

But I'd done it.

The run-in with Blair's ghost had me feeling weak and powerless—like I had when I was a teen and new to all of this. Now, I didn't feel so... inept.

Well, until Tabitha opened the double swinging doors to the main holding area.

"Well, are you just going to stand there?" she asked, her voice not unkind, but also *not* kind, either. It was like she was trying not to be a bitch, but the inclination was far too strong.

And right behind her, hovering just to her left, was Blair's ghost.

16

"Dr. Holmes," J exclaimed, startling me out of my dumbstruck staring at the ghost hovering at Tabitha's shoulder. He stepped in front of us, allowing me to shake off my shock and put my mask of indifference back in place.

Holy shit. Blair was here. She'd been in this building, unable to get to me when I'd called her. But that didn't make sense, either. If she couldn't get to me, then how had she been able to hurt me?

"Yes, Dr. Holmes. We need to see the body once more," Bishop announced, elbowing me in the arm behind J's back so Tabitha wouldn't see. "A few of the photos didn't capture certain aspects of the scene, and I would like to see the body for myself."

I shook myself, trying to pay better attention to the conversation.

Tabitha gave Bishop a guileless smile. "Absolutely. Captain Stevens called me early this morning to let me know you'd been granted access. I hope there are no hard feelings. Procedure, you know?"

If I couldn't see Blair, if I didn't know better, if I didn't get the heebies every time the woman spoke, I might have been fooled. But the fact that Blair was here made it hard to deny that there was something up with Tabitha Holmes. Something big. I just didn't know how to handle it.

Tabitha led us into the holding area—which was a nice way of saying the room was a giant refrigerator that stored cadavers before they were released to funeral homes. She already had Blair on a slab, her face uncovered—the grotesque twisting of her mouth and swollen tongue difficult to look at.

"What do you make of the slashes at her chest? Were they made with the knife she was holding or something else?" I needed her to pull down the sheet so I could see Blair's chest but had to do it in a way that wouldn't arise suspicion. The last thing I needed was her to figure out I was on to her.

Tabitha nodded, her face a solemn mask as she pulled back the sheet to show us the slashes. "The injuries are consistent with the edge and thickness of the blade. Blair's blood was found on the weapon as well, so it is likely the same one that made the wounds. But you and I both know that isn't what killed her. This poor woman was poisoned."

Tabitha hardly ever spoke in absolutes. It was one of her few redeeming qualities. Granted, it didn't make me like her, but still. Under normal circumstances, she would never give a cause of death until she knew for certain. And the only way she'd know for certain was if we'd gotten the mass spec reading back from Knoxville.

I frowned, and J asked the question that flashed like a neon sign in my brain. "Toxicology is back already?"

Tabitha hesitated, her gaze whipping to J. "Um, no." She tucked a strand of hair behind her ear, rushing on. "But it's obvious. Plus, the wounds were made post-mortem."

All true, but her demeanor didn't check.

J nodded as if he believed everything coming out of Tabitha's mouth, but I saw the difference in his face—it was the mask that fell over his features when he'd pegged a suspect and was waiting for them to trip them-selves up. "Very true. Hey, could you show me the report? I missed a few lines on the scan, and I'd like to have a hard copy."

She seemed to breathe a sigh of relief. "Sure, J. Come with me."

Only when her back turned did I let my gaze fall to Blair's exposed skin. I practically had to bite my tongue so I didn't gasp and draw her attention to us. Hands shaking, I dug into my bag for a pad and a pen.

"Do you see them?" Bishop whispered, careful not to move his mouth too much. He read J's and my reaction to Tabitha, or maybe he had suspected her all along. Either way, I was grateful I wasn't the only one who thought she'd had a hand in this.

I gave him a jerky nod, my hands closing around my pad and pen. It was tough not to just whip it out of my bag and start jotting the sigils down. Why I hadn't done that when I'd first inspected the body, I couldn't recall. Maybe I thought they would show up on the pictures. Maybe they were spelled so I couldn't record them. The possibilities as far as the arcane went were endless.

"I'll help J distract her. You get them down on paper. We need to know what she's doing," Bishop instructed. Like I wasn't already doing that, but whatever.

Like a good little cop, I covertly sketched the sigils in my notepad, copying the curves and loops, the hard slashes, and lines. They weren't like any runes or sigils I'd ever seen before. And I couldn't stop myself from muttering to Blair—whose ghost was still hovering near her feet. "What are they using you for? Do you know anything that can help?"

Blair hadn't said a single word to me since I'd entered, and when she didn't answer me, I glanced up at her ghostly face. Her lips pressed together, and she shook her head "no." The motion reminded me of another ghost I'd met who'd done the same thing, but I couldn't remember where I'd seen her. For some reason it made me feel like the two ghosts were connected.

I stifled a groan and finished drawing the markings, racking my tired brain for the image of the ghost shaking her head at me. Shoving my pad and pen back in my bag, I suddenly felt cold. Blair had moved closer, her hand reaching out to me. My body remembered the last time Blair had "touched" me and I instinctively avoided her touch, shoving her away like Hildy taught me.

But that was my morsel of power, and now it was gone. If I didn't leave now, I might never get out of this building.

"Well, Tabitha, I think we've taken up enough of your time. Gentlemen, if you wouldn't mind?" I announced, pushing through the doors in lieu of a goodbye. Already, I could feel the heat of my nose starting to bleed, the last bit of my lacking strength giving up the ghost. Pun totally intended.

There were too many specters drawing on me, too

many lurking around corners and filling the corridor to bursting. At thirty feet to the door, I started to run, shoving out of the double glass doors like my ass was on fire. The coldness crept at my heels until I was through the entrance, the hot wash of the Tennessee spring hitting me like a wave. A big, beautiful, welcome wave.

But I didn't stop on the stairs—even though navigating them took far too much concentration. I didn't stop until I made it to my Jeep where Hildy was waiting for me. I practically fell into the driver's seat once I'd found my keys, but I left the door wide open so I could bask in the warmth of the day—even though I was doing that with a paper towel on my nose so I wouldn't drip blood all over my clothes.

"What happened in there?" Hildy asked, his concern noted.

I swallowed once, twice before giving up and taking a swig of water. Once that was down, I re-plugged my nose and gave him the skinny, barely managing not to shudder at Tabitha's obvious involvement.

"She's part of this, Hildy. She's part of this, and she's dating my dad."

Hildy was solemn, his incorporeal form flickering just a bit. "I figured, lass. When I couldn't get into the building, it didn't make sense for that to be the case unless whoever was here was doing something they shouldn't. Did you get a copy of the sigils?"

Wearily, I pulled out the pad, turning it so he could see. I was glad I looked up to watch his face because he had a blink-and-you'd-miss-it emotion skate across his features that chilled me to the bone before his whole damn face closed down. At least I knew where I got that from.

"Get rid of that paper, Darby."

After all the trouble I'd gone through to get it? "I don't think so. How about you tell me what it means, and maybe I'll think about it? I know this means something, Hildy. Cough it up."

Hildy rose to his full height. "I most certainly will not. And never you mind what it means. This is some dark magic that you want no part in. Don't look at the markings. Burn that paper. Burn the whole fecking notebook while you're at it."

I sat up straighter, noticing the guys headed my way out of the corner of my eye. "No, I won't. Tell me what I'm dealing with."

Hildy held tighter to his cane, his fingers closing over the skull head as the eyes grew brighter. Hildy seemed to become more solid for a moment, and then he snatched the pad of paper right out of my hands. Before I could do anything, he threw it down on the ground, and with a snap of his growingly translucent fingers, he lit the whole pad on fire.

It didn't matter if we were in public or if anyone could see us—both of which were true. Hildy just grew solid and then... and then...

"What the fuck, Hildy?" I hissed. At the same time both J and Bishop skidded to a stop, J's eyes on the smoldering pad of paper, but Bishop's were on the space where Hildy was.

With another snap of his fingers, the fire was out. "I told you, lass. This is dark magic. I swore to your mother before she left you that I would keep you safe. I swore. I don't break promises. It's high time for you to let this death dealer work out his case on his own. You'd best be listening to me, lass. This is not something you need to be sticking your nose in. Leave it alone." His words ended on a growl, a sound so inhuman, it chilled me to my bones. This was not the Hildy I'd come to know and love.

No, this was the grave-talker version. The almost-villain version. Keeping me safe or not, this was a Hildenbrand I did *not* want to know.

My face must have said as much because his expression turned hurt before he spun away, striding down the sidewalk until he disappeared from sight.

"What the fuck was that?" Bishop breathed, his big

body somehow in the space of my driver's side door. He'd taken the paper napkin from my fingers and pressed it to my nose.

"That was Hildy being an asshole," I muttered, my voice all wonky since my nose was now plugged. "He said that the sigils meant something bad. That we shouldn't even look at them. When I wouldn't burn the notebook, he—"

"Became solid and then did it for you? Yeah, I saw. That makes no sense, Adler. None. I've never seen a ghost do that."

I snorted—which hurt since my nose was plugged, and it created some kind of weird honking vacuum. "You can't see ghosts at all, so what do you know?"

Bishop held in a grin—barely—and replaced his hand with mine on my nose. "I can see ghosts when I summon them for spells. When I control them. Not once have any of them gone solid."

J shoved his way into the conversation. "I've never been so happy that no one comes to this side of the building. No one saw, I don't think."

Well, that was one less thing to worry about. I peered over the side of the Jeep to inspect the ruined pad of paper. Pile of ash was more accurate.

All that work for nothing.

Now what?

17

Despite evidence to the contrary, I wasn't a big crier. This fact didn't stop me from staring at the pile of ash on the pavement and wanting to burst into tears. Luckily, I was still pinching my nose, so by some kind of miracle, I managed to keep the salt water in my head where it belonged.

Bishop cleared his throat, bringing my attention back to him. "If Hildy won't—or can't—help, maybe someone else can. Do you have any witch friends?"

He knew full well I had witch friends. I had a whole damn coven of witch friends. That didn't mean I wanted to ask them about this. Something told me keeping this shit under my hat was the best course of action if I didn't want to end up a ghost myself. But I could call someone who'd remain mum on this whole thing.

"I have someone I can call," I groaned, letting my head fall back on the headrest. This was going to go sideways. I just knew it.

The coffee shop in Knoxville proper was a tiny little thing. Cozy in the extreme, it sported velvet couches and reclaimed wood tables. Nothing matched and yet everything went together. Shiloh St. James—the coven leader of the largest group of witches in Knoxville—sat in a quaint corner booth, the semi-circular couch a deep emerald green. At her table was a giant cup sprinkled with cinnamon and nutmeg, an odd choice for the middle of spring. Tennessee wasn't cool this time of year, but she drank the hot coffee like she was freezing.

Dark-haired and olive-skinned, Shiloh was a level of effortless beautiful I could only wish to be. Her dark eyes and angular features told of Italian or Greek lineage. Given she could speak both languages, it was possible she was both. Either that, or she just loved to study. She had a slew of rings on each hand, an inordinate number of bangles on her wrists, and a curtain of charms at her neck—a look I couldn't pull off, ever. She paired all of that with a mahogany leather jacket—yes, in this heat—a tight, black top, skinny jeans, and tall boots.

She didn't wear a stitch of makeup on her face, but she didn't need it.

It was tough not to be jealous of Shiloh. She knew who she was—what she was—and she had a whole family full of people who were there for her. But then I remembered what happened to the last coven leader and failed to suppress my shudder. Maybe being on my own wasn't exactly a bad thing.

As one of the first people I'd met in the arcane world, Shiloh had helped me stay under the radar. At least I'd thought she had. After five years without so much as a peep from the ABI, I'd thought we'd succeeded.

Given our past, it wasn't too unexpected that she didn't seem too pleased with my company. Bishop and J had refused to let me go in alone after the death mage blabbed about the last time I'd had dealings with this coven. Why, oh, why did Bishop have to tell *that* story? I was way more comfortable with J thinking those witches we'd caught last year were fake Satanists instead of what they really were.

Weaving through the tables, I managed to put a hand up before she could start yelling.

"I know this looks bad." Not exactly the best start to asking for a favor, but here we were. "But they wouldn't stay in the car. Look, I need your help. Please just listen, okay?"

After all I'd done to keep her coven out of the human spotlight, she owed me. Big time.

This was why she settled on glaring at me instead of what I suspected she wanted to do, which would likely be yelling her head off at me.

"Go on." She crossed her arms and legs in the perfect bitch stance. "Darby, please explain why both a human cop and an ABI agent are here. This is not what I agreed to."

That was true. On the phone I'd implied I'd be coming alone. Bishop and J coming was not only a breach of trust, it made me a liar, too. Goodie.

"You know J's my partner. He's just gotten a crash course in what we're dealing with and I trust him. Bishop, however, is nosy and won't leave unless this case is finished, so here we are. He isn't a threat to you —especially since you haven't done anything wrong. It's me in the hot seat, not you."

Shiloh pursed her lips. "Fine, but if I even get an inkling he's getting too nosy, I'm out of here." She said this not looking at me, but leveling Bishop with a glare that spoke of curses and unfortunate ends.

Bishop threw up his hands. "I fully plan on never coming back here after this is through. No need to start lopping off chicken feet or whatever it is you witches do."

Shiloh uncrossed her legs and arms and sat forward in her chair. "I don't need chicken feet to put you in your place, death mage. And don't you forget it."

Was it just me, or were Shiloh's fingers sparking just a little? And was Bishop standing firmer, ready to throw down?

Why, yes. Yes, they were. Fuck.

"Whoa, whoa, whoa there," J rumbled, his calming cop voice in full effect. "No need to get our feathers up. Let's just sit down and have a polite conversation." He slid into one side of the booth and sat down.

Shiloh seemed to be appeased for a moment, so I, too, sat down on her other side, leaving Bishop to sit across from her in the lone chair.

"I'm sure you heard by now that there was a spell done in Haunted Peak—one that had a shock wave reach all the way down here. Well, that spell drew the eye of the ABI, which is why Bishop is here. As soon as we catch the killer, he will be on his way, and honestly, we want him gone posthaste. Something is going down up there, Shi, and it's bad. Bad enough to have my ghostly companions running for the hills."

She sighed, running a hand through her waves as she sat back. "We heard about it. It has quite a few of my people running scared, too. That kind of magic isn't used for happy things, but when we looked into it from our end, we couldn't find who'd done it. There are a few of our coven members up there, and no one has said so much as a peep."

That was what I'd figured. I didn't have an "in" with the Knoxville coven members that resided in Haunted Peak. The two I knew of were reclusive and unfriendly. Granted, there could be more of them that I *didn't* know about. Shiloh wasn't freely doling out a shit-ton of information, much to my dismay.

I nodded. "There were sigils drawn on the body. They don't show up on camera, and I seem to be the only one who can see them. If I drew a few for you, could you tell me what the spell is used for?"

Shiloh's brow pulled into a frown. "Maybe? There has to be cloaking magic on them if you're the only one who can see them. It makes me wonder why you and no one else."

Shrugging, I pulled a paper napkin from the dispenser and began to draw what I could remember. After the first sigil, Shiloh slapped the pen out of my hand and dumped her coffee on the napkin.

"Don't write that ever again. Do you hear me, Darby?" she hissed before shoving at J until he got up. "Move, damn you!"

In the commotion, our table upended, the shattering of the cup ringing through the little shop. She weaved through the tables faster than anyone had a right to, and then she was out the door. All three of us were on her heels, but it was me who somehow caught up to her, snagging her jacket before she could get into her car.

"Please," I huffed, still trying to catch my breath. "Tell me what's going on!"

Shiloh shook off my hand but didn't get into her car. "That magic is too dark to speak of. You know how people say if you speak the devil's name he appears? Well, what you wrote isn't the devil, but the magic in that sigil alone is bad enough."

I stood straighter. "That was carved into a dead woman's chest, Shi. I need to know what's going on so I can stop it."

She moved back, opening her car door. "You can't, D. As reluctant as I am to say this, it might be time to call in the cavalry. I don't want the ABI anywhere near us, but if it's what I think it is, this isn't something you can do on your own. Stop digging, and if you had any sense, you'd get the hell out of Haunted Peak."

"I can't," I whispered. "They know about me. All about me. They see me as a threat."

She knew exactly who "they" were. One of the first things Shiloh had drilled in my skull was that the ABI were bad news. Magic's very own version of the Gestapo. They might believe they were the good guys, but she and I both had seen plenty of regular members of the arcane just poof out of existence, all traces gone at the ABI's hands.

There was nowhere I could go. Nowhere I could run to if they decided I was a threat. Not without doing some shady-ass shit that would likely send me straight to hell.

Shiloh groaned, tossing her head back and stomping her foot three times. I knew what that meant. She'd just cast a working that made anyone around us conveniently disinterested in what she was about to say. That meant she was going to spill real dirt.

"If you absolutely have to do this, I'd take a gander at Whisper Lake and the people who live there. I'm sorry, but that is as much as I can tell you." She reached out and squeezed my shoulder. "Be safe, Darby. And think about calling the cavalry, would you? There's brave and there's dead. Don't be both."

With that, she slid into her two-door sports car and got the hell out of there, leaving me freaking the fuck out in the coffee shop's parking lot. I knew someone who lived on Whisper Lake. A someone with ties to Blair.

But why would Suzette want to kill her best friend, and moreover, what ties did she have to the arcane world?

In the middle of my freak-out, Bishop and J moseyed on over, likely hanging back to make Shi more comfortable.

"Did she tell you anything?" J's words seemed hesitant, like he almost didn't want to know.

I huffed out a laugh. "Yeah, she did. But you aren't going to like it."

I honestly didn't want to tell him. I had an inkling of what I'd have to do to get the info I needed—the info that would get the ABI off my back and Bishop the hell out of my life. Not that having him around was too much of a hardship. If he didn't work for the magical version of a nefarious governmental agency, we'd likely be BFFs. Well, that was a stretch, but I wouldn't overtly hate the guy.

But I was about to have to do some shady shit, and I gave enough of a crap about J to want him to have plausible deniability.

"Because you aren't coming, Jeremiah. Not if you want to stay on the right side of the law."

I never called J by his given name. He claimed it was too biblical, and I just thought it was a mouthful. Still, he knew I meant business.

Too bad he wasn't going to listen.

18

"What do you mean I'm not coming?" J thundered, his voice echoing off the nearby brick buildings and drawing eyes to us.

I moved closer to him, shushing him as best I could. "I'm about to do something that will get my badge yanked out of my hands faster than I can blink if I get caught." I swallowed hard. It was a wonder why I was a cop at all. Half the things I did, no good cop would be able to stomach.

I had a healthy respect for the law, sure. But I cared more about people. I cared more about what was right. Sometimes laws were put in place to keep people down rather than build them up, and I just wasn't that kind of cop. Neither was J, but this was different.

"And how much of that shit have you done without me? Doing things you shouldn't because it meant people were safer?"

That wasn't a question I expected him to ask. Not at all.

"How many times have you gone out into the fray without me watching your six, D? I thought..." He trailed off, shaking his head, his fingers clutching at his hair. J's lips turned down, his bottom lip heavy with emotion. "How many times have you gone out there alone, unprotected, because you wanted to save me an uncomfortable conversation? Or save my job? Or my fucking ego?"

The answer? A lot. Nearly every case we got nowadays had something to do with the arcane world. More and more, that world was colliding with ours—it was almost more than I could keep hidden.

I didn't say that, though. J was quietly tearing himself up, and all it took was one inane comment from Bishop to make him see.

"I'm not letting you go out there alone again, Darby. I know I haven't been a good partner for you. I know I've been too up my own ass to see that you were struggling. That stops now. I'm coming with you. Maybe... maybe I can actually do some good."

I was about to tell him that he could come if it was

that important to him—a bitchy comment to be sure, but I didn't do emotions too well—when my phone vibrated with a text. Huffing, I yanked it out of my back pocket. I'd missed several texts and a few phone calls from Jimmy, but there was one that caught my eye before I could read his.

Dad: 911. Get to the house. Right now.

A flash fire of dread skated over my whole body. Dad never called for a 911 unless it was an actual emergency.

Instead of speaking, I flipped the phone to show J. "I have to see what he needs. How about you guys go and talk to Suzette. Make it a little more of an interrogation and less polite conversation this time. Shiloh said something was up with Whisper Lake and the people who lived there. I got the straight-up heebs when I was in Suzette's house, and the ghost in her den pretty much said her alibi was bullshit. Get her to talk. When I'm done with my dad, I'll meet up with you."

Hope bloomed across J's features, and I let it warm me for a second before I turned to Bishop. "I don't know what's got everyone running scared, but it has to be bad if Shiloh won't even talk about it. If you can't get Suzette to talk, we may need to call in your friends."

Bishop gave me a grave sort of chin tip—like he

respected me and knew I was willing to call in the cavalry—as Shiloh had referred to them—if need be. Even if it meant I wouldn't be safe.

"You watch out for him. If he gets spelled on your watch, I'm sending Hildy after you. You got me?"

Bishop laid a hand over his heart. "I give you my word. I will do everything in my power to return your friend to you."

I supposed that was as good as I was going to get.

The drive up to Haunted Peak was quick—either because I wasn't following the posted speed limit, or the traffic was just nil—and I pulled into my childhood home's driveway less than an hour after my father's text. Before I even got out of my car, I could tell this 911 call was about to turn into some bullshit. Tabitha's silver BMW was parked beside my dad's Lexus, the shiny sports car a blight on an already shit day.

Like walking the damn gallows, I trudged to the front door, wincing at whatever I was going to find.

Please don't be naked. Please don't be naked. Please don't be naked.

But the door opened without a hitch, and there were exactly zero ass cheeks on display. No, Tabitha and my father sat in the front room, their hands clasped together.

I swear to god, if they're announcing an engagement, I will vomit all over this floor.

"Come in, Darby," Tabitha cooed like she had a right to. Why the fuck was she telling me to come into my own damn house?

Still, I did what I was told, my hand itching to reach for my service weapon. I didn't trust Tabitha on a good day. After all I'd seen at the ME building, after Blair? That trust was in the negative.

Even though their hands were clasped together, even though they were sitting there like everything was sunshine and roses, just one glimpse of my father's face had me aching to shoot Tabitha in the head on general principle.

Killian Adler was a blond powerhouse. At over six foot three, he usually towered over most people, his solid bulk intimidating whether he was in a suit or in jeans. His bright-blue gaze was typically laser-focused, like he was seeing everything you would ever be with one glance. But he didn't look that way now.

No, his face was gray, his eyes dimmed, his shoulders hunched. And he wasn't holding Tabitha's hand, she was latched onto his. Tabitha had either spelled him, poisoned him, or something else.

"I said to come in here, Darby," she ordered, her voice harsher than I'd ever heard it, but it was laced in threads of a command that meant she couldn't possibly be human. Especially since I couldn't stop my feet from moving at her insistence. Without another option, I walked further into the room, my eyes darting to all the exits and windows, plotting an escape. As much as I wanted them to, my fingers refused me, failing to reach for my gun, failing to do anything but hang listlessly at my sides.

Tabitha tsked at me, her tongue clucking like I was a naughty child. "No need for that. I'm not going to hurt you. I just need to make sure we understand one another is all."

Her voice took on a Southern accent, one that had never crossed her lips before. I tried to think of when Tabitha had come to town. Had she always been here? Had she moved here? Where was she from? "You've been a busy little bee, haven't you? Palling around with that silly little ABI agent. I appreciate you keeping him busy for me. It made getting everything in order smooth as butter. You know, I had no idea you were as powerful as you are until you copied those sigils down in your little book."

It was tough to figure out what to be most afraid of. On one hand, we had Tabitha who was either the grand poohbah of witches or she was something bigger, older, and far more dangerous. On the other, she was spewing arcane shit right in front of my dad. A dad that might be spelled but could still hear her since he flinched like she'd electrocuted him when she started talking about me.

"You seem to know all about me, but I'm at a disadvantage. What are you, Tabitha? A witch? A mage? A succubus?"

She tossed her head back and laughed at the last one, her curls bouncing around her shoulders. Succubi were rare, a lower-class demon with limited powers of persuasion, they feasted on the sexual energy of those around them. Which seemed harmless until you figured out that they also incited sexual energy in their victims, too, and sometimes their feedings turned deadly.

"No, I'm not some low-class demon. You poor, uneducated child. This is what you get when you don't do your research."

Condescending as ever.

"Enlighten me, then," I shot back, my tone probably way too big for my britches, but it was all I had. My feet still wouldn't unstick themselves from the floor, nor would my legs move even an inch.

Tabitha shook her head. "Better not. It'll spoil the surprise later. I called you here for a reason, Darby."

"Well, get on with it then. If you're going to kill us, I'd rather not suffer through a monologue if you don't mind."

Tabitha's smile widened like I'd said something truly funny. "Oh, I'm not going to kill you. There's no call for it. After this is all over, the ABI will do my dirty work for me, keeping my hands pristine. No, I'm here to keep you occupied." With that, she stood, her abrupt motion startling me enough that I managed a single step back.

I yanked on my feet with my mind, but they wouldn't move. Neither would my hands.

The tell-tale sound of a knife being pulled from its sheath had me trembling in my frozen stance. Tabitha yanked a curved, crescent-shaped blade from a hidden pocket of her skirt, the wicked knife stamped in familiar sigils.

"You said you weren't going to kill us," I accused, as if the murdering woman would keep her word.

Tabitha's giggle was the thing of nightmares. "Oh, honey. You really must pay attention. I said I wasn't going to kill *you*. I said nothing of your father. Really, it's a shame. Killian was such a good lover and a fabulous little birdy in my hip pocket. It was so easy to pin death after death on unsuspecting people with him on my side."

My dad managed to lurch away from her, his back

hitting the back of the sofa. But he didn't manage much else, still frozen in her thrall.

Tabitha grazed the knife down my dad's cheek, not drawing blood, but showing she could if she wanted to. "Oh, don't beat yourself up, lover. They actually committed the crimes you charged them for, they just required a little incentive is all. I couldn't be doing my own dirty work, now could I?" She turned to me with a sickly-sweet smile. "Well, I did put your business card on Blair. That kept you and your little friends busy for a short while."

Before I could respond, she pressed a kiss to my dad's lips, like she was kissing him goodbye. When she lifted her head, she gave him a sad sort of smile. "It really is too bad." She sighed.

And then she slashed at his chest with that wicked knife, the blade digging deep as a red "X" bloomed over his starched shirtfront.

I couldn't hold back the scream that clawed its way up my throat. "Dad! Daddy! Please!"

I vaguely recalled Tabitha giving me a little finger wave as she practically skipped out of the room, her thrall lifting almost as soon as she left. As much as I wanted to go after her, there was no way I could leave my father.

His big body slumped back, his wounds pouring

blood—far more than I would expect from their placement. I yanked the blanket off the back of the couch, pressing it to his chest as I tried to figure out what to do.

"Jaysus, Mary, and Joseph," a welcome Irish accent called, and I spared him a glance before turning back to Dad.

"You're going to be all right. Okay? You hold on for me. I'm calling for help." I practically laid on him to press the blanket into his wounds as I reached for my phone.

"Lass," Hildy called. "Lass!"

"What?" I shouted, my shaking fingers slipping on my touchscreen as I tried to dial 911.

"You don't have much time. Say goodbye to him, lass. He isn't going to make it to a hospital."

A wave of aching despair slammed into me. I couldn't lose him, too. I couldn't.

"Please, no. Please don't make me," I sobbed, my fingers sliding more on the touchscreen and failing to dial the correct numbers.

A cool hand rested on my shoulder, and I stared up at Hildy's somber expression. "There's nothing to be done for it, lass. He's leaving. You can feel it, too. Hug him. Say what you need to."

I let my gaze meet my father's, his face gray with

blood loss and shock. He was scared—like everyone was when they were dying, I suspected. "It's okay," I whispered, trying to be brave for him. My voice trembled, but I figured he didn't mind. "There's nothing to be scared of. Once you move on, you'll see Mom again." *Unless he stayed here.* No. He shouldn't have to stay. I wouldn't let him linger. He had to move on. "I'll be okay. You don't have to worry about me."

Dad shook his head. "She's not..." He trailed off as a wet-sounding cough bubbled up his throat. "Can't go. She's... not..."

Dad's eyes rolled back in his head, his body lurching like he was being electrocuted.

Then he was still.

And that's when I started screaming.

19

"**G**et Bishop."

How those words came out of my mouth, I could only guess. How I even had a voice was a mystery. How the whole of the police force wasn't busting down the door, or the world wasn't burning down around my ears was, too. How did everyone not know just how much had gone wrong in such a scant amount of time?

How was I breathing right now? How was the world turning?

"What do you mean, lass?"

My head whipped to Hildy. "You know good and well what I mean, Hildenbrand. Get. Bishop. He can fix this."

Hildy shook his head, his face resolute. "I won't do

that. He can't bring him back without a price, Darby. He must exact a cost for something like that."

Heat and rage and the urge to set fire to everything and watch it burn suffused me. "I don't care." I seethed through gritted teeth, still holding onto my father like I could prevent his soul from going anywhere if I just hugged him hard enough. "Get him. I know you can. I know you can do more than you've ever shown me. Get. Him."

"You don't know what you're asking, lass."

"And whose fault is that?" Hildy's visage went blurry as tears swam in my eyes. "Bring him to me. Now. Or so help me, Hildenbrand, I never want to see you again. You and my mother can just fuck off into the great beyond together."

Shock colored Hildy's face, and he reared back like I'd wounded him. He shook that off soon enough, bowing slightly to me. "As you wish."

Then he blinked out of sight. I didn't know if he was actually moving on or if he was doing as I'd asked. Either way, I hugged my father closer, burying my face in his cooling neck as I sent a prayer to whoever was listening for help.

I couldn't say how long it was until I heard the running of feet. Minutes? Hours? Days? All I knew was that my father was cold in my arms, and I'd stopped crying at some point.

"Darby?" Bishop's voice filtered into my brain before a pair of hands pulled at my shoulders. "Are you hurt? What happened?"

He pulled me harder, yanking me away from my father's cold body as he assessed me for injuries.

"I need your help," I croaked. "Ta-Tabitha did this. She..." I couldn't finish that sentence. "I need you to bring him back. I don't care what it costs. I don't care what I have to do. Please." I latched onto his strong hands, mine sticky with my father's blood. *"Please."*

A knowing sort of expression flowed over his face and was gone in an instant. "That's what he meant," he muttered. "I can't do that, Darby. Not without a cost."

I shook my head, my fingers tightening on his. "I don't care what the price is. I'll pay it. Just tell me what it is." For a brief moment, I wondered how many times he'd been asked to bring someone back. I wondered how many times someone had used him the same damn way I was right then. "I know this is big. I know. But she took him. It wasn't his time. He doesn't deserve this."

I was pleading now, spouting nonsense. Didn't everyone deserve death's cruel hand? Wouldn't everyone feel it one day? I knew that better than anyone, and yet I

198 | ANNIE ANDERSON

was still here pleading for my father's life as if it were mine to bargain.

"The price is another life. To restore him completely, you would have to kill someone, Darby. A life for a life. This is why I don't do this—why I haven't in a very long time. I won't ask that price of you."

Shakily, I wiped my face with the back of my hand as I reformed my code of honor in my head—molding it to what I was now. Something new, something altered, something vengeful. I let it still me, let it wash over me like a caress. I could be this new thing. I could toss everything that I was away and be this person.

"How much time do I have?"

Bishop sat back on his heels. "For what?"

I chuckled wetly, my mirth as fake as Tabitha had been. "To take the life. How much time?"

And then it was his fingers tightening on mine instead of the other way around. "You're going to kill her, aren't you?"

Damn straight I was. How many people had she murdered right under our noses? Five? Ten? Twenty people? A hundred? "She's been spelling people to kill for her for who knows how long. She murdered my father right in front of me. She set this up because she's going to do something up at Whisper Lake. Fuck knows what, but it has to be big. If cold-blooded mass murder is beneath her, what the fuck do you think she's up to up there? Knitting booties and scrapbooking? She has to be stopped. Before it was going to be handcuffs. Now it will involve a bullet. How much time do you need?" I repeated my earlier question with far more force than necessary when asking for a favor.

I knew Tabitha's life wouldn't be the only price I'd have to pay. It might also mean my own.

Bishop blew out a breath and stood, striding away from me only to come right back. "If I do this... No one can know, okay? If someone at the Bureau finds out, I'm dead. Like all the way, soul put in a mystical shredder with zero chance of saving me, dead. You, too. This is major—fucking with fate on an epic scale, major—and if you think I won't require a favor from you, you're dreaming."

My smile was sad as I nodded. "I knew that before I asked."

"More like demanded, but whatever. If I can't revive him before midnight, I won't be able to bring him back. That gives us eight hours—tops. And if someone finds the body..."

"This whole thing goes tits up, yeah, I got it." With more relief than I likely had a right to feel, I stared at my father's motionless face. "Can you hide him? Can you make it so no one will find him? Just until..." I didn't finish that sentence, but the meaning was there. Until we either stopped Tabitha and got him back or lost everything.

"Yeah. I can do that."

I wanted to look at him one more time, but I didn't get the chance. Bishop's magic rose within him, the crackle of it high in the air as swirls of black and purple raced over his hands. In a flash, my father was gone—his blood, his body, everything. Just gone. Even the blood on my hands was hidden from view.

"The spell won't last for more than twelve hours, so don't expect it to be pristine tomorrow. Also, you should change and get cleaned up. Humans won't be able to tell, but all it takes is for one member of the arcane to sniff you out, and then we have a whole other mess of problems. And I'm driving. Hildy popped into J's car and just yanked me out. Even if he didn't wreck his freaking car, he's on his own. I don't want him walking into an ambush."

Nodding, I got up and handed over my keys. Time was not a luxury we had.

I didn't exactly remember the drive to my house, but I figured that was to be expected. Time jumped in fits and starts, until I found myself under the spray of my shower. Only then did I really get my shit together enough to focus. After setting a land-speed record for the fastest shower and change in history, I met Bishop back in my living room. I'd barely cleared the entryway when he tossed a necklace at me. I just managed to catch it before it smacked me in the face.

Not exactly the best start if I was about to go kill a murdering bitch, that was for sure.

"What is this?" I examined the black beaded necklace, the pendant a glowing purple diamond-shaped stone.

"Power. You don't have any. Hildy won't tell you how to get some, and we need as much as we can get if we're going to stop this woman. Or women. I have no idea if Suzette's involvement was coerced or not. And even if it was under duress, she's likely still a threat."

These were all the same thoughts I'd had when I relayed what I knew from my run-in with Tabitha. The flash of her blade still streaked across my brain every time I thought of her name, and I had to shake my head and push past the memory—for now. I had to remind myself that if we made it out, Dad would be alive again.

He would be here, and she would be gone.

I just didn't know what was so important about that damn lake.

"Did you call J? Is he safe?" I looped the amulet over

my head. Immediately, aches I didn't know I had, eased. I wasn't a hundred percent, sure, but the damage Tabitha had caused wasn't going to be erased with a piddly little necklace.

"It's going straight to voicemail. What kind of weapons do you have in this joint? Guns are great and all, but if we're going up against witches with enough juice to stop a grave talker in their tracks, we're going to need more than bullets."

Damn Hildy. Damn him straight to the fiery depths of hell. "I don't know what you think I can do, but bullets are all I've got. I can see the dead, and sometimes I can push them away from me. That's it. Whatever Hildy could do in his hey-day is not on my list of skills. I have guns. I have a few knives that are blessed by a priest, and a rosary that seems to have lost what little power it had. Other than that, I'm out."

Bishop pinched the bridge of his nose like I was giving him a headache. "How in the hell you've survived this long is a fucking mystery. What was Hildy teaching you all this time? How to twiddle your thumbs?"

I sighed, my breath coming out in a loose interpretation of a chuckle as I checked the mag on my service weapon before moving to my backup. "Hildy hasn't taught me much. Mostly, he just sat there running commentary on my life and making funny faces at J. I think he was watching out for me. Who the fuck knows? I sure don't."

"If this is the best you've got, it's going to have to be good enough. Let's go before he gets into trouble. I can't believe Hildy just ripped me out of the car and left," Bishop griped, his hand closing over the door handle.

I shoved my service weapon back in its holster, checked my backup, and then tucked the amulet under my T-shirt. But when I glanced up again, Bishop wasn't headed out the door.

No, he was backing up. A dark-haired woman had her finger in the center of his chest, like one wrong move from him was going to bring the fires of hell as her wrath.

Her pale-bronze skin practically gleamed in the low light, her brown eyes flashing like winking bits of amber as her ire rose around us.

Bishop let out a nervous chuckle. "Hiya, Sarina. How's tricks?"

Sarina's eyes narrowed on him like she knew exactly what he was doing and *exactly* what he was going to do —which was likely the case since she was a damn psychic.

Sarina turned her irritated glare onto me. "You two are in way over your heads."

Tell me something I don't know.

20

"**I** could have sworn I told you that my ass would be on the line if you fucked up down here. That I could be demoted or *worse*."

Sarina removed her finger from Bishop's chest, but that didn't stop him from taking a giant step back from the tiny powerhouse of a psychic. Or oracle. Whatever, I just didn't want to piss her off. I had enough problems.

Bishop huffed, crossing his arms like a petulant child. "It's not like I had a choice. You try working with this one." He jerked his thumb at me. "I spent more time trying to keep her alive than I did investigating."

It was tough not to be offended. I had been on this case a day and a half and I'd already found the woman—or women—responsible.

All it took was her revealing herself and murdering your father. No big deal, right?

My inner voice was a real bitch sometimes.

"Don't even," Sarina shot back. "You had nothing to go on. Darby did all the legwork on this case, and you know it." She met my gaze again, hers sad this time. "I'm sorry for your loss, Detective Adler."

My eyes welled, and it was all I could do not to flop on the floor and start bawling.

You don't have time for this. J needs you, and Tabitha needs to pay. Get moving.

"Are you here to stop us?" Yes, that question was valid, but it was also said like a threat. The tone of my voice was enough to warn her not to. I didn't even have to say that if she tried, it wouldn't go too well for her.

A ghost of a smile flitted across her lips as she tucked a shoulder-length strand of hair behind a heavily pierced ear. "You know, Adler, I like you. I think we're going to be friends."

"Super," I deadpanned. "We can braid each other's hair and talk shit about people later. I need to go kill a bitch and save my human BFF from certain death. You standing in my way or coming with us?"

She snorted, and Bishop groaned. "Oh, she's coming all right. She wouldn't miss this shitshow for the world. Right, Sarina?"

Sarina chuckled before turning on the heel of her combat boot. "Of course. You know how much I like watching things explode," she tossed over her shoulder.

"Explode?" I squawked, my hand landing on my sidearm without much thought on my part.

Bishop shook his head. "Don't ask. She won't tell us the future and it'll only piss you off. Trust me. I ignore her about ninety percent of the time."

I had a feeling that was to his own detriment, but who was I to judge?

Following Bishop out of the house, I turned to lock the door, the mundane task enough to nearly make me cry. How did everything get so fucked up that turning a key in a lock was enough to bring me to tears?

We didn't have time for that.

I didn't have time for that.

I swallowed hard, stuffing all my emotions down into an iron ball in my gut where they damn well belonged. If we made it through this, I could cry later.

"Please tell me you're going to do that death mage, voodoo shadow-walk bullshit. I've been dying to try it," Sarina insisted, latching onto Bishop's sleeve like they were besties. Just a day ago I was marginally jealous of the faceless Sarina. Now with her here, all I could think about was that her current chipper mood made me want to smash shit. I didn't even think it was jealousy at that point.

It was pure despair and fear.

"What do you call it again?" She tugged him by the sleeve to the side of my house, away from the street.

"Shade jumping," he muttered. "But it's daytime."

Sarina rolled her eyes at him. "You know full well you can conjure darkness. Quit being a baby and do it." Her gaze drifted to the side, like she was listening to something far off. "We don't have much time."

Abashed, Bishop nodded before his irises began to glow with the light of his magic, the swirls of inky black and deep purple wafting up his arms as he reached for the sky. All at once, storm clouds formed overhead, ready to burst and drench us all. Then he reached for us, latching onto our arms as he pulled.

My entire body felt like it had been doused in glacier water, as we leapt from one bit of shade to another—moving faster than anyone ever had a right to. The world raced by us as we jumped, the trees and buildings blurring into one big blob of color.

When Bishop finally let me go, I fell to my hands and knees, retching when my stomach failed to catch up with the rest of my body. A flash fire of adrenaline hit me, my skin too hot and too tight, and the world too slow and too fast around me. Like when Blair had cut me, I was holding onto tufts of grass like they would keep me on the earth. Only this time, they actually did, the cool blades a welcome to my now-overheated skin.

"I never want to do that again," I croaked, the world spinning just a little too fast for my liking.

"What in blazes are you doing with a psychic, lass? I brought you one agent, and you return with two?"

I glanced up at Hildy's concerned-yet-judgmental face and promptly flipped him the bird. "I'm finishing what I bloody well started."

"There she goes again, flipping off air," J muttered, and it was a toss-up if I wanted to flip him off, too, or hug him because he was alive for me to hug. At least he was breathing and unhurt, and Tabitha's murdering, sadistic fucked-up ass hadn't taken him, too.

I went with option two.

"Thank god," I whispered into his shoulder as I attack-hugged him, squeezing him tight enough for him to grunt.

"What's all this? I swear this day could *not* get weirder. First, Bishop just disappears into thin freaking air. Then, the car just freaking died and I had to pull over. After which, a no-shit tree branch came swinging at me out of nowhere, shoving me back into the tree line. What kind of random-assed bullshit is going on here?"

My chuckle was wet as I squeezed J tighter, my carefully crafted strength cracking with relief.

"I came back to watch out for him, lass. I didn't want you to lose him, too." Hildy's face was grave, a clear reminder of everything that had transpired over the last hour.

I mouthed a "thank you" over J's shoulder before letting the big lug go. "That was Hildy keeping you out of trouble. This isn't a picnic we're walking into, J. It's bad. Real bad."

I couldn't go on, the tears raced up my throat faster than I could stop, and I had to walk away for a moment. To his credit, Bishop stepped up to the plate and told J what I couldn't. He told him what Tabitha had done—to my father and to the people in this town. I tried to compartmentalize. I tried shoving it down. But I was failing miserably.

Dad was all I had left.

The sob that left J's throat was a thing of nightmares. The arms that wrapped around me from behind less so. "We'll get her, Darby. We'll get her."

Fucking right we will.

I sucked in a huge breath. "Did Bishop tell you what I want to do?"

"He sure did. We're getting him back, D." I felt more

than heard J's answer, his permission. It gave me that little bit of strength I needed.

I stood taller, pulling away from my childhood friend. "Then, let's go."

"I wouldn't go that way," Sarina called, her voice pitched low, but carrying all the same.

J and I turned back to her, listening to a psychic was a new thing, but we had a habit of bending an ear to people who knew more than us.

"What do you know about Tabitha? Do you know what she's planning? How we can stop it?"

Sarina's smile was rueful as she shifted from foot to foot. "Yes, but a lot of it's classified." She threw up a hand to stop me before I even opened my mouth. "I know it's bullshit. I know. But there are parts of this case I cannot speak of. As in, if I do, I could die. The ABI does not like whistleblowers or secret-spillers, and I've been spelled to never divulge. However, I will tell you what I can."

The ABI spelled her so if she told a secret, she would kick the bucket. That seemed harsh. Why not just spell her so she couldn't utter a secret instead?

Sarina plucked that thought right out of my head and answered my question. "Oh, I'm spelled that way, too, but if I ever work around it—by word or deed—it's curtains for me. If I tried just telling you, I'd end up puking my guts out and passing out face-first in the dirt. Trust me, they make you try just to make sure the spell works, and it is a gaggle of giggles, let me tell you."

I blinked really hard at her, super uncomfortable that the psychic was also a telepath.

"Sorry," she mumbled. "Force of habit."

"Quit stalling, Sarina. Tell us what you can so we can stop this bitch from taking any more lives. We're on a time clock here." Leave it to Bishop to get us back on track.

"Right! So, the most I can tell you is that Tabitha is an ousted member of a regional coven. Ousted for reasons I cannot divulge, by the way. Anyway, she is trying to raise a being from the depths. And I think that's about as much as I can tell you."

I blinked really hard one more time before my brain started functioning again. "You mean like a demon?"

Sarina sighed. "I can't say. Not because I don't know, because I do, and if you knew this tea you would be losing your shit. But really. I can't say."

Hildy sidled up next to me. "Can she say how to stop Tabitha? Because that would actually be helpful."

Again, before I could open my mouth to ask, Sarina began answering me. As weird as telepathy was, it was a mighty time-saver.

"Yes and no. I know we'll need to interrupt her spell,

but how we're going to do that is fuzzy. The outcome isn't set, so I can't tell you how it all goes down. It's probably because you're involved, but..." She trailed off, shrugging.

If she could read my thoughts, why couldn't she see my future? And why did Bishop tell me I was blurry to Sarina? Did it matter right now?

I stared past Sarina and Bishop, catching a glimpse of gray silhouettes weaving through the trees. Beyond them was the tree line, and past that was the road that led to Whisper Lake. A lake that hadn't even been there until I was a child.

What could Tabitha be raising? It had to be a demon, right? And how in the blue fuck was I supposed to fight a demon? It wasn't like I could shoot the son of a bitch.

I strode closer to the incorporeal gray figures that flitted through the trees. The specters were headed in the direction of the lake.

Whatever Tabitha was doing, it was there. But we knew that already. She had to be calling them to her, right?

And what was she going to do with the ghosts when she got them?

21

"What is Tabitha?" I stared at the mass of specters traipsing through the forest like see-through zombies. "A witch, a demon? What?"

"A sorceress," Sarina answered. "With a major affinity for the dead. Or at least that's my best guess. She's not registered, so she's never been tested. When she was with the local coven, she was under a false identity. A pretty good fake one, too, if they didn't catch her right away."

Sorceress, enchantress, whatever. They were all just pretty words for "witch," with a little razzle dazzle thrown in. And witches could be stopped—their spells, too, with enough power tossed into the break. I nodded to Sarina who'd started chuckling to herself.

"Razzle dazzle," she muttered, shaking her head. "I'll have to remember that one."

"Keep out of people's private thoughts," Bishop scolded, narrowing his eyes. "We talked about this."

"It's not my fault they aren't warded. It's like hearing a radio on full volume. It's bad enough she's blurry as fuck, but she's also loud as fuck, too. Excuse me for taking some pleasure in her humor. Jeez."

"If everyone could stay on task," J growled as he pinched the bridge of his nose. "Darby, why are you asking? And no, Sarina, I want to hear it from her, not you."

Sarina snapped her mouth shut, huffing.

"There are ghosts everywhere, headed toward the lake. I think she's going to use them for something, drain their power, maybe?" I was spitballing, but that theory made the most sense.

J nodded, but it was Hildy who spoke up. "She's trying to raise a being that shouldn't be. She'll need the dead to power the spell, and then he'll eat whoever's left to become whole again. Jaysus, Mary, and Joseph. Why can't they just leave well enough alone."

If tapping my foot or threatening Hildy would do any good, I would have, but I knew it would do exactly fuck all. He knew a lot more than he was saying, yes, but I couldn't dwell on each tiny betrayal. No, I needed to know what to do.

He wanted to keep his secrets? Fine.

"Can I convince the souls to leave? Can I shove them away like I did in the ME building?" I tried to work a problem that seemed to have no real answer.

"It's possible, lass. You'd have to get closer without her seeing, though."

I nodded, relaying Hildy's vague solution to the rest of the gang. I was tempted to tell J it was time for him to bow out, but one look at his face told me not to. Like Sarina, he seemed to read my mind, and shook his head at me.

"I might not be like you," he began, stating his case before I could contest it, "but I can do some good. I'll stay out of the way, D, but you need backup. I don't trust anyone but me to watch your six."

How in the fresh hell was I supposed to say no to that?

"Fine, but if you die, you'd better not haunt me," I huffed before wrapping him in a hug so tight he grunted.

Bishop and Sarina took point, the pair of them leading us through the forest as we stayed parallel to the road. They planned on moving faster than us around the lake to get the lay of the land. That, I had no problem with since the thought of doing another shade-jumping jaunt made me want to hurl.

J and I moved at a steady clip at first but had to slow soon enough. Specters were everywhere, their grayed-out see-through bodies filling the open spaces, so much so, it was hard to walk around them. Soon they filled every space, and I couldn't go any farther, the peak of Suzette's cabin mansion visible just past the trees.

Beyond that was the lake and whatever they were trying to raise from the depths.

But being around this many specters was starting to take a toll. Already my nose was dripping blood. And, I was now near the point of passing out from the pull of so many so close.

"I can't go any further," I croaked, my knees nearly buckling under the strain of all the spirits.

"Ya can, lass. All you need is to go a little bit more, then you can push them away like I taught you." Hildy's cold touch pulled at my arm as he dragged me closer to the cabin. I felt the power from his grip, the slight bit of energy filtering into me as I took another step. I could feel J at my back, ready to catch me if I fell.

My feet found themselves on the edge of the black-top, the mountain road crumbling at the edges as it fought against nature encroaching on its space. I was in a sea of spirits, their faces turned toward the lake as they stood silent, waiting.

"Try, lass. Push them all back like I showed you. In your mind, tell them to leave, to go back where they came from."

And I tried. I did. But when I closed my eyes, all I saw was Blair. Her swollen tongue, her purpled mouth, the sigils carved in her chest. My eyes flashed open, and I took a step back.

"I can't." Shaking my head, I stumbled backward, aching for the cover of the trees. "Blair is in my mind." I tapped my temple with a shaking finger. "She's in there, waiting for me. What have they done?"

"Fecking witches and their blasted games. They've made Blair into their shade. Witches used to do that ages ago when they needed a protector to help them carry out their spells uninterrupted. Did she cut you, get your blood?"

We both knew that Blair had cut me, the healed flesh of my cheek practically burned with the memory. My hand flew to my face.

"Lucifer's bleeding heart. She did. Damn and blast. And I can't do this for you, because if I get too close to that damn spell, I'm done for." Hildy latched onto my arm again, pushing a little more power into me so I could stand on my own two feet.

"I thought I told you to get out of town?" a woman's voice called from behind me.

I was lucky it was a voice I knew. Shiloh St. James stood atop a fallen log, her high-heeled boots gone, replaced with laced-up combat-style shit kickers. Her collection of amulets glowed in the low light, their magic shining with use. At her hips were a pair of daggers, and across her back was a legit, honest-to-god, double-sided ax. I had yet to see Shiloh roll into battle before, and the sight was equally awe-inspiring and terrifying at the same time.

At her sides were two women, both similarly attired—only sans the ax. At her left was an Amazon of a woman, her bronze bald head adorned with the thick lines of tribal tattoos. Banded across her front was the string of a bow, a quiver at her back. At Shiloh's right was a redhead with skin so pale it practically glowed in the dark. Red had a lighter in her hand, and she kept clicking it open and flicking it closed like she was aching to light something ablaze.

"Sorry, I couldn't fit it in my schedule." That joke probably would have landed had my voice not sounded like I was gargling glass.

"This is witch business, Darby. I kind of figured my warning would be good enough."

I almost wanted to start laughing. Did she think I would be here unless I didn't have a choice?

"I take it Tabitha was the sorceress ousted from your coven, then? I really wish you would have told me when I fucking asked you, Shiloh. I really wish you had." Grief bubbled up my throat as tears stung my eyes. Quickly, I blinked them away, shaking my head as I stood taller, turning so she was at my back.

I had to figure out a way to get these ghosts out of here without Blair slicing me to ribbons.

"Killian—her father—is dead." I heard J murmur, his hand tightening on my shoulder as I stared out at the cabin. "Tabitha killed him right in front of her. We need her alive, so if your plan doesn't include that, I'm afraid you'll have a fight on your hands."

I chuckled mirthlessly. As if a fight from us would do any good against a whole coven.

I had no illusions that just Shiloh and her two friends were the only witches in this forest.

"I'm sorry, Darby. I didn't know about her being here until you showed me that sigil. We—my coven—buried a dark entity here almost two decades ago. Dumped a whole lake on him to keep him down. Had houses built so no one could live here, aside from those of us sent to make sure he stayed down. It's our job to make sure he doesn't rise. I can't say any more than that, I'm sorry."

That tracked with what little information Hildy and Sarina had provided. But that also meant that Suzette—or her husband, the mayor—were potential members of Shiloh's coven.

"I don't need to know what he is. I don't need to know why he's here. I need to know how to stop her while keeping her alive so I can kill her at the appropriate time. That work for you?"

Shiloh blinked at me. "You're trying to bring your father back?" She seemed shocked, but I had no idea why. She knew full well he was all the family I had.

I didn't answer her, letting my silence speak for itself.

She gave me a stiff nod. "We'll do what we can. I make no promises, Darby. If it comes between keeping her alive or keeping him down, you know which way I'm going to go. Letting him rise will start the end. There is no room for failure."

I could accept that. Don't get me wrong, I didn't want to. But the logic of it all was too much to ignore. I was selfish enough to want Tabitha dead and my father back. I was not so selfish to let everyone else die, though.

"What I want to know," J began, his voice a low growl, "is whether or not Suzette Duvall is a member of your coven. You said all the people who live on this lake are your people, right?"

Shiloh hopped off the log, her compatriots following her. "Yes, both she and her husband are our people."

"Then I think you've got an internal problem," he drawled, pointing at Suzette's front door where a bound and gagged mayor was trying to run away. Both Suzette and Tabitha bounded out of the house, catching up to the poor man without much effort. The pair of them shoved and prodded and outright kicked him until he went where they wanted him to go, which seemed to be toward the water.

"Huh. Well, fuck," she muttered, drawing her ax. "That explains some things."

I snorted. "Shiloh, when all this is done, and the ABI aren't breathing down both our necks, you and I are going to have a conversation."

Shiloh's grip tightened on the handle of her battle ax. "Sure. I'll pencil you in after we stop the end of the world. Cool?"

Assuming we lived that long.

22

"What's the game plan here?" I asked, my gaze locked on the fleeting backs of the struggling trio.

It was tough not to chuckle at the utter absurdity of the situation. J and I were the cops, and Shiloh and her friends weren't. But I knew I was without a doubt outgunned in every aspect of this shit. I was pretty sure J knew it, too.

"That depends on who you ask," Bishop piped in, drawing my eyes to him. He and Sarina stood at the tree line, seeming to pop in out of thin air. Likely the case if he was shadow jumping or shade walking or whatever the hell he called it.

Red, Shiloh's right hand, began snarling at the death mage. "We don't need your kind here. We're already doing what we said we would. Take your stupid badge and go back to your bullshit holier-than-thou sandbox and kindly leave us the fuck alone."

I wanted to laugh—I really did—but the world was going dark. Wait. No, I wasn't passing out. Storm clouds ballooned out of nowhere, blanketing the setting sun as the thunder rolled in.

Startled, Bishop stared up, glanced down at his magi-cless hands, and then turned to the lake. "Look, I don't mean to be the mansplaining asshole of the group, but do you see those clouds? Do you hear that thunder? That isn't me. Their spell is already starting, and we're dicking around out here instead of stopping them. So how about we work together so we can all go home, hmm?"

Lightning crashed into a nearby tree, sending us all diving for cover. Half of the obliterated pine hit the dirt not a moment later, the smoldering carcass nearly hitting our little group.

"Whatever ya'll have planned, you'd best be getting started," J muttered.

"But be careful," I warned. "Tabitha made a shade out of Blair and she has my blood. I can't stop the spirits from gathering. I'm figuring that's a bad thing."

"She shouldn't be here at all," Red muttered in Shiloh's ear. Well, muttered was a strong word for the blatant way she said it like I wasn't freaking there. But it wasn't like I could blame her. I mean—what purpose did I serve?

"She's the only one who can see the dead, Katrina. We need her," Shiloh's bald coven sister insisted. Again, like I wasn't there. I was tempted to look down at myself to check if I was actually invisible.

Hildy moved in front of me, stealing my attention. "Ya can't make it through, lass. Whatever these witches are doin' you can't be part of it. You need to leave. You don't have the power to make it through."

I wiped at my nose again, chuckling at the ridiculousness of it all. "You either need me to help keep him down, or not. You either need me here, or not. I can either help, or I can't. Fucking pick one, Hildy. And when you do, why don't you tell me how I'm supposed to go in there with no power against a sorceress with hundreds of souls to power her spell? Moreover, how am I supposed to live with myself when these people get blown to kingdom come? Riddle me that, you ghostly fuck?"

Hildy opened his mouth to probably spew some bull-shit, but I stopped him before he got started. "Don't. Unless you have a way out stashed away in that damn top hat of yours, you may as well save it. I'll figure this shit out on my own."

Gathering my meager strength, I flitted my gaze to the swarm of souls gathered around the lake before turning to Shiloh. "Start whatever it is you're going to do. I'm headed that way." I jerked a thumb over my shoulder. "I'll push back the souls I can, take the heat off of you and yours."

Hildy, J, Sarina, and Bishop all squawked at me, but I didn't listen. No, I was too busy wading through the icy touches of specters, their ghostly arms grabbing at my skin, my hair, my arms. They clung to me, pulling, scratching. Their touch eroded my strength, my nose dribbling blood as I felt the cloying, coppery tang hit my tongue.

It didn't matter if I had Bishop's amulet around my neck or the blessed rosary, either. The ghosts were angry, and their touch was so cold it burned like acid.

"Bloody well fine, then!" Hildy barked, his form so close to me his words echoed in my ear. "If you're going to be a child about it." I heard a boom, boom, booming of power hitting the ground, the warm tendrils of it filtering up my boots, through my toes, filling me with fresh air and life.

And then I could move. No, not move. *Move.*

Breathing the first real bit of air since I stepped foot in this forest, I darted toward the water, following the lightning strikes and swirling clouds to the shore of

Whisper Lake. The beach was filled to the brim—with not just ghosts.

Oh, no, that would be too damn easy, wouldn't it?

Dotting the sand were people I knew—townsfolk I'd passed in the street, people I was friends with in passing, and a few assholes thrown in for some spice, I guessed. Each one stood motionless, alive, and breathing but turned off like someone had scooped out their brains somehow.

They all faced the water, their hands at their sides like they were waiting for something.

As soon as my feet hit the silty sand, I figured out real quick what they were waiting for.

Me.

The man closest to me let out a primal scream once my boots hit the sand. Reaching for me, the pudgy, bespectacled man raced my way, ready to tackle. I'd started out as a beat cop—we all did—so I was familiar with this kind of attack. Honestly, one would be surprised at how many drunk men tried to full-body tackle a female cop.

But I didn't want to hurt the man too much. I mean, I was pretty sure this was my butcher. No way was he part of this. I couldn't just shoot the dude. Instead, I let him come, catching his arm as he almost passed me and tossing him over my hip. He landed flat on his back in the sand, and I felt good about myself for about half a second. Then, I got knocked to the ground by the next guy, his attack slightly more stealth since I was dealing with Butcher Dude.

I ate sand, the weight of him shoving me into the wet shore before I could get an arm free to knock his lights out. Scrambling up, I nearly got mowed down again when J came to my rescue—his football glory days being put to good use as he flying-tackled what looked like a legit frat boy in a U of T jersey.

"Please explain why we're doing nonlethals," he huffed, shoving himself up from the sand.

I fought the urge to roll my eyes. "Because these people are likely spelled to do her bidding. Just look at their faces."

By faces, I really meant eyes. Each of the people we'd taken down had all-black eyes, the whites of the sclera gone. Even the unmoving ones that I assumed were knocked out, still had wide-open eyes as if they were frozen like that.

A banshee screech heralded the approach of a woman, her mom-bun and lounge pants a testament to the fact that Tabitha had called her right out of her morning routine. And then it wasn't just us clashing with the people on the beach. Both Bishop and Sarina tackled them, blowing white powder in their faces.

As soon as the powder hit their skin, the towns-people dropped like stones, their all-black eyes open, yet unseeing.

With the living problem squared away, I could finally concentrate on the dead one—or rather dead *ones*. The spirits waited, their ghostly eyes fixed on a point at the center of the lake. I, too, cast my gaze that way, not at all shocked to see Tabitha and Suzette at the center of all this mess.

Situated in the middle of the small lake was a floating dock, a tiny fishing boat moored to a post. And atop that damn dock, just barely visible in the low light was a circle of dead flowers with the damn mayor in the center.

There had never been a time I did not remember Dunstan Duvall being Mayor of Haunted Peak. He'd been in charge of our town since I was a kid. My mother had even been his right hand once upon a time. Now that I knew he was an integral member of the local coven, it wasn't much of a surprise that he and my mother were friends. He'd been a young mayor—maybe thirty when he first got the post—which would make him in his fifties now. He wasn't exactly a looker, which meant—at least to me—that Suzette either married him for his money or there was another reason.

Given the fact that she was currently anointing his

body with oils like she was going to freaking sacrifice him, I had an inkling what that other reason was.

All at once, I could hear the faint strains of chanting filtering through the trees. Whatever the coven was doing, they'd started their work. In response, Tabitha reached for the heavens, pulling power from thin air as she gripped an unseen force and pulled it down. Like she'd struck a match, the flowers in the center of the dock and all the water in the lake ignited, a sea of flames reaching for the heavens.

J and I stumbled back as the fire lashed at us, the damp beach now an inferno. The water receded inch by inch, slowly at first and then a little faster as the flames burned up the lake. But after my ass hit the dry sand, I became entranced by the fire, watching it dance and play.

For some reason I wanted the water gone. I wanted to meet the thing they were trying to free. I wanted to tell him my secrets.

Sarina grabbed my arm—she and Bishop yelling in my face as they tried to tell me something. Only when J dead-armed me did I shake the cotton out of my head.

"What the fuck was that?" I croaked, struggling to focus on J's face.

"You can't wait any longer," Sarina insisted, talking

to Bishop as she held me up. "Tell her what Hildenbrand will not. He cannot be set free."

Sarina and Bishop locked gazes, seeming to have a silent argument as I hung from Sarina's grip.

"Tell me what?"

Bishop blew out a breath, his face a frantic mess. "I know how you can draw power—from the souls. If you take the souls from Tabitha, she can't draw on them. There isn't another way."

The debate that warred in me was quick. On the one hand, it needed to be done and the logic of it was sound. On the other... I'd be painting a target on my back—or at least a bigger one.

I didn't exactly plan on much past getting my father back, so I supposed it didn't really matter.

"Go for it. Tell me what I'm supposed to do."

Hildy's Irish burr sounded in my ears. "I'll be asking you not to do that, lass." He moved then, shoving Sarina and Bishop away from me as I crumpled in the sand. "Listen to me now. If you do this, there is no goin' back. You will lose everything you love—everyone you love. You will consume it all and burn yourself up. Please don't be making me break my promise, lass. Please."

"I have to," I whispered, pleading for him to understand.

Hildy nodded at me, crouching himself so he could

look me in the eye. "Then I'll be the one teachin' ya," he insisted. "Go to that quiet place in yourself, the place where there is no fire, no light. No sound. Call to the dead. Tell them to come to ya, to fill ya. Ask them to be at peace. Draw them in. When the cold goes away, stop." His eyes filled then, his cold hand cupping my cheek. "That's all I can tell ya, lass. I hope when I see ya again, you're still breathin' on this side."

And then he faded out of sight, leaving me to choose my fate.

23

The sand caressed my skin as I dug my fingers into the shore. Latching onto anything I could reach, I felt little comfort in the fragile grains that shifted with my every movement. I wanted something a bit more substantial, but like everything else in my life, the moment I had it in my hands, it was gone.

I watched the fire of the lake dance for a single, solitary moment before I closed my eyes, mentally reaching for the souls that littered the beach like debris. Hildy had said to clear my mind of sight and sound, but that was impossible. One never thinks of it, but fire was loud. The world itself was loud. Even so-called quiet had a noise to it, like a ringing or a calling—a singing of a song I could never really make out.

There was no such thing as silence.

I beckoned the woman closest to me, her tiny frame and clothes telling me when she'd passed. I saw her clearly in my mind, like she was waiting for me to call her. She abandoned her perch at the water's edge, coming to me without question. She reached for me—which I usually hated and ran away from—but this time, I managed to stay put. Instead of touching me—she seemed to fall into me.

It felt like being electrocuted and healed all at the same time. Power raced down and out from my chest, filling me, fixing things I hadn't known were wrong, healing aches I hadn't even known I'd had.

A litany of her life slammed into my head. Her name. Her favorite thing. How she'd died. And all the rest. Helen loved her little sister and her garden, but hated her cousin, Zachariah. He was mean, and cruel, and hurt small animals for fun. He'd hurt Helen, too: murdering her in her garden and burying her under her heirloom roses.

But Helen wasn't the only one to hear my call.

The woman who reached for me next was a mother who'd died of sepsis a few days after she'd given birth to her third son. June named him Michael after her father, and her favorite smell in the world was the scent of Michael's hair after his first bath.

A man fell into me after June, a sour soul turning my stomach. Linus had never been married, never wanted a family, and given his life as a child, I was glad for it. His favorite pastime was to accost women on the streets, and if one were walking unsupervised, he would make her regret it. I gagged when he filled me, the rotten core of his soul making me taste bile.

The next was a soul of an older man, Geoff, who'd lived to a ripe old age and passed surrounded by his grandchildren and great-grandchildren. He was following his wife to the hereafter, but no matter where he looked, he couldn't find her. He hoped wherever he was going, he'd see her there.

And then Blair found me, her swollen tongue, her blackened lips. She slashed at me with that cursed knife, but somehow, some way, I managed to catch her. At my touch, the fight fell away, and then she, too, fell into me. Blair hated her husband and her mother. Hated Suzette and everything she stood for. Blair hated a lot of things. In fact, there wasn't too much on this planet she did like except for driving with the windows rolled down and the radio blasting. She'd always wanted out of this town—where people didn't know her or her family. Where she didn't have to keep up the façade of queen bitch. The whispered words of "thank you" hit me as she sighed in relief, grateful she wasn't being used anymore. By anyone.

Quickly, the next soul found me, and on and on it went until it felt like I was burning up from the inside. What had Hildy said? *When the cold goes away, stop.* Well, I'd stopped feeling cold after the first soul, and I'd lost count of how many souls had followed the first. Twenty? A hundred? Two hundred?

I was without a doubt certain I had just royally fucked this up. My insides felt like the surface of the sun, the power roiling under my flesh aching to get out. If I held onto it, I was positive I would burn up just like Hildy had warned.

This was too much power for anyone. And whatever this thing was that they were trying to raise, it needed this much to become whole.

My eyes flashed open, the world brighter, the sky closer, the wind whipping in a maelstrom around the lake as the fire raged on the surface. Trees broke in half, sand pelted my skin, and J, Bishop, and Sarina were holding onto the earth as if any second, they might blow away.

And I was floating.

The air around me, along with gravity, were no match against the energy coursing through my veins. My hands all the way up to my biceps were glowing white, like an iron in a too-hot fire. J and Bishop were screaming at me, telling me to stop whatever it was that I was doing, but I wasn't the one doing this. Okay, the floating and glowing thing, yes. But the wind and fire and rapidly evaporating lake? Definitely not.

No, Tabitha's spell was working. Meaning, I hadn't taken all the souls for myself, no matter how full of power I was. I'd only taken the ones left over after she'd done what she'd come to do. I could sense the dark energy at the bottom of the lake, buried under sheets of limestone and granite. I could feel him stir.

I could feel other things, too. The witches surrounding the lake were close to death, their counter-spell failing them just like their bodies were. I'd never felt it when someone was near death before, the sensation like a summoning, a calling.

No. They were singing to me.

I didn't want to hear their song—especially if it meant what I knew it did.

Something wrenched inside of me, the burning getting too hot, too big. It had to get out. I couldn't say what the thought process was for what I did next. Maybe it was basic math or just dumb fucking luck—I was going with option two—but instead of trying to keep all this burning-hot agony inside, I shoved it out.

With barely a thought of direction, the power flowed

from me like the most natural thing in the world. Like this was how it was supposed to be used. I only needed so much, but everyone else around me was dying, losing their fight against Tabitha and Suzette and their damned spell. So I gave it back, feeling the song of death die with each person the power touched. I felt Shiloh's sigh as the power hit her like a fist, filling her up so she could go on.

So she could stay breathing.

The covens' spell ramped up harder, the break, the undoing, hitting the whole of the lake all at once. It raked across my skin like knives, the spell catching those of us on the beach in its thrall. My feet hit the sand—my legs barely able to hold me up as I let the last vestiges of the souls' power race through me. And I pushed, adding my power to the break Shiloh's coven was trying to hammer down onto Tabitha's spell.

But it seemed too little too late.

A whirlpool sprouted in the center of the fiery lake, the swirl funneling down to the center where I knew *he* was. Whoever *he* was—even with all this power at my fingertips, I still didn't know who we were fighting. Still didn't know why no one would tell me.

The secret failed to matter at the moment as the earth rocked under our feet. The whirlpool widened, and I knew the second the man under the lake, under the stone, under the earth woke up. It felt like the whole world was exploding, the blast throwing me off my feet. I landed on the grass with a crash, nearly fifty feet from where I started, air failing to flow into my lungs.

I tried to gasp but nothing was helping, it was as if all the air everywhere was gone. As if I'd been shoved into space without a helmet. A hand shot out to latch onto me, yanking me to my feet as another hand slapped my back. Upon impact, I sucked in a scant bit of air, the rest flowing as soon as my lungs finally figured out how to work.

And then my breath was gone again as a form rose out of the whirlpool. He was hard to see at first, blending in with the blackness of the night. Long dark hair covered his face, his skin ruddy with dirt and bits of rock. His clothes were black as well, torn pants and a shirt, yet they did nothing to hide just how freaking big he was.

Nor did it hide just how unhappy he was to have been woken up.

The demon—or whatever he was—seemed to unerringly find the persons who summoned him. Scanning the shore until he landed upon Tabitha and Suzette, it was like the earth broke open when he began to speak. Rage coated his words even though I couldn't understand them. He was speaking a language I didn't know, all guttural words full of consonants.

But Tabitha understood.

Shock suffused her face as she dropped to a knee, seeming to plead with the man in the same language. Suzette just seemed shocked that the spell worked, and poor Dunstan Duvall was dead—his throat a wide-open maw of wound. The risen man yelled at Tabitha, a chastisement if I ever heard one, and she began to cry, dropping to both knees as she started to beg.

For forgiveness? For leniency? For her life?

I didn't know.

The man touched down on the floating dock, his shoulders practically vibrating with rage. He reached out a single hand, touching Suzette's cheek. The color drained out of her face, out of her hair, and then she started screaming as her hands began to disintegrate before her very eyes.

She died quickly but painfully, her soul standing where she once did, confused. I called to her, not wanting the man—or thing, or whatever the hell he was —to take even one soul that could make him stronger. Suzette seemed almost relieved, zooming toward me while he focused on Tabitha. She reached me, falling into me faster than the others. Suzette was still confused, her life a bevy of polarizing moments. She was superior and cruel, but at the end of her life, she'd tried going against Tabitha and failed, falling victim to her thrall. She was scared, too, worried about where she would end up. But her misgivings were gone in an instant, the power of her letting me breathe again.

The dark man spoke again, this time in English. "I left this earth for a reason, and if you did not have a purpose, I would take you, too. Your life is hers, but your power is theirs. Give it back to them, or I'll take you to the depths with me."

None of that made any sense, but I didn't have the time to dwell on it. Shaking with fear, Tabitha nodded before a brilliant white light bloomed on her chest. Soul after soul escaped, each one reaching for the man, but failing to do so. He rebuffed them all, the specters falling around him and reaching for me instead.

I wasn't even calling to them, but they raced for me, filling me so fast I couldn't differentiate one soul from the next. The heat hit me like a flash fire, filling me to bursting. If I held it in, it would kill me.

Booming words reached my ears, making no sense at all. "Put me back where I belong, child."

My eyes flashed open. My whole body was glowing white, the power so much greater than it had been before. I reluctantly let my gaze fall on the man in black, his scraggly hair covering half his face. One of his eyes peeked through the fall of hair, the color a piercing blue against his weathered skin.

"Let me go home to my rest, child. I was not meant to return here. Send me back. Send me home."

I'd never heard of a demon requesting to go back to Hell, and as much as I couldn't help but think this was a trick, I couldn't hold onto this power any longer. Not unless I wanted to die.

Unlike when I'd given it away, I wielded the molten-hot energy inside me like a sword: sharp and cutting, it tore through the air. It whipped from my fingers, hitting the man in black in the chest, shoving him back toward the whirlpool. He went willingly, falling to the depths until the water crashed in, and the fire fell away, and the wind calmed.

Water bubbled up from the center, returning the lake that had evaporated in the maelstrom, tossing the floating dock until Tabitha hit the surface. A wave formed out of nowhere, carting the sorceress to my feet, washing up on the beach like an offering.

One I wasn't going to refuse—no matter who gave her to me.

The man in black was right; Tabitha did have a purpose.

24

Staring at Tabitha's face, it was tough to remember that I needed her alive—at least for the time being. It was a struggle not to reach down and wrap my hands around her skinny throat and squeeze the life right out of her. Said hands were still glowing faintly, the power in them—in my entire body—too much for my skin to contain. It didn't burn anymore, though, so at least that was a plus.

I was debating whether or not I should just break Tabitha's neck or suffocate her or cut her open like she did my dad when a pair of hands closed around the top of my arms. On instinct, I struggled, the strength in my limbs far greater than I'd ever experienced before. Unfortunately for the person who grabbed me, I had no idea just how strong I was until he was face-down in the dirt.

"Bishop?" I recognized the agent immediately. *Yeah, buddy, probably should have announced yourself.* "You idiot, I could have killed you."

He groaned in response, gingerly pushing himself up from the beach. "So noted."

Beside him, Tabitha began to stir.

"Oh, no, you don't," Sarina warned, taking a handful of white powder from a pouch and shoving it in Tabitha's face. "That ought to hold you down for a while."

Tabitha instantly went to sleep, an indelicate snore ripping from her lips with every breath.

"Well, that was," J began from behind me, "that was something. Holy shit, Darby. You just put that thing down like it was a regular Tuesday. You didn't even flinch." J swallowed hard, blinking at me like I was some alien lifeform that had beamed down from Saturn or something. "Holy shit."

I shook my head at him, confused about his recollection of the events that just transpired. "I didn't really put him down. I have a feeling if he didn't ask me to send him home, the outcome would have been much different."

"What?" Bishop croaked, his forehead a wash of furrowed brows and confusion.

I was starting to get uneasy. Didn't they see the same thing I had? Did they miss it with everything else going on? "He asked me to send him home. He went willingly. He didn't want to be summoned at all."

Bishop and J shook their heads at me. Sarina was just staring at me like I was talking crazy. "He didn't say anything at all, Darby. His mouth never moved once."

But that didn't make any sense. I watched him talk to Tabitha—yell at her. I heard his voice, that deep, gravelly pitch of a command that quickly turned soft and pleading.

I'd heard him.

"I told you to take a few souls. Not so many you lit up like a Roman fecking candle," Hildy griped, appearing out of thin air like he was wont to do. "But I'm sure glad you're breathing, lass, even if you were glowing so bright you could've been seen from space."

"Did everyone make it?" I asked, but I knew the answer to that already.

None of the coven fell to Tabitha's spell. There were no souls lingering around here, and no imminent death, either. No, the closest dying person was five miles away, but it would be weeks if not months until she was released from this life.

Cancer.

Why did I know that? Moreover, how did I know that? Swallowing hard, I schooled my features, waiting for someone to answer the question so I didn't have to process.

"Everyone but Suzette and the mayor," Shiloh said from behind me, her presence catching me by surprise. "You saved our asses, D. I thought we were done for."

I didn't think Shiloh realized just how close she and her coven had been to death. Or maybe they had. "You were, but then again, so was I. Giving you that power saved us all. I was going to burn up if I hadn't."

Shiloh chuckled, "Be that as it may, this coven owes you. Again. If there's anything you need, let us know. But..." She hesitated, her gaze falling to the still-snoring Tabitha before continuing, "Make sure she stays dead, yeah? We didn't just kick this one out a decade ago. Maybe with a necromancer in the mix she'll actually stay dead this time."

"Oh, don't you worry," Bishop growled. "I'll make sure of it."

Dad. I stared up at the cloud-free sky, the moon full to bursting and right overhead. *Shit.* I pulled my phone out of my back pocket—how it was still there a mystery for the ages. It refused to turn on, so it was probably toast, the magic and power frying it most likely.

"Anyone got the time?"

Several shaking heads responded, and I could feel the fear rising in my belly. What if we ran out of time? Bishop reached down to snag Tabitha, tossing her over a shoulder in a fireman's carry. "I have a promise to keep, right?"

I hadn't recalled Bishop making a promise to me. At most it was a vague "maybe" followed by a "we'll see."

"Time to go. Grab onto me, we'll need to make this quick," he instructed. Sarina, J, and I all latched onto Bishop as he yanked us through the shadows, flitting faster, the world blurring with incredible speed as he carried us where we needed to go.

I hadn't even been able to say goodbye to Shiloh or tell Hildy where we were going.

All of a sudden, our movement stopped, the quick halt jarring me enough that I fell to my knees on my father's back deck. I'd told myself I was never going to shadow walk or shade jump or whatever the hell that was again. Now I was sure of it. Next time—when my father's life wasn't hanging in the balance—I was for sure walking.

J puked in my father's hydrangeas, half-tangled in the bush, and it was all I could do not to laugh at him as I helped him out of it. It was weird for something to be funny right now, but I quit thinking about what could go wrong. Instead, I assisted my friend to his feet and followed Sarina and Bishop through the sliding glass door inside.

My childhood home was silent save for Bishop's feet on the hardwoods, his footfalls heavier with Tabitha on his shoulder. He walked through the kitchen and down the hall to the front room—the room where she'd killed him. My forward movement halted, and both Sarina and J went on ahead.

Reluctant to admit it as I was, I was scared for Bishop to remove the spell hiding my father's body. I was scared to do the spell that would bring him back. Afraid of what it would mean, if my father would be changed, if this thing that we were doing had more consequences than I could fathom. I wanted my father back, but the price—not Tabitha's life because I didn't care about that—might be bigger than just becoming a murderer.

My gaze fell on the kitchen table. It was where I drew pictures as a kid, where I'd studied as a teen. Where I'd eaten dinners and breakfasts and everything besides. I didn't remember living anywhere else except for this house, and even in the silence, even with her gone, the touch of my mother was still here. Wherever she was, I hoped she'd think I was doing the right thing.

I hoped I was doing the right thing.

With nervous feet and wringing hands, I made it to the front room, the nightmare of blood and my father's body on display for all to see. My father's skin was gray now, his lips almost blue from blood loss and rigor, the blood around him nearly black. Bishop had laid Tabitha next to him, and at the sight of her sleeping body so close to his made me want to vomit.

How long had she used him? How long had she hurt him, twisted him, made him her puppet?

From who knew where, Bishop produced a black bag the size of a satchel. From it, he pulled several items including a smaller bag, candles, and an honest-to-god sickle, it's wooden handle dark from age. Just then, it occurred to me that I didn't know how old Bishop was. According to Hildy, my mother had been pushing a century and a half when she'd died. Bishop could be the age he appeared to be, which was about thirty- to thirty-five, or he could be older.

Much older.

Bishop handed Sarina the candles, and me, the small bag. "I need a circle of candles and salt. Hurry, we're running out of time. She won't stay asleep much longer."

Fear that this would all be for nothing, my feet moved fast as I poured the black granules from the bag in a circle around the two still forms. When that was done, Bishop instructed me to stand on the inside of the circle between the pair of them. I couldn't stop my gaze from falling to my father's motionless body, as the weight of all that had happened crashed over me like a wave. Struggling to breathe, the faint shimmer of my still-glowing skin ramped up, my hands lighting up like a damn Christmas tree.

"Darby," J called, his voice barely able to pull my eyes from my father. When I finally met his gaze, he gave me a tremulous smile. "It's all going to be okay, D. Just breathe. Let Bishop do his thing, okay?"

Inexplicably, twin tears fell from my eyes, their hot tracks burning more than all the power of the souls at the lake. Bishop could fail. My father could stay dead. This could all go to shit. What would I do then? How could I breathe? How could I go on?

But I nodded anyway, letting J's confidence fill me— even if I knew it was just for show.

Bishop handed me Tabitha's knife—the curved blade carved in familiar sigils. "When I tell you to, cut her like she did your dad. Don't get cute, either. Exactly the same. Do you remember?"

As if I could forget it. No, I'd have that memory even if we brought my father back. I'd remember it until the day I died.

My Latin was rusty, so I had no idea what Bishop was

saying as he began the spells needed to bring my father back. Okay, I didn't know any Latin, but I recognized the language when I heard it. With a wave of his hand, all the candles in the circle flamed alight, the wicks flaring so high it was a wonder the smoke alarms didn't go off. He cut into the palm of his hand with the sickle, dotting his blood along the salt line as he chanted. The power of his blood raked across my skin, nearly as hot as the power in my hands.

Bishop's cadence was precise, exact—he enunciated each word like he was reading it from a book, even though there was no book around.

Hardly ever performed the spell, my ass.

But even as the light in my hands and arms dimmed when I tried shoving the power down, I could feel the death around us stirring, my father's soul lingering, hiding. I refused to call to him, worried that if I did, he'd fall into me just like all the others had, and I'd lose him forever. This power beneath my skin fought with me, begging me to answer the call of the soul with one of my own. Gritting my teeth, I fought with it, refusing to give in.

"Now, Darby, now!" Bishop yelled, screaming at me from the edge of the circle. How long had he been shouting? How long had I just been standing here fighting with myself?

Not wasting any more time, I knelt at Tabitha's side, taking the blade in my hand like she had, looping my thumb through the hole in the grip and spinning the blade just as she'd done. Sucking in a single breath, I brought the blade down in an "X," watching as the blood bloomed over her lake-wet shirt, the red staining the damp fabric like ink.

And then the real fun began—if by fun, you meant torture. Tabitha's soul sang the loudest of all the souls I'd consumed, and it was the darkest, too. I didn't have to let her fall into me to know that she'd done monstrous things. Things I never wanted to know.

Unlike all the others, Tabitha's soul was dark and slimy as it tore like a beast from her body. It thrashed and ripped, her blood falling on both me and my father but not leaving the circle. Only when her soul was free from her corpse did my father's appear, wisping in the air like he'd been searching for his body this whole time.

He seemed scared, seeing the twisted form of Tabitha crouching low next to her eviscerated corpse, but with Bishop's command, he fell back into his body, his wounds knitting back together before my eyes. Tabitha's soul screamed, trying to reach for my father's before she was yanked back by an unseen force.

That force pulled her by the feet, shoving her into the barrier of the circle. Tabitha's scream was deafening as the wall of magic began to burn her up, her entire form erupting in flames. She went up like a flash fire until she was nothing but dark motes in the air—those, too, winking out of sight.

After the last mote was gone, I heard a gasp at my feet. My father shot up to sitting, his hands checking his chest for the wounds that used to be there. His gaze fell to the body formerly known as Tabitha—the parts strewn all over the circle. But when he met my gaze, I knew. He knew exactly what this circle was, exactly who the corpse next to him was.

"What have you done?" Censure and judgment were both ripe in his tone, both biting hard enough to draw tears. I wanted to hug him, but I didn't think he'd let me.

"She saved your stupid life is what she's done," Bishop growled. "You're welcome."

"You don't understand," my father muttered, shaking his head. "You shouldn't have done that." He lifted his gaze to mine, the sorrow in them opening a cold pit of dread in my belly.

Then there was a great big boom as the front door blew in, shards of wood flying everywhere. Three men in suits walked in, each one had hands alight with swirling magic. Behind them a woman trailed, her suit a brilliant cranberry red. The men parted, and I got a good look at a dead woman.

Or at least she was supposed to be dead.

Mariana Adler, my mother, marched toward our little tableau, her face a prettily painted blank mask. She spared her husband a glance, an emotion flitting over her face quick and gone in an instant. Then she looked at me, her gaze trailing over my dimmed skin and blood-covered hands.

"Take them. All of them. Even the humans," she said before turning right back around and walking out the ruined door.

25

My ass was planted on a hard metal chair as I sat handcuffed to a table in a generic interrogation room that smelled of fear and spent magic. The only thing less comforting than the fact that this room had no cameras, no mirrors, and a door made of spelled iron so thick it would take a bomb to get through, was how I'd gotten here.

As soon as my mother snapped her fingers, those three men—and a whole host of others—grabbed us all. Cuffing Sarina, Bishop, and I, and taking both my father and J by the arm to a black transport van with a sliding door and no windows. Wedged in with three agents, my feet were zip-tied, and a hood was thrown over my head. Granted, they hadn't taken my weapons or frisked me, just cuffed. Interesting.

We drove what seemed like hours, and no one was allowed to speak. Bishop had found that out the hard way when he'd tried to explain himself, and his words were abruptly cut off into a pained "*oof.*"

The only upside I could see in this whole thing was that I still had Hildy, the ghostly specter of my grandfather was yapping away in the van, telling me exactly where we were and how to get home. Not that the information would be helpful if they freaking killed me as soon as we stopped, but hey, info was info.

Seeming to read my thoughts, Hildy scoffed at my dire attitude. "They aren't goin' to kill ya, lass. You just did them a favor, putting that man away. Their whole coven was fightin' Tabitha and couldn't do feck all. If Tabitha had done what she was goin' ta, she would have leveled the whole fecking mountain. No, lass. Just stay quiet, they'll be coming to you with bleeding gifts if they know what's good for them."

And so, I did. I stayed quiet the whole ride to the building—even though I wanted to know what the fuck was going on with my "dead" mom. My father's words before he died made a whole hell of a lot more sense now than they did then. When I was trying to comfort him, he was telling me she wasn't dead after all. But before my mouth betrayed me and I started talking, we made it to wherever the hell they were taking us.

The activity suggested it was a headquarters of some kind. I couldn't hear anyone exactly, but something about my new and improved senses made it so I knew how many souls were in the building. The musk in the hallway also telling that we were underground, beneath water or a river of some kind, which explained why Hildy was no longer yakking my ear off.

Only when I made it to this room, was I unhooded, a burly man shoved me into the chair so hard it nearly tipped over. My teeth clacking together, I rocked back until he caught me, earning a searing glare from me. Burly guy didn't say anything, but his expression of contempt was enough to speak volumes. Swiftly, he cuffed me to the table and left, slamming the ten-inch-thick door with enough force to rattle the whole room.

I stayed put for a long time, the silence welcome. The spelled door and bevy of water meant Hildy couldn't follow me here—most definitely done on purpose, I figured—but it was fine. I'd done what I said I would. I brought Dad back. I stopped Tabitha. If I lost everything else, at least Dad was alive.

I worried about Bishop and Sarina and J while contemplating just what they would do to me as punishment for Tabitha's murder. Though I totally agreed with Hildy, as bonkers as he was. I'd definitely done them a favor by taking her out. Shuddering at the mental image of her clawing her way out of her body, I tried to think of what Tabitha might have really been. I'd never seen a human soul do that.

Granted, I'd never absorbed a human soul before today, nor had I seen a necromancy ritual performed, either. Truth be told, nothing that had happened today made any lick of sense to me.

Not Tabitha and her motives. Not the ABI. Not Shiloh's coven. Not what I'd done.

None of it.

I was missing a piece of the puzzle. A major one.

I mean, how did I go from seeing ghosts one day to the glowing and floating being that helped those specters move on? That was what I'd done, right? And why did they need to fall into me to move on? Couldn't they have moved on before?

Was something stopping them? Yeah, I was missing a big piece of the puzzle and I didn't like it one bit.

Plus, I was still stewing on the mom bullshit. I wanted to believe there had to be a good reason for it, wanted to give her the benefit of the doubt. But also, I kinda wanted to punch her in the face and mess up those perfectly painted red lips of hers.

At my ire, my hands started glowing again. Perfect.

Doubly perfect? The door picked that moment to

open, said Mommy walking right through. Burly guy gave my hands a cursory yet angry glance before shutting the door behind her.

"My friend out there bet me fifty bucks you'd try to shoot your way out of here," she began, setting down a rather thick file folder on the table and pulling up a chair. "He's very put out you remained so honorable."

Damn near twenty years since I'd last seen her and that was what she opened with?

I wanted to smash something, but just like I had before, I shoved it down, willing my stupid hands and their damned glow to calm the fuck down. I could not, however, stop myself from cracking my neck, the action making my mother shudder. She'd always hated that I could do that. Even as a kid, I could pop my neck just by tilting my head to the side.

Telling her to kiss my ass was off the table, but that? That I could do.

"Well, you told me then, huh?" She chuckled. "Was that Darby speak for fuck off? If so, dear, well done."

I'd never been a sullen teenager—not until I was left on my own to deal with seeing the dead everywhere. And even then, I was never mean to Dad. I did my chores, I tried to focus on my homework. I'd been a good kid.

Because she was gone, and he was hurting and there was nothing else to be done about it. She'd left us to grieve, and here she was, breathing. She wanted me to tell her to fuck off? Well, I could do that.

"There would be no point in trying to escape," I said, the first words I'd spoken in hours. "There are too many agents here; I'd never make it to the surface. And never mind about J or Dad, right? I mean, if I didn't get shot as soon as I walked out of this room by the three agents you have stationed outside, I'd still meet the other ten you have around the corner and the twenty you have on standby. Let's not forget about the sniper on the roof. I mean, it's not like Grandpa could come and tell me when the coast was clear—not with being under a river and surrounded by iron. So really." I paused for effect. "All there was to do was wait."

I'd expected her to appear mad or afraid or *something*. I did not expect for her to smile.

"You remind me of your father. Not Killian," she clarified, "Your real father. He could tell when souls were near, too."

As quickly as she tried to slide it by me, I still caught her meaning. I could tell when souls were near. My father could as well, but I had a feeling she could not. That was *not* comforting at all. What the hell was my dad if not another grave talker?

"Your skills are formidable, your actions brave, however, my darling daughter, you are in some deep shit."

Tell me something I don't know.

"You were part of an illegal necromancy ritual; you murdered a woman—"

"That was no woman," I insisted. "You didn't see her come out of that body. If that was a human soul, I'm a fairy princess."

My mother smiled at me before continuing, "Be that as it may, you took a life that was not yours to take."

"She murdered my father right in front of me. I had every right to take that life. It was owed to me," I growled, my hands once again lighting up like fucking Christmas.

"Ah." She nodded as she sat back in her chair. "That does allow you a bit of leeway, but the ritual? That is riddled with sanctions for a reason. Agent La Roux knew this, and yet he allowed it. Why?"

Looking back, there was no way Bishop should have allowed it—not if it rained down this kind of hell on us.

"I don't know why he did it. All I did was ask him." I shook my head. "No, not ask. I demanded he bring Dad back. He probably felt sorry for me."

I refused to think of what motives he might have had —not with my likely imminent death in the cards.

"Interesting. Very interesting."

She was quiet for a long moment, the time ticking by as she waited for me to fill the silence. Using that particular interrogation tactic wouldn't work on me. I didn't actually like talking, and silence was just so rare, I relished every little bit of it.

So we sat, and I could tell she was getting more and more amused by me as the silence stretched.

"Very well, my darling daughter, you have convinced me. It's time to make a deal."

Wait, what? A deal? I was waiting for her to cart me off to the gallows and she wanted to make a deal?

I didn't say any of this. Instead, I schooled my expression and sat back in my chair. "I'm listening."

My mother's painted red lips stretched wide as a smile flitted across her face. She was about to drop a bomb on me, I just knew it.

"Tell me—what do you know about the Angel of Death?"

Darby's story will continue with
Dead and Gone
Grave Talker Book Two

Want to binge the sister series?
Don't miss **Night Watch**!
Available on Amazon & Kindle Unlimited!

DEAD AND GONE

Grave Talker Book Two

There are few things worse than being on the Arcane Bureau of Investigation's naughty list.

To keep myself out of hot water, I've made a deal with the devil—using my skills as a grave talker to help the ABI solve some very cold cases.

But there is something mighty amiss in this task—especially when quite a few of these cases lead me right back to my home town of Haunted Peak and the secrets buried there.

Grab it now on Amazon!

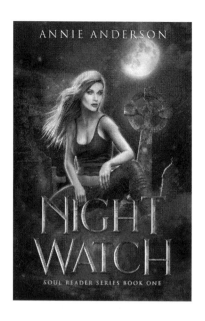

NIGHT WATCH
Soul Reader Book One

Waking up at the foot of your own grave is no picnic…
especially when you can't remember how you got there.
Cursed with powers she can't name, Sloane Cabot has
vowed to catch the Rogue who turned her into a
monster and killed her family. Too bad a broodingly hot
mage is bound to keep her on the straight and narrow.
Whether she likes it or not…

Grab Night Watch today!

THE ROGUE ETHEREAL SERIES

an adult urban fantasy series by Annie Anderson

Love the Grave Talker Series?
Then You'll love Max!

Come meet Max. She's brash. She's inked. She has a bad
habit of dying... *a lot.* She's also a Rogue with a demon
on her tail and not much backup.
This witch has a serious bone to pick.

Check out the Rogue Ethereal Series today!

THE PHOENIX RISING SERIES

an adult paranormal romance series by Annie Anderson

Heaven, Hell, and everything in between. Fall into the realm of Phoenixes and Wraiths who guard the gates of the beyond. That is, if they can survive that long...

Living forever isn't all it's cracked up to be.

Check out the Phoenix Rising Series today!

JOIN THE LEGION

EXCLUSIVE SNEAK PEEKS, GIVEAWAYS, BOOK DISCUSSION. COME FOR THE BOOKS. STAY FOR THE MEMES.

To stay up to date on all things Annie Anderson, get exclusive access to ARCs and giveaways, and be a member of a fun, positive, drama-free space, join The Legion!

ABOUT THE AUTHOR

 Annie Anderson is the author of the international bestselling Rogue Ethereal series. A United States Air Force veteran, Annie pens fast-paced Urban Fantasy novels filled with strong, snarky heroines and a boatload of magic. When she takes a break from writing, she can be found binge-watching The Magicians, flirting with her husband, wrangling children, or bribing her cantankerous dogs to go on a walk.

To find out more about Annie and her books, visit
www.annieande.com

Printed in Great Britain
by Amazon

Intermittent Fasting for Beginners

How to Lose Belly Fat with Intermittent Fasting Strategies for Men and Women, Simple Ways to Look Younger, Stimulate Autophagy, Weight Loss and Rejuvenate Cells

BY
KENNETH STERLING

Finally, any of the content found within is ultimately intended for entertainment purposes and should be thought of and acted on as such. Due to its inherently ephemeral nature, nothing discussed within should be taken as an assurance of quality, even when the words and deeds described herein indicated otherwise. Trademarks and copyrights mentioned within are done for informational purposes in line with fair use and should not be seen as an endorsement from the copyright or trademark holder.

Table of Contents

Introduction

Congratulations on purchasing *Intermittent Fasting A Beginners Guide to Weight Loss and A Healthier Lifestyle: Everything you need to know to incorporate Intermittent fasting as a weight loss and health rejuvenation tool* and thank you for doing so. Making the choice to change your eating habits for the better is an important decision and one for which you should be applauded. Unfortunately, it is also quite often easier said than done which is where this book comes into play.

The following chapters will discuss everything you need to know about intermittent fasting in order to ensure you have what you need to get started on the right foot, starting with an overview of basics of intermittent fasting and how it can lead you to look and feel better than you have in years. While intermittent fasting has many proven benefits, it's not for everyone which is why the next chapter will discuss who should and who shouldn't consider intermittent fasting as a new long-term lifestyle. With the basics out of the way, you will then learn all about the different types of intermittent fasting that are at your disposal.

From there you will learn about why you would want to do all this hard work in the first place with a breakdown of intermittent fasting's many benefits. Next, you will find a variety of tips to help you eat properly while fasting as well as the things you can do to maximize your weight loss once and for all and additional tools to help you ensure that you are able to turn intermittent fasting into a new lifestyle.

With so many choices out there when it comes to consuming this type of content, it is appreciated that you've chosen this one. Plenty of care and effort went into ensuring it contains as many interesting and useful tidbits as possible, please enjoy!

CHAPTER 1

What is Intermittent Fasting

Intermittent fasting is a method of eating to make sure that you make the most out of every meal you eat. The core tenets of intermittent fasting mean that you don't need to change what you are eating; instead, you have to change when you are eating it. Intermittent fasting is a useful viable alternative to traditional diets or simply cutting your daily caloric intake, which can help fasters lose weight and body fat without many changes to calorie consumption in a day. As you will find, the preferred method of intermittent fasting is to simple consume two meals every day instead of the more traditional three (or more) meals in that same period of time.

Are you one of those that has trouble adhering to diet plans? Intermittemt fasting might just be the solution as it only requires you change one small habit as opposed to wholesale changes in diet. The beauty in intermittent fasting is in its combined simplicity and effectiveness. The key to understanding why intermittent fasting is such an effective weight loss/muscle building tool all boils down to the differences in your body during a fasted state versus a fed state and the important changes that will come across as a result of changing habits and sticking with it.

During the process of digestion and absorbtion of food, the body is in a fed state. Depending on how long you take to digest a meal, the fed state starts approximately five minutes after your first bite and continues until three to five hours after food consumption. A fed state, in turn, leads to higher levels of insulin which make it much more difficult for the body to burn fat. The period directly after the fed sate is referred to as the post-absorptive state which is the period of time where the body is not actively processing food and its insulin levels begin to fall. This state lasts for between eight and twelve hours and directly precedes the fasted state.

Intermittent fasting is seen more as a way of life rather than a diet. There are few rules about which foods you should eat but, rather, when you should eat. There are different protocols of this kind of fasting with each protocol splitting a day or week into eating and fasting periods.

A lot of women have taken to intermittent fasting and turned it into a lifestyle. Think about having a switch that can balance your metabolism and perform a deep cleanse without using costly detoxification kits. The body has an excellent mechanism that can achieve this. This mechanism is known autophagy, and it is simply another term for intermittent fasting.

What is autophagy? It is your body's ultimate recycling system. Autophagy replaces damaged and worn-out parts of your cells with new ones, thereby helping to preserve tissue health. The cells in your body create membranes that hunt down diseased, dead, and worn-out cells and then consumes them, using the resulting molecules to make new cell parts and for energy. In the process, the cells also consume harmful organisms such as disease-causing bacteria.

Thus old and worn-out bits are consumed by the cells within your body which creates fuel as well as parts for new cells. Cells in your body sometimes digest proteins to release amino acids and provide much-needed energy. This process, known as autophagy, is essential as it promotes metabolism and slows down the aging process.

Fasting for medical reasons: Patients are required to abstain from eating food before their blood, cholesterol, or glucose levels are tested and before they are screened for diabetes. That is because food can interfere with test results. A partial fast that only allows clear liquids to be consumed is required just before a colonoscopy.

Patients must not eat before having a major surgery that involves the use of anesthesia. If a patient eats just before surgery, he could vomit, inhale the vomit and die while he is unconscious. Regurgitation while under anesthesia is rare, however, so fasting may no longer be required of surgery patients in the near future.

A long history

Great healers, thinkers, and philosophers in history used fasting to heal and reach general health. Let's look at this a bit more closely.

Ancient medicine and philosophy: Galen, Aristotle, Socrates, Plato, and Hippocrates were all in favor of fasting. One of the most famous participants in Western medicine, Paracelsus, said that fasting is our access to the inner physician and the greatest remedy we have available to us. Early arts centered on healing recognized the rejuvenating and revitalizing powers that fasting offers to us.

Fasting in spirituality and religion: Early spiritual and religious groups utilized the act of fasting in their rites and ceremonies, usually during fall and spring equinoxes. These days, each well-known religious practice uses fasting to gain spiritual benefits. Here are some examples of traditions using it today:

- Indian traditions in North and South America.
- Hinduism.
- Buddhism.
- Islam.
- Gnosticism.

- Judaism.
- Christianity.

Each of these traditions uses fasting in some way, whether for sacrifice, mourning, paying penance, or to reach spiritual visions and purification. Many different faiths use fasting on a regular basis to stay clear of and heal gluttony. In America, the religious groups most commonly tied to fasting are Jews, Roman Catholics, and Episcopalians. In addition, practices in yoga often involve fasting and go back many thousands of years. Many yogis believe that fasting is the most natural and quick way to heal the body.

In the Bahai Faith, fasting is practiced each day for most of the month of March and includes a fast from liquids as well as foods while the sun is up. Every member of the faith between the ages of 15 and 70 are asked to look inside themselves and commit to the practice. Additionally, fasting can be seen in the Muslim faith during the holy time of Ramadan. In addition to this month long daytime fast where even water is prohibited, the prophet Muhammad was also known to encourage fasting throughout most of the week as well.

Fasting is also a crucial part of Hinduism and it asks that followers observe many different kinds of fasts depending on their local customs and personal beliefs. It is common for many Hindus to fast certain days of each month including Purnima, Pradosha or Ekadasi. Additionally, individual days of the week are also dedicated to fasting based on which deity the practitioner is devoted to. Those who worship Shiva typically fast on Mondays, followers of Vishnu tend to fast on Thursdays and followers of Ayyappa typically fast on Saturdays.

Fasting is also common on specific days in certain regions of India. In northwestern as well as southern portions of India they often fast on Tuesdays. In the south, this is a fast that is dedicated to Mariamman a goddess who is, in turn, one form of the Goddess Shakti. This fast is a daytime fast where only liquids are permitted while the sun is up. In the northwest, however, this fast is dedicated to Lord Hanuman and those who adhere to it allow themselves nothing but fruit and milk while the sun is up.

Additionally, it is common in the northern parts of India for those who follow Vrihaspati Mahadeva to fast by fist listening to a story. They typically also wear yellow on this day and prefer food that is also yellow when they do break their fast. Thursday is also a fast day for those who follow Guru. Fasting is also common on many religious holidays and festivals including some that do not even allow the faithful to consume water during the day. This is especially common during Navratri and lasts for nine days in April and then again in either November or October.

Rules to follow

While intermittent fasting has been known to produce real results in a wide cross section of individuals, it only works for those who are able to follow its generous rules. These include:

1. Always run a calorie deficit: While many diets emphasize this idea, it is crucial when it comes to intermittent fasting as if you are not careful you can easily overeat once you break your fast, and as a result mitigate all your potential results in one fell swoop. Keep in mind that you need to work off 3,500 more calories than you eat every week to stick with a healthy 1 pound of weight loss per week. It doesn't matter how that calorie deficit appears, all that matters is that those calories aren't tallied at the end of each week.

2. Always be in control: If you are interested in intermittent fasting then the first thing you need to ask yourself if you are going to be able to go without food for a minimum of 12 hours each day as any

inbound calories during this period will reset the cycle and minimize the amount of fat you can effectively burn each day. Keeping your appetite in line is crucial to maximizing success as a single missed meal doesn't provide that generous a window for the next if you hope to maintain a 500 calorie deficit per day.

3. Stick with it: To see the best results when it comes to intermittent fasting, you need to get in the habit of following a set schedule on a regular basis. Only once your body gets into the right sorts of habits moving forward will you begin to see the types of reliable results you are looking for. If you switch between fasting schedules, or, even worse, different diet plans then all you will achieve is causing your body to get confused and cut all weight loss until it can figure out what is going on. Consistency is key when it comes to maximizing your weight loss potential.

If you decide to switch back and forth between multiple types of intermittent fasting, or if you switch back and forth from doing it at all, then rather than enhance your body's ability to build muscle and lose weight, you will instead find yourself in a state of limbo while your confused body tries to determine what exactly is going on. This means that instead of losing more weight, your body will desperately try to cling to every single calorie until your eating habits settle down. If you hope to see real results, the only reliable way to do so is to find a schedule of eating that works for you and stick with it no matter what.

4. Be safe: While intermittent fasting is scientifically proven to have many positive results once your body adjusts to the idea, that doesn't mean that it is going to be the right choice for everyone or that the first month or so isn't going to have its share of side effects. You will likely experience some amount of dizziness, irritability, lightheadedness, and nausea as diarrhea or constipation while your body adjusts to the fact that you are not eating as much as you used to.

5. Likewise, it is important to avoid binging after a fast, not just because it will ruin all of the benefits associated with cutting calories, but also because it can have numerous negative side effects as well. Finally, before you start any new dietary plan it is important that you discuss your plans and goals with a dietitian or healthcare professional to ensure that you aren't accidentally doing more harm to your body than good.

Intermittent fasting myths

Intermittent fasting impedes brain development: This is a widespread myth about intermittent fasting that our brain cells need glucose for functioning effectively. The human brain can also utilize ketones as a significant source during prolonged starvation phases, thus conserving the body's protein like skeletal muscle. Again, if glucose were solely responsible for the functioning of the brain, we really wouldn't survive. Fat is the human body's system for accumulating food energy in the long run, while glucose is a more short-term solution.

Think of it is like this when short term reserves are utilized, the human body effortlessly knocks on the door of its long haul reserves. Thus, the lack of glucose does not mean the brain does not derive the energy from anywhere. It dips into other long term energy sources to perform its functions effectively.

Intermittent fasting breaks down your muscles: This is entirely false. If that were the case, why have so many bodybuilders, whose professions rely on muscled bodies, practice Intermittent Fasting? When you see the incredible muscles on trainers who fast intermittently, the logical conclusion is that it doesn't break down one's muscles. So, why do people believe it does?" People find this to be true because they've heard the repeated warnings made by people, not in the know, and they have chosen to believe the voice of the ill-advised.

In truth, what breaks down muscle is inactivity. This is why older, less active people lose muscle tone and definition. It's not even age that causes muscle loss. Go to any gym, and you'll see many older people who are fit and their bodies show it. They are muscled to the max, and many of them practice intermittent fasting on a regular basis. What causes flabby, out-of-shape bodies is that individuals fail to take preventative measures by exercising regularly and eating healthily. You can do that as you fast, and you won't break down your muscle mass. In fact, many fitness gurus put on muscle mass when fasting because they continue to practice their regular workouts as well as take advantage of all the benefits of Intermittent Fasting.

Intermittent fasting lower's a man's testosterone level: There is some truth to this myth, but it's misleading if the statement is left to hang on the unfinished fact that fasting lowers testosterone levels. During long-term fasts, testosterone levels are temporarily lower.

However, at the end of the fast, they jump up to higher than they were before starting your fast. Although you will notice a difference in more extended fasts, Intermittent Fasting doesn't usually see that much difference in testosterone levels. Because the fast is short-lived before eating once again replenishes the body, testosterone levels are rarely an issue.

Intermittent fasting isn't safe for women: There is plenty of debate about the side effects of intermittent fasting on women. A majority of research conducted in the area has shown a non-existent co-relation between fasting and fertility issues. However, if you are going to increase your fasting durations to consume next to nothing for 24hours every other day, that is an invitation for trouble. It may end up wrecking your hormones and ultimately fertility. Fast for shorter durations or once a week.

Studies have also pointed to the fact that despite several metabolic alterations in your body while fasting, even a

72 hour fast is incapable of having a negative impact on the menstrual cycle of healthy women.

If you are already in a disturbed state of mind, your fertility and menstruation are affected, and if you go on begin fasting during this potentially negative stage, it only ends up worsening your psychological condition, and thus leads to even more stress, hormonal imbalances, and infertility issues. The issue here is not intermittent fasting. It is the idea of fasting at the wrong time that can cause these unfavorable conditions. Otherwise, there is no direct co-relation between intermittent fasting and menstruation or infertility.

However, extended fasting periods may affect the cycle of very lean women, with body fat quotient under 20%. Limit fasting to 24 hours once or twice a week or practice the 16-8-hour intermittent fasting method, which is fairly easy, to begin with. Studies have revealed that compared to men, women find greater success with shorter fasting durations. Gradually, increase the duration of your fast as you get comfortable with the idea of fasting.

Eating small meals controls blood sugar: It is commonly claimed by dietitians and health "experts" that eating smaller meals throughout the day will provide you with a stable energy source, prevent hunger pangs, and keep your brain sharp and focused. This is believed to be due to the effects of blood sugar. Contrary to popular belief, in healthy people, blood sugar is actually quite well controlled. Unless you are eating highly unbalanced meals, such as bowls of ice cream, your blood sugar is not likely to spike up and down throughout the day. Going a few hours without food, or even a full day, is not going to make a healthy person's blood sugar drop.

Maintaining blood sugar is a high priority of the human body, and due to this, we have efficient pathways that will keep it stable, even under extreme conditions. Studies show that even if you were to fast for 23 hours and then go on a ninety-minute run, your blood sugar would not drop. It would take at least three days of fasting in order for your blood sugar to drop enough to affect you mentally, and by that point, your body will adjust and start fueling off of ketones in place of glucose. One study revealed that even after fasting for two full days, the blood sugar is maintained steady within normal ranges and cognition levels were not negatively affected, either.

While correct that blood sugar does affect hunger, "low" just means "lower range" in healthy people, and when their blood sugar is signaling to eat, it is not an actual low. More important than blood sugar, is your regular meal patterns, which affects the hormone ghrelin and other metabolic hormones. The release of ghrelin will make people extremely hungry and likely to eat much more than they otherwise would. When you eat at irregular intervals each day, the secretion of ghrelin will not be well controlled making you more likely to overeat. The cells that produce ghrelin have a circadian clock that synchronizes in the anticipation of food with metabolic cycles. This means that if you set up regularly scheduled eating times that your body will adjust to you eating at those times and you are less likely to feel hungry at other times.

CHAPTER 2

Is it Right for Me?

Of course, everyone doesn't start intermittent fasting to lose weight. While it is one of the most effective means of losing weight, there are many other reasons why one might consider it.

Detoxification: Fasting forces the body to shed anything it doesn't need to survive. If you have a toxic buildup either from poor diet choices or because of overeating, the body gets a break from trying to break down those foods and is able to cleanse its digestive tract.

Hunger management: If you have a tendency to overeat sometimes and is always feeling like you're hungry, it is because your blood sugar levels have dropped and your brain is telling you it needs more glucose. When you are fasting, however, your body will be forced to burn its fat stores and so it will turn off that hunger triggering hormones. This automatically will reduce the hunger pangs and you will be less likely to have to cope with different food cravings that tempt you to overeat.

Lowers your risk of developing type II diabetes: When you are fasting, your body burns up all its glucose before it turns to fat, and it keeps the blood sugar levels from increasing. Consistent low blood sugar lowers your risk of developing Type II Diabetes. As a caveat, IF can also help to improve your body's sensitivity to insulin, which can also be very effective in controlling diabetes.

Lowers risk of cancer: While most people do IF to shed weight, there have been recent animal studies as well as several preliminary human trials that so far have shown promising results in lowering the risk for cancer. While still in the early stages, initial reports on these studies give some indication that this is most likely the result of regular fasting.

So far, it appears to lower the production of blood glucose, triggers stem cells to regenerate the immune system, and increased the body's ability to produce tumor-killing cells. While the jury is still out, and the studies have yet to be completed, the initial reports do show some pretty impressive and promising results.

Muscle gain: It is also very effective in helping to build muscle. It is important to point out that this can only happen if you do it in conjunction with healthy nutrition designed to minimize fat gain and exercise. Muscle growth is the result of a progressive overload of the tissues and continued repair. There is no way to avoid this. However, if you have a good strength building program to work along with IF, there is clear evidence that you can build muscle.

Fitness: Fitness means different things to different people. However, in this sense, we can define it as getting your physical health to optimum levels. Being fit is not just about physicality though, it can also apply to your emotional and mental well-being as well. So, once you begin to see improvement by losing weight and gaining a little extra muscle, you'll feel better about yourself both emotionally and mentally. As a result, you'll start to want to participate in more things that you enjoy, and your overall level of fitness will automatically improve.

Weight loss: By large, the majority of people who practice intermittent fasting are doing it for weight loss. Considering that the average person is walking around with five to twenty pounds of food clogging up their intestines, fasting is a great way to relieve some of that pressure. When you fast, the body will have time to work on eliminating much of those compacted contents on its own. This kind of weight is in addition to the extra fat and water you may have retained as well.

Determine the right fast for you: How many calories you should intake during your fast if any, and how often and long you should fast depend on your personal needs and limits. There are many ways to fast you can choose from, as no size truly fits all when it comes to health.

The most important factor to consider is your own endurance. Activity level, lifestyle, and any health concerns or illnesses all need to be considered before you commit yourself to any fasting plan. You should pick a plan you feel you can realistically – not ideally – complete without really regretting it when you are famished, drained, and overexerting yourself. Exhausting yourself from an over-ambitious fasting attempt does not do your body or your state of mind any favors.

Generally speaking, every type of intermittent fasting is relatively flexible and can be adapted to fit your everyday life. Do not forget to consider work, school, household duties, or any other commitments that might interfere with your fasting plan. Also, be aware that some of these plans are geared toward those who regularly exercise, others are not. This will make a drastic difference in how the fast goes. Only choose a fast that is suited to your activity levels. If you exercise regularly, choose a plan designed for those who are very active (generally those with shorter fasting periods). If you are a mostly sedimentary individual and do not exercise regularly, choose a plan designed as such (generally those with longer fasting periods). Typically it is best to start off small, with achievable beginning goals that you can later build up on if you so choose.

People who should avoid intermittent fasting

Athletes: Athletes need a consistent intake of calories in order to be able to perform. This is especially true for those who train, practice, and perform outdoors in the heat. Not having a consistent supply of energy from food can cause athletes to feel week and underperform. After a certain point, their bodies will begin to consume muscle tissue for energy. This is the exact opposite of what athletes need as well as the benefits intermittent fasting is supposed to provide. Athletes need to eat three main meals and three smaller meals or large snacks throughout the day.

Pregnant women: Growing a person requires a steady supply of calories, significantly more calories than non-pregnant women normally consume. When following an intermittent fasting plan while pregnant, you will run into at least three problems. The first problem is that you will not be able to get as many calories as you need because, by definition, intermittent fasting plans will reduce your caloric intake. For example, the alternate day diet will cut your overall calorie consumption nearly in half. You can ensure that you fulfill your entire calorie need by consuming large quantities of junk food, but this will have an adverse effect on your health and the health of the baby, as well as undo any of the benefits that intermittent fasting may bring.

The second problem is that you will not have the steady stream of calories that you and your growing baby need.

The third problem is that you will not be able to follow the intense exercise programs that are prescribed. While exercise is usually advised during pregnancy, the kind of exercise that is commonly advocated is cardio, not resistance training or lifting weights. Intermittent fasting could seriously harm you and your baby.

Diabetics, especially type 1: One of the much-touted benefits of intermittent fasting is that it lowers insulin levels. This makes it seem like a great option for people who are diabetic. However, intermittent fasting has not been studied enough in diabetics in order to ascertain what the long-term effects are. Type 1 diabetics in particular need to follow a carefully structured diet in order to maintain their health, especially because intermittent fasting will significantly lower blood glucose levels.

Women and intermittent fasting

In women, calorie restriction due to lifestyle changes like fasting can alert the body to interrupt fertility. Anytime you suffer a low-calorie or low-fat diet, your body adopts a defensive mechanism which is only discarded when sufficient nutrition intake resumes. While fasting can affect your hormones, intermittent fasting does support proper hormonal balance leading to a healthy body and weight loss the right way.

There are many reasons why women fast. Most of these reasons relate to weight loss, better health, improved physical appearance, and fat loss in certain areas such as the tummy and waist. Some women chose to fast to lead a healthy lifestyle and others to manage different medical conditions like high blood pressure, diabetes, and even cancer.

<u>Fasting challenges that women experience:</u> Some women who fast regularly experience a number of

challenges. For instance, some women claim to experience problems such as metabolic disturbances, early-onset menopause, and missed periods.

When a woman's body suffers hormonal issues and fertility problems, this could lead to hair loss, pale skin, a lack of energy, acne, and similar challenges. Fortunately, you do not have to suffer any such challenges as a woman. You can tailor your eating and fasting periods so that they match your lifestyle and enable you to avoid the issues and challenges that affecting fasting women.

Fasting and your hormones: When done incorrectly, intermittent fasting can result in hormonal imbalances in women. This is because women are extremely sensitive to what scientists refer to as signals of starvation. When the body senses that it is being starved of important nutrients, it produces excessive amounts of the hunger hormones ghrelin and leptin. It is the production of these hormones that causes fasting women to experience insatiable hunger.

Scientists are not 100% sure why women's hormones are affected so much compared to men's. However, suspicion points to a protein known as kisspeptin. This molecule is used by neurons for communicating with each other. It is also super-sensitive to insulin, leptin, and ghrelin, which are all hormones that control hunger.

It is interesting to note that women have more kisspeptin neurons than men. More of this molecule means greater sensitivity to alterations in energy balance. This is probably the reason why fasting causes the production of this molecule to dip, hunger hormones are not as properly regulated.

Scientific studies: It would be ideal to reference to a study of experiments on human beings to properly illustrate the scientific evidence that appropriately explains the interaction with hormones within a woman's body while fasting. However, there are none. Instead, the most biologically correct studies have only been performed on young female rats and how their reproduction cycle is negatively impacted by intermittent fasting. In one particular study, the subjects of the experiment are ten female and ten male rates.

Throughout the twelve- week experiment, half of the subjects were allowed to eat whenever they wanted to, while the other half were only provided with food every second day. Between the eating cycles, the second half's food was taken away and the rats were forced to fast. The twelve- week study for the rats equivalates to ten years in human life. At the end of the twelve weeks, it was recorded that the female rats who fasted have lost approximately nineteen percent of their body weight, has lower blood sugar levels, and their ovaries had shrunk. The overall conclusion was that the intermittent fasting study had affected the female rats' hormones significantly more than it did the males'.

Although the experiment found that kisspeptin production was reduced in both fasting male and female rats, the females additionally had significantly depleted LH and heightened estradiol levels that were four times higher than the average level. Estradiol is a hormone that interrupts GnRH in human beings. Furthermore, the hunger hormone leptin was six times lower for fasting female rats than it was for females that ate every day. It took approximately ten to fifteen days for the scientific study to completely inhibit the females' reproductive cycle. In the result of intermittent fasting, the female rats' hormones with both appetite regulation and reproduction regularity were completely thrown off.

Now, all of this science talk only has to do with rats; so, what does this mean for women? Because of the limited data of female human relationships with intermittent fasting, it is hard to tell how the body will be affected in the long run. Considering what is known about the change in diet in regards to the HPG axis, leptin levels, insulin levels, kisspeptin, and the females' ultra-sensitivity to environmental factors, it is possible that fasting will have a similar effect in female human beings.

Why this matters for women: If you do anything that makes your estrogen levels drop, you might eat more due to being hungrier than you would usually. Yes, estrogens is a plural word because estrone, estradiol, and estriol (estrogenic metabolites) are shifting as time goes on. When you are pre-menopausal, estradiol is most prominent, while after this time period, estrone remains the same and estradiol drops down. Estrogens are, therefore, very important regulators of metabolic processes and functions in the body.

The precise roles of each of them are not entirely clear, but some believe that estradiol dropping could lead to increased storage of fat. Why does this occur? Because estradiol is made with fat. That's why certain females have a hard time keeping weight off after they go through the change of menopause. This also could give women a concrete reason to think about your health in terms of reproduction, even if they don't want to have children anytime soon.

Why are women designed this way? You may be wondering why these differences exist. It may even seem unfair. Men have an easy time getting a six-pack while women struggle and struggle. But the fact is that women may not have as much of a need of this. Diets low in energy can lead to a drop in fertility if you're a female. Being too thin gives you a disadvantage, in terms of reproduction, if you're a woman. Women's bodies are tunes exquisitely to threats in fertility and energy levels, which does make sense in terms of evolution. Female humans are unique as far as mammals go. Nearly every other mammal can terminate their pregnancy at will, but human females cannot.

In human females, the mother's blood vessels are breached by the placenta, giving the fetus control over the situation. The baby is able to block insulin action in its mother to give itself more glucose. The baby can also cause dilation in its mother's blood vessels, getting more nutrients to itself. The baby will be determined to live even if the mother doesn't survive. Scientists even compare this to the relationship between a host and a virus. As soon as a woman is with child, she cannot convince the fetus to cease growing.

CHAPTER 3

The Different Types of Intermittent Fasting

As you will see, there are many different ways to do intermittent fasting. The secret here is to keep in mind your eating window. The more you fast the better the results will be. As previously discussed, the goal is to restrict the calories so that the body will be forced to burn fat when the glucose runs out. The only way to accomplish that is to shock the body into complying.

When you are fasting, it is very important for you to remember to truly fast. Even a small nibble of something during the fasting hours could trick the body into thinking that it is getting sustenance. If you can avoid eating during the fasting periods, your body will automatically reset and do what it is supposed to do, burn fat.

Identify your ideal eating window

The eating window is simply the time period set aside for your meals. For example, if you fast using the 16/8 schedule, then you will fast for 16 hours and the eating window will be eight hours. You are free to set your eating schedule for anytime you want. So, if you want to start your window at 7 AM, then you can eat your meals anytime between 7 AM – 3 PM. Some prefer to start later in the day. Whatever time you set your meal time, all of your food needs to be consumed during those hours. Once the eating window closes, you start fasting again.

The trick here is to define your own eating window based on your life and time schedule. There are several methods you could consider when setting up your eating window. Since all of our lives are very different, you need to find the method that best suits your personal lifestyle. One is no better than any other; the key here is to find the one that works best for you.

The Crescendo Method

One of the most popular methods of fasting is the crescendo method. It is great for beginners because it allows you to ease into fasting without putting your body into shock or throwing your hormones off whack.

With crescendo fasting, you do not have to fast every day but only two or three times a week. You might want to try starting with a Monday, Wednesday, Friday schedule and then build up. You can start with an eating window of about 12 hours and then gradually reduce it to 8 hours over time.

First and foremost, it is important that you don't fast more than three days a week for the first month and never fast for more than 24 hours at a time. During these fasting periods you are going to want to fast anywhere between 12 and 16 hours, it is very important that you never exceed more than 16 hours of fasting at a time if you can help it. On the days that you do fast, you are still going to want to exercise, just do something light or wait until after you have broken your fast to get started.

While you are fasting you are still allowed to consume water, coffee, and tea as long as you don't add anything with calories into them. If you know you are going to be pushing up against the 16 hour limit then you may want to add some coconut oil and grass-fed butter to your coffee. This approach to fasting tells your body that it is time for the cells to burn fat to obtain energy and to clean house. Crescendo fasting is a game changer for women. It will additionally boost your fertility and attractiveness. Within a couple of weeks, you will note the following benefits;

- Radiant skin
- Healthy libido
- Shiny hair
- An energetic demeanor
- Appropriate body weight

If you are over the age of 40 or are more than a few pounds overweight, then you might want to consider adding grass-fed collagen to your coffee on your fasting days instead. Collagen can reset your leptin levels which will help combat hunger. During fasting days it is important to keep both your fructose and sugars levels to a minimum as this will help to optimize leptin levels in the body. You can also add it to simple warm water if you don't prefer coffee or tea.

This more modified approach has lots of benefits, especially for women.

- It is easier on the body and keeps the hormones in balance.
- It's a great way to lose weight quickly.
- It keeps your energy levels high, so you are less likely to tire out quickly.

If you choose to use the crescendo method, there are some pretty basic rules that need to be followed:

- It should always be done on alternate days of the week, not consecutively.

- Start small with only two days a week and gradually build up.

- Do not start with the eight-hour eating window, start with a bigger window and gradually decrease it.

- On the days when you are fasting, include some lite cardio exercises.

- When you are not fasting, you can try a more intense workout program.

- During fasting periods, make sure you keep hydrated. Drink plenty of water but you can also drink unsweetened tea or coffee.

- Wait two weeks before adding another day of fasting.

- On fast days, take 5-8 grams of branch-chain amino acids to make sure your body is getting enough nutrients. You can buy them at any health food store or online.

If you follow the crescendo fasting method, you teach your body how to stop unconscious eating and can quell many of the cravings that most people struggle with. You'll learn to eat smarter while you reap the benefits of IF.

16/8 Method

The 16/8 method means that you fast for sixteen hours a day and cut your eating window down to only eight hours. Most people opt to skip breakfast or put it off until lunchtime, so they include the hours when they are sleeping as part of their fast. It is considered one of the most optimal ways to get your body to work more efficiently.

This method is a little more extreme than the crescendo method but many people like it because it is much easier to stay on track than the other methods. While on other diet programs, there are very strict rules to follow; 16/8 just restricts you to a very specific eating window. You are free to repeat it as often as you like so newbies start with doing it only one day a week and build up over time until they achieve the goals they have set.

16/8 has been very effective in speeding up weight loss, keeping your blood sugar under control, and even improving your brain function. It is very flexible and convenient as you set your own eating window, so you can set a time period that works best for you.

Additionally, two larger meals in an eight to ten-hour span is enough to leave the average person feeling completely full for about 12 hours which means you then really only have to get your body used to not eating for those remaining four hours.

It doesn't matter how many meals you eat during your non-fasting period, it only matters that it totals your complete calorie intake for the day and that the chosen amount is healthy enough to sustain you for a full 16 hours. Remember, once you start a pattern of eating, always stick with it throughout the trial period for the best results.

A common way to utilize the 16/8 fasting plan is to eat a large and filling dinner around 7 pm before not eating for 16 hours and then eating lunch as normal. This isn't the only way the split can work, however, and you can break your fast as early in the new day as you like, as long as you then stop eating early enough to repeat the cycle again tomorrow.

For the best results for those who are either already overweight or have a mainly sedimentary lifestyle, cutting out most, if not all, starchy carbs from your diet are also recommended. It may be difficult at first to cram all of your caloric requirements into this time period, but it will get easier with time. Most practitioners of this type of intermittent fasting either split their calories between 2 extra-filling meals or between 3 regular-sized meals and you should try both to see which works best for you. Whatever you decide on, it is important to keep in mind that consistency is very important to your long-term success.

A study done by the Obesity Society found that the most effective fasting period is between 10 pm and 2 pm, for men, and 12 am and 2 pm for women. Having your first meal at 2 pm has been shown to reduce feelings of hunger for the rest of the day while also maximizing fat burned throughout the entire day as well.

If you find yourself in a situation where you will not be able to realistically break your fast as you normally would, it is important to prepare for this fact as best you can and do whatever is in your power to keep your new normal going as much as possible. With that being said, it isn't the end of the world if you happen to eat a single meal outside of your standard eight or ten hours. If this occurs simply start your fast as normal at the end of the day and keep yourself on track as much as possible.

Again, the specifics of when you fast are not nearly as important as ensuring that you fast for the same period of time as regularly as possible. If you vary your fasting period too much it can lead to an erratic change in your hormones which among other things can make it much more difficult for your body to shed any excess weight.

If you are exercising as well as intermittently fasting it is important to ensure that you are eating more carbohydrates than fats while you are working out while on days you are not exercising the opposite is true. It is important to ensure that every day you keep your protein intake at a steady level and stay away from processed foods whenever possible.

The biggest benefits of this type of fasting is that it is extremely flexible so that it will work for a wide variety schedules. Most people find it helpful to either eat two large meals during the 8 or 10-hour period feeding period or split that time into three smaller meals as that is the way most people are already programed.

On days you are exercising as well as fasting it is important to try and always break your fast with a mix of protein, vegetables, and fruit. If you generally go to the gym directly after you have broken your fast, it is important to include enough carbohydrates to give your muscles the energy they need to get the most out of your workout. If you are planning to exercise it is generally best to start the early afternoon off right with a medium calorie meal and then exercise within three hours before then eating a larger meal soon afterwards. In this larger meal, it is important to add a larger portion of complex carbohydrates and you can even have a little dessert as long as it is in moderation.

On days you do not plan on exercising it is important to adjust your caloric intake appropriately. Start by limiting your carbohydrate intake and instead focus on eating lots of protein, dark green, leafy vegetables and fruit in moderation

24-Hour Fast

This type of fasting revolves around a few 24 hour fasts per week but don't let the name scare you the 24-hour fast is much easier than it sounds. Most people do it by having dinner one day, sleeping at night, and then fasting throughout the next day and then having dinner the following day. How often you do it depends on your ability to push through the fasting period.

If you have started with the crescendo method, then you can gradually build up to the point where you can follow the 24-hour fasting method. Frequency should be based on your level of activity though. If your lifestyle is more sedentary, then you might want to have 24-hour fasting periods more often than someone who is very active.

It is a well-known fact that we eat mostly when we are stressed, or feel lonely, frustrated, excited, confused, or even when we are happy. This means that we humans tend to eat in response to our emotions which is not the best approach to health, diet, or food intake. With this approach, we tend to feed our emotional hunger rather than psychological hunger.

Fortunately, the 24-hour protocol helps you to identify the difference between the two. For instance, if you have your last meal of the day at 8.00 pm one evening, then you will not eat anything for the next 24 hours. You do not have to follow this protocol every single day of the week. Instead, you can practice it once or twice each week.

Some people are unable to fast for 24 hours straight. Fortunately, these programs are flexible and so fasting for 18 or 20 hours is also acceptable. The main aim here is to find what works best for you and then learn to live with it.

As you fast, you are allowed to drink a cup of coffee, black or green tea, and any other non-calorific beverages. If you are following this protocol for weight loss purposes, then you should maintain your regular eating habits.

Nutrition experts prefer that you perform this fast once a week. Find the day of the week when you are most sedentary then plan to fast that entire day. For instance, if your fast day is Tuesday, then start fasting on Monday after dinner. Do not eat any food all day until dinner time on Tuesday.

The main challenge about this protocol is that many people are unable to maintain a fast for an entire 24-hour period. If this is you, then you do not have to fast for an entire 24 hours in the beginning. You can start with 14-16 hours then increase the hours until you can fast for a full 24 hours.

Sometimes participants get angry and hungry. Those with conditions such as diabetes may not be able to cope with the 24-hour protocol. In such instances, participants are encouraged by health experts to modify this protocol or to choose a different one. This way, they will still be able to enjoy the benefits of fasting.

Eat-Stop-Eat

If you are already relatively health conscious when it comes to what you put into your body, but are still looking for a way to bump your weight loss into high gear, then the eat-stop-eat method of intermittent fasting might be what you are looking for. This type of intermittent fasting requires participants to go without food for a full 24-hour period 1 or 2 days out of the week. During the fasting period you may only consume, 0 calorie sodas, water, 0 calorie gum, and coffee, but only if it is consumed black. It is important to always break these days up and to never try and go 48-hours without eating in a row. Ideally, putting 3 days between each day of fasting is recommended.

Ideally, during this period, you would manage to not consume a total of 3,500 calories which means that once you break your fast you are simply able to go about your eating habits as normal, within reason of course. Especially when following more prolonged periods of fasting such as this, it is extremely important to break your fast with something relatively small and simple to prime the pump for the more significant meals to come. Failing to take into account the proper preemptive period can lead to serious gastrointestinal stress.

Likewise, when following an eat-stop-eat cycle it is important to not allow yourself to fall into a habit of binging and fasting as this is too much variance for your body to handle easily. This cycle only works for those who are able to practice controlling themselves and consuming in moderation, not just on fast days but every day. For the best results, resistance-style weight training is also recommended, though only on the days you are not fasting.

If you don't like the idea of being completely passive during your fast days, then a mild yoga session or some light cardio is all that is recommended. While you might not feel it at first, anything more than that will make it much more difficult to see you fast all the way through to the end. During this period, it is common, especially at first, to experience feelings of anxiousness, anger, headaches or fatigue. Understand that these feelings will pass as your body adjusts to your new dietary habits.

On the days that you are fasting, you will want to limit yourself to water, diet soda, tea, and coffee. On the days you are eating regularly you are going to want to feel free to eat what you will, within reason. Make it a point of adding plenty of high quality fruits and vegetables to your diet.

Additionally, you are going to want to aim for at least 200 grams of protein per day to give yourself enough to ensure that your body continues functioning properly during fast days. Aim for 50 grams every 3 to 4 hours. Using high-quality protein powders to ensure you hit this amount is recommended.

Some people will not be able to adapt to such a strict type of fasting, you will know that it is not for you if you continue being irritable during fast days after a month or so and if you continue to experience periods of dizziness or headaches. With that being said, the benefits to this intermittent fasting method are undeniable and it offers the freedom to alter when you are fasting based on need. Whatever you do, however, it is important to never fast for 2 consecutive days and never fast for more than 2 days in a single week.

The Warrior Fast

The warrior fast sets the eating window at night in a similar fashion to ancient military fighters who fought battles throughout the day and only had meals after the sun went down. This is a very strict program where the eating window is cut down to our four hours in the day. If you follow the warrior fast it is very important that you consume a lot of calories when you eat so that you have enough to get you through the next twenty hours.

This plan was formulated by fitness expert, Ori Hofmekler, who studied how the lean and muscular ancient Romans and Spartans ate. If body building is your thing, this should be your intermittent fasting diet of choice.

This diet is similar to the 16/8 style of fasting except you eat very small portions of food for 20 hours every day and then eat a lot of food during a period of just four hours every evening. Even this diet needs to be eased into because the dieter can experience the same symptoms of hunger as if they didn't eat anything at all for all of those hours. Skip breakfast once or twice a week. Skip breakfast three or four times the next week. Move into skipping lunch and work on up to skipping all breakfasts and lunches every day.

You nibble on raw fruits and vegetables, eat small amounts of protein, and drink fresh juice during the days. This maximizes the "fight or flight" response from the sympathetic nervous system. This response promotes alertness, boosts energy, and burns fat.

When you break your fast at night, you must eat particular food groups in a particular order. First, you eat broth, then vegetables, protein/meat, and then fat. You can eat carbohydrates at the end of your four-hour feasting period if you are still hungry.

Eating at night maximizes the parasympathetic nervous system, which helps the body to recuperate, become calm, relax, digest while the body uses the nutrients for growth and for repair. It may also help the body to produce fat-burning hormones that work on your fat the next day.

Another aspect of this diet is to do strength training during the days. Do squats, pull-ups, high jumps, press-ups, frog jumps, and sprints. Select three of these activities, doing two sets of five minutes each during a thirty-minute period of time that you set aside every day. Drink a protein shake before you exercise.

5:2 and 4:3

For this plan, you would eat a regular diet for five days. For the remaining two days, you will eat approximately 500 to 600 calories. The baseline of the calorie ingestion is 2,000 for women and 2,500 for men. A few famous names swear by the diet including Jennifer Aniston and David Cameron. These are some of the ways of how to manage the 5:2 diet plan; just remember carbs don't mix with your fasting days.

Health benefits include asthma relief, reduction in heart arrhythmias, insulin resistance, menopausal hot flashes, seasonal allergies, and much more. After twelve weeks of fasting using this method; these are the results from a small study group:

- Fat mass reduction: 3.5 kg with no muscle mass changes
- Body weight reduction: Over 5 kg
- Increased LDL particle size
- Reduced blood levels: 20% reduction of triglycerides
- Leptin levels: 40% decreased
- Levels CRP: Reduced levels (inflammation marker in your body)

The 5:2 intermittent fasting choices are much simpler than the 4:3 plan because you are more restricted. You will be intermittently fasting for three out of the seven days. You should not eat processed/sugary/refined foods for four of the days. If you do, your body will crave the supplementary fatty acids you need to thrive.

If you consume junk on those four days, you will defeat the purpose of the plan. Just remember, not to over-indulge. As you train your body by eating a well-planned diet; your body will adjust to the routine, and you won't feel as hungry. The 4:3 plan acclaims you skip the morning meal, and it recommends you check your weight daily. However, this can be disheartening if your weight fluctuates.

It is important not to overindulge on the days that you are eating freely as it can be easy to go over your calorie limit and defeat the purpose of the entire exercise. With time, you can train your body to expect a well-structured diet and you won't feel as hungry during the fast days. The 4:3 plan also recommends that you skip breakfast and measure your weight daily. For those whose weight tends to fluctuate more than average this is not recommended, however, as it can be disheartening.

Sample meal plan

- Breakfast: Skip it. If you enjoy a morning meal then you will need to eliminate the snack during the day. You may also skip lunch instead.
- Lunch: Lentil, leek or chicken soup with a small snack such as a tangerine.
- Dinner: A small portion of fish or fillet of grilled chicken with a side salad with lemon juice and seasonings as dressing.
- Snack: Carrot sticks to fill out the remainder of your calories.

Other Types of Fasting

36-hour fast: This is probably the most difficult eating window to practice. It requires you to forego nourishment for a full day and a half. It requires that you sleep two nights in a fasted state before you can eat again. Most people start it the same way as the 24-hour fast, by having dinner and then going the entire day without eating. Instead of having dinner the next day though, they go to bed again and eat lunch on the second day. If you follow the basic rules of fasting, after you get used to it, you won't feel any extreme hunger.

Breakfast and dinner fast: An easier fast to consider is almost a 50/50 fast. You wake up early in the morning and have breakfast, then go throughout the whole day and have a late dinner. This fast almost divides the day in half with twelve hours of fasting and a twelve-hour eating window. Some are even able to do this twice in a single 24-hour period.

Alternate day fasting: One of the ways you can start fasting is by using a method called alternate day fasting. Known as one of the best practices to see a decreased risk of chronic diseases like diabetes, cardiovascular diseases, and many others, in human studies, it has shown to bring up "good cholesterol" which led to lower risk of heart diseases.

In animals using this method has proved to lower cancerous cells, so without a doubt, this fasting method will be ideal for you if your goals are to prevent the risk of having these diseases. Just like most other fasting methods, it will also help you with goals like fat-loss and other aesthetic purposes that you might have, but this method is more known to lower risk of diseases and used by people who have that goal in mind. This method can still be used with success if you have the goal of losing weight and looking good. Just like others have used this method to lose body fat or put on muscle. That being said let us talk about how this method is to be used.

Well, the name says it all, you will be fasting for one day and then eating a regular healthy diet like you should be the next day. Now on your fasting day, you are not going to be completely restraining yourself from food, you should still have one-fourth of the calories that you have on the non-fasting day. So if you have two thousand calories a day then on fasting days you should be consuming five hundred calories a day on your fasting days, you would instead have one meal on your fasting day which should cover your daily requirement for approximately five hundred calories. Some people have also seen some great success with having small snacks throughout the day to equal their calorie need for the day.

Fat loss forever: This form of intermittent fasting combines elements of several other styles of fasting to create something rather unique. The good news is that you get a cheat day every week, the bad news is that it is followed by one and a half day fast with the remainder of the week being split between 16/8 and 20/4 fasting. For this diet, it is important to schedule your exercise rest days for the second part of the 36-hour cycle but otherwise, it is important to stay as busy on these days as possible in order to help combat your hunger. If you find it hard to control yourself on cheat days, then this form of intermittent fasting may not be for you as it requires you to go from 60 to 0 quickly and regularly.

In addition, it is important to not try and last 36 hours without food all at once, you will need to build up your body's tolerance for fasting. As such it is usually better to start with another form of intermittent fasting and work up to the Fat Loss Forever method after your body has already gotten out of the habit of eating every three or four hours. Remember to always fast responsibly and never push your body to the point where you feel physically ill.

For this one to work, you should save your longest fasts for those days when you are really busy. This makes it easier for you to focus on being productive and getting things done, rather than focusing on the meals that you are missing. This type of plan can also include some training programs, so you can lose as much weight as possible.

According to the ones who started this type of intermittent fast, while everyone does do a little fasting each day, such as when you are sleeping, most people do it in a sporadic way that does make it harder to get the rewards. This program offers you a seven day schedule of fasting so that the body can get used to this new timetable and can get the most out of the fasting periods. Plus, it adds in a cheat day that a lot of people like.

CHAPTER 4

The Benefits of Intermittent Fasting

The benefits of intermittent fasting are wide ranging and reach far beyond simply losing weight while at the same time building muscle. Intermittent fasting also leads to a simplified routine ensuring you don't have to worry about one whole meal every day, usually breakfast. You will be surprised by how much time and money you save by not eating one meal every single day. It turns out that eating larger portions of existing meals, even if the caloric count is the same is cheaper than purchasing additional smaller meals. While it may seem odd at first to completely give up on breakfast after you give it about a month you will find that you don't even miss it.

In addition to making your life easier and cutting down on your food budget intermittent fasting also helps you live longer as the body sees itself as starving and does everything it can to prolong basic biological functions as long as possible. Intermittent fasting is quite a bit different than starving however and if you eat two large meals a day, you won't even by too much hungrier than normal come your mid-day meal once your body has adjusted to the change. Nevertheless, waiting for as little as twelve hours between meals has been proven in mice to cause many of the same benefits the body sees during starvation.

Weight loss: While the benefits of intermittent fasting are numerous, the most obvious benefit is weight loss. When your body runs out of glucose it will have no choice but to turn to the fat stores that you have accumulated over the years to pick up the slack. As a result, you will literally start to burn fat while you are doing nothing more than sitting around waiting for your next meal, sleeping, or some combination of the two.

Intermittent fasting does not just help you lose weight, but it helps you to lose it in one of the most stubborn places - your stomach. Because intermittent fasting inherently restricts your meals to a certain time, you are already lowering your daily caloric intake. When you do that, you end up losing weight. However, what makes intermittent fasting more effective is that fasting causes your weight loss hormones to rev up. When you are in a fasted state, your body gets energy from your body's fat stores and not the food you eat.

This, in turn, increases your metabolism rate. So what is your metabolism rate? It is the rate at which you lose calories. You can lose calories by either eating less food or getting your body to use your stored fat, which is what intermittent fasting does. Additionally, intermittent fasting does not cause you to lose muscle as true starvation would. When you still have some type of muscle on your body, your muscles work harder than fat to increase your metabolism, and so you are losing weight while doing limited activities.

The hormones that help you lose weight while doing intermittent fasting are numerous. One of the hormones that increase when you fast is called the human growth hormone. This hormone is important in weight loss because it helps your body to burn more fat and it also helps increase your muscle which helps you lose more weight as well. Another hormone that is affected by intermittent fasting is leptin. This hormone tells your brain when you are hungry. If you are obese, this hormone is overactive. When you intermittently fast, it helps improve your leptin sensitivity so it is more accurate. It sends your brain more measured indicators of your hunger so you are not overeating.

Helps diabetics: There is evidence that daily intermittent fasting, as well as alternate-day fasting, is an effective way for those in danger of contracting type 2 diabetes to lower their glucose levels steadily in just six months. These same studies, however, show that in animal testing weight loss was not always seen in addition to the other benefits if the animals overcompensated on the days and for the meals they were eating. The same can be said for humans and it is important to remember to not overdue it on the meals you do eat if you want to maintain a steady weight loss.

However, you must be aware that there may be differences in how this works between the genders. One study that was done in women showed that control of blood sugar actually got worse after they followed 22 days of an intermittent fasting protocol. More studies would have to be done on this, and it may just be a factor of changing around how long you fast for women to get the same benefits as well.

Reduces inflammation in the body: Oxidative stress is hard on the body and it can be one of the risk factors that come with aging and other chronic diseases. This kind of stress is going to involve a lot of free radicals, or molecules that are considered unstable, reacting with some of the important molecules that your body needs. These important molecules can be things like DNA and protein in the body. When free radicals react with the important molecules, they will end up causing damage.

There have been several studies that show how intermittent fasting is a great way to enhance how your body resists oxidative stress. In addition, there are other studies that talk about how intermittent fasting is important for fighting off inflammation. Inflammation can be hard on the body because it is going to be the key force behind many other harmful diseases in the body. With the help of intermittent fasting, you can effectively reduce the amount of inflammation that is in the body and get your health back on track.

Reduces the risk of cancer: Besides general lengthening of the lifespan, intermittent fasting has also been shown to reduce the risk of cancer and cardiovascular disease while also lessening the effects cancer patients felt after undergoing chemotherapy. Current studies show that restricting your daily caloric intake by as little as fifteen percent can improve a person's tolerance to glucose and increases inulin action which in turn helps to lower blood pressure and benefits a wide array of other bodily functions including things like increasing the amount of oxidative resistance things like DNA, protein, and lipids all have which in turn helps your body be more resistive to things like spontaneous or induced cancers, lower rates of kidney disease and an increased period of reproductive function.

While the exact reason for this interesting tidbit is not yet clear, scientists believe it may relate to both the decrease in stress the body receives and also that after a period of restricting your diet regularly for a prolonged period of time the body begins to increase its resistance to a variety of stressors which broadly allows the cells a greater chance to protect themselves from injuries that can occur to portions of the digestive tract including a number of crucial organs.

Boosts brain function: While most of the studies on brain function and fasting are on animals, and more human studies are needed, the results are promising. One study in mice found that intermittent fasting for eleven months improved both brain function and structure. Another study found that fasting may improve overall brain health, as well as increasing the generation of nerve cells, and enhancing cognitive function. Fasting has also been shown to possibly have beneficial effects on neurological conditions such as Parkinson's disease and Alzheimer's disease.

Fights heart disease: As you might know, heart disease is one of the biggest killers when it comes to conditions. Intermittent fasting has also been shown to reduce the risk of heart diseases; the way it works is pretty simple. Intermittent fasting reduces the levels of LDL, which leads to heart attacks. Intermittent fasting has also been shown to lower blood pressure levels, and high blood pressure is also one of the many reasons why people tend to have heart complications.

There are many other fitness experts and professional doctors claiming that intermittent fasting works to reduce the risk of heart diseases. Even though there have been studies to back these claims up, they were done on animals. To confirm these claims, we need to make sure that these studies have been backed up with human studies.

Nonetheless, there is still some considerable evidence to follow intermittent fasting if your goal is to reduce the risk of heart diseases. One way intermittent fasting can help you to reduce the risk of heart diseases is by lowering the amount of sugar present in your bloodstream, and this has been shown to decrease the risk of heart diseases in humans, making it a plus point of intermittent fasting. So, if you are looking to lower the risk of heart diseases in the best way possible without following any diets, then intermittent fasting is the answer for you. But make sure you consult with your physician before you start any plan.

Improve cell-life: Likewise, limited your caloric intake has been shown to cause your mitochondria to work in a limited energy utilization mode which in turn means your cells will experience less oxidative damage over your lifetime. A third theory is that the creation of artificial scarcity leads to a general slowing of certain key metabolic actions including the rate at which cells divide which in turn makes each cell live longer than then would otherwise. This theory has gained credibility in recent years as it correlates to recent experiments done on yeast cells.

Despite the wide variety of health benefits perhaps the best part of intermittent fasting is just how easy it is to get into the habit of doing. When most people diet they tend to go directly from zero to sixty when it comes to changing their routines and their eating patterns which quickly ends with a reductive mindset where the smallest slipup is enough of a cause to get them to turn back to their previous unhealthy eating habits with open arms. Because intermittent fasting is not a diet it is much easier for people to see it for what it really is, a small change with big results.

In fact, studies show that even in obese individuals, those who tried intermittent fasting were nearly three times as likely to keep at it for a period of three months compared to those who are dieting in a more traditional fashion. What's more, the amount of weight loss between those who completed a 90-day intermittent fasting plan and those that completed a traditional diet were about the same. Even better, four months after the initial test those on the intermittent fasting plan had still lost more weight than the dieting group; and not only that, they showed improvements to their memories as well.

Normalizes hormone function: It has been demonstrated that this lifestyle regulates your hormones and provides better hormonal balance in your body. When you fast, your internal organs, including your liver, get to rest and this allows hormones to balance naturally.

Insulin is a hormone that regulates blood sugar levels. It is released by the pancreas. As you fast, the body begins to convert fat within your body into glucose in order to provide energy. As the levels of stored fat decrease, you start to lose weight. In the process, your cells and muscles become more responsive to insulin in the blood. This way, insulin becomes easily absorbed by the body.

When the body absorbs insulin efficiently, it is then better able to regulate blood sugar levels. This is crucial because it prevents conditions such as type II diabetes. Anyone searching for a natural way of managing insulin sensitivity should definitely think about intermittent fasting.

There are individuals who suffer insulin resistance. This situation occurs when there are excessive amounts of glucose in the body. Insulin resistance is often viewed as a precursor to diabetes. Pre-diabetes is a term that means your blood sugar levels are higher than normal but not too high to be diagnosed as diabetes. When you begin fasting, all the glucose stored in your body gets consumed and turned into energy. This allows your body to function normally again.

This is a hormone produced in the body that stimulates cells to divide and multiply. The human growth hormone or HGH boosts collagen synthesis in the joints, tendons, and skeletal muscles. HGH boosts the immune system and also helps to improve physical activity even as it breaks down lipids or fat cells. When lipids are broken down, the fats in the body are reduced rapidly.

The hormone cortisol is also referred to as the stress hormone. It is released in the body anytime you are in a highly stressful situation. The main purpose of cortisol is to trigger a flight or fight response. It also works closely with the sympathetic nervous system.

Intermittent fasting helps with the regulation of cortisol by regulating insulin. Insulin is a cortisol antigen so when it is properly regulated, there will be very little cortisol in the body.

CHAPTER 5

Eating Properly

One mistake that many people who are new to fasting make is assuming that just because they are fasting they are now free to eat anything and everything they want. The reality of the situation is that this could not be further from the truth as eating properly is key to making all that fasting worthwhile.

You need to understand what your daily calorie needs will be to adopt a realistic diet plan and maintain a new desirable weight. The use of an adult BMI and Calorie Calculator will be an essential tool if the calories are not indicated in the recipe. Most products you purchase will have ingredient panels listing the counts, so you will have a general idea of how to plan your menu around your intermittent fasting plan.

You will need to enter your sex, height, weight, and age into the calculator. You will also need to provide the calculator with your daily activity schedule (such as daily—more than an hour—less than an hour—or rarely. The BMI will indicate your BMI score and the number of calories necessary to maintain your current body weight. It will make your goals simpler to map by providing you with the tallies from your calculations to lower your counts.

Maintain a healthy diet plan: The components for a healthier eating pattern using intermittent fasting methods will account for all of the beverages and foods within a suitable calorie level. A good plan for a healthy fasting pattern will include the following:

- Whole Fruits
- Oils
- Grains (a minimum of half should be whole grains)

- Protein foods such as eggs, poultry, lean meats, seafood, nuts, seeds, and soy products.

- Varied veggies from all of the main subgroups include—starchy legumes (peas and beans), red and orange, dark green and others.

Health concerns in the United States are focused on fundamental elements that should be limited when using the intermittent fasting diet plan. They recommend you do the following:

- Consume less than 10% of your daily calories from saturated fats.

- Eat less than 10% of your daily intake of calories from added sugars.

- Sodium consumption should be less than 2,300 mg (milligrams).

- Moderation must be accompanied if you consume alcohol products. You should have no more than one daily if you are a woman and only two each day if you are a man.

Foods to avoid

As a general rule, the following foods should be avoided or at least limited as much as possible.

Processed Meats: While protein is an undeniably important part of a healthy diet, seeking your protein from meats which have been processed will stuff your body so full of chemicals that any benefits the meal might have had are otherwise lost. In addition, these meats tend to be lower in protein while higher in sodium, preservatives that can cause a variety of health risks including asthma and heart disease than the quality of the cuts of meat found in most grocery stores.

Non-organic potatoes: While starch and the carbohydrates it contains are an important part of a balanced meal, non-organic potatoes are not worth the trouble. They are treated with chemicals while still in the ground before being treated again before they head to the store to ensure they stay "fresh" as long as possible. These chemicals have been shown to increase the risk of things like autism, asthma, birth defects, learning disabilities, Parkinson's and Alzheimer's disease as well as multiple types of cancer.

Farm-raised salmon: Much like processed meat, farm-raised salmon are the least healthy type of an otherwise healthy meal choice. When salmon are raised in close proximity to one another for a prolonged period of time they lose much of their natural vitamin D while picking up traces of PCB, DDT, carcinogens, and bromine.

Non-organic milk: Despite being touted as part of a balanced diet; non-organic milk is routinely found to be full of growth hormones as well as puss as a result of over-milking. The growth hormones leave behind antibiotics which in turn makes it more difficult for the human body to counter infections as well as causing an increased chance of colon cancer, prostate cancer, and breast cancer.

White flour: Much like processed meats, by the time white flour is done being produced it is completely devoid of any nutritional value. When eaten as part of a regular diet white flour has been shown to increase a woman's chance of breast cancer by a shocking 200 percent.

These are just a few of the reasons that processed foods should be considered a scourge on the modern world. Processed foods can be considered any which contain preservatives, chemical colors, flavorings or additives or chemicals which change their texture. An additional extremely important warning sign of unhealthy food is when an item contains a large number of carbohydrates in their refined form.

The cliff-notes version is this, the sooner you begin to take the time to read labels and check ingredients the sooner you can start getting the most out of the meals you eat in between intermittent fasting sessions. Making a real, consciousness effort to do so may very well be the difference between life and death.

Don't forget supplements

Reasons to use supplements: There are three primary reasons why people reach for supplements on the keto diet. It is highly extreme and goes against nearly everything you've been taught before. This could put your body into a state of shock while it is adjusting to this drastic change. Supplements are a great way to help your body through this difficult period of transition. Most of the supplements recommended here are used to help with the common withdrawal symptoms and problems that many people suffer when they begin on their keto diet:

Low energy: You can have both low mental energy and physical energy. You will feel drained if you're not keeping up with your macros. Supplements can be very effective in keeping your energy levels up while your body adjusts and can help your physical performance remain up.

Deficiency of micronutrients: If your meal plan does not include a sufficient amount of micronutrients, you can also find yourself not functioning at optimum levels. Supplements will be the key to helping you to manage that balance while you tweak your diet until you get it right.

MCT oil: This is a unique tasteless oil consisting of medium chain triglycerides. These are the kind of fats that are more easily absorbed by your body. MCTs are extracted from coconut or palm kernel oil and is often used as a treatment for digestive system disorders, seizures, and other illnesses. MCT Oil can:

- Enhance ketone production
- Improve weight loss efforts
- Give you a quick supply of energy
- Aid in appetite control

One of the reasons MCT Oil is so effective is because it doesn't require digestive enzymes or bile to break it down. Instead, it travels directly to the liver from the small intestine, so it can be used to provide an instant energy boost either from fatty acids or ketones. It can also aid in weight loss by controlling the genes responsible for fat storage.

To use MCT Oil, you can simply use it in your recipes. Because it is tasteless, you can add to anything including your coffee or smoothies. Add it as a base for your salad dressing or just take a spoonful of it when you can. It is odorless, so it won't alter that taste, aroma, or any other element of the things you consume.

The best time to take it is in the morning when you first wake up and just before you start a workout.

Collagen peptides: Collagen makes up about 30% of all the protein in your body. It is an essential element for your bones, cartilage, skin, tendons and any connective tissue. Your body is perfectly capable of producing its own collagen, but it can also be taken in the form of collagen peptides, which are merely a hydrolyzed form of it. It can be used to help.

- Make your skin look and feel younger.
- Strengthen the larger muscle groups.
- Improve joint health.
- Strengthen Bones.
- Reduce inflammation.
- Help recovery after a workout.

But the main reason why you want to take collagen peptides is they are the kind of proteins that are the least likely to take you out of ketosis.

When getting collagen peptides, make sure you're getting them without fillers or any artificial ingredients. Avoid any that contain caloric sweeteners. The best sources are from those produced from grass-fed cattle, pigs, and fish.

To take them, add them to your drinks like coffee or tea; include them in your smoothies, or simply add a spoonful to your water and drink as usual. You can even add it to any recipes you make. The taste is very mild, so it is not likely you will even notice it. Try to take it around 30 minutes before or after a workout. If you add it in your morning coffee, then you can get the added benefit of increased appetite control and an energy boost as well. Some add it to their lunch, so they can stay full longer. Just make sure that you don't go beyond the recommended daily limit allowed.

Electrolytes: As soon as you start your keto diet, you will begin to lose fluids. As you do, you will also lose essential electrolytes, which is one of the key triggers for the keto flu, so having electrolytes on hand will go a long way in helping you to get over the initial phase quicker.

Electrolytes are essential minerals or micronutrients. The most important to have are:

- Sodium, which you can get from table salt, bullion, and soy sauce.
- Magnesium, which can be found in leafy greens, nuts, and mineral water.
- Potassium can be found in avocados, fish, and spinach.
- Chloride comes from table salt.
- Calcium, eggs, leafy greens, and dairy.

Fiber: Because you are going to be so low on carbs, you'll also be low on fiber, the indigestible part of carbohydrates. Without an adequate supply of fiber, you can start to feel bloated and constipated. In addition, the higher amount of fat you take in can be hard on the digestive system, which can create a condition of fat malabsorption where the body struggles to absorb the fat. Good sources of fiber include:

- Psyllium Husk – found at a local pharmacy or supplement store.

- Acacia Fiber – a water-soluble fiber used to treat constipation or diarrhea. Works very well in treating IBS and high cholesterol.

- Ground Flaxseed – comes in both soluble and insoluble form. Insoluble fiber gives bulk to your stool, so it is easier to pass. But you will need to grind it first to get the benefit. Flaxseed is also very rich in omega-3 fatty acids, protein, thiamin, and folate.

- Chia Seeds – an insoluble form of fiber-rich in omega-3 fatty acids and calcium. They're low in net carbs but are also very high in fat.

Other excellent sources of fiber include:

- Nut Flour
- Coconut flour
- Nuts
- Seeds
- Leafy greens

Fish oil supplements: For omega-3 fatty acids, fish oils are the absolute best source. These are acids that your body can't make on its own but are essential for good health. It is used to build up cell membranes and to help the molecules to produce energy. Omega-3s help to control inflammation and can protect the brain.

- Fatty fish
- Eggs
- Avocado
- Walnuts
- Broccoli
- Flaxseed
- Chia Seeds

These supplements are also very good at helping your body to get into ketosis and stay, something that you will appreciate as you go into your keto fast.

Healthy eating tips

Don't expect results overnight: As previously discussed, it will take some time for your body to fully adjust to your new dietary patterns and for it to start reflecting these new results. Try intermittent fasting regularly for at least a month before rendering judgement.

Try Branched Chain Amino Acids: For those on a low calorie diet such as intermittent fasting, studies show that a BCAA supplement will stimulate additional fat loss while at the same time preventing lean muscle from being consumed as the body tries to feed itself.

Start slow: If you find that you are having difficulty starting the transition to an intermittent fasting program full bore, instead of trying simply moving your breakfast time back one hour each week. Before you know it you will have reached a 16/8 (14/10) split without even trying.

Start the day of with a belly full of liquid: Often times the signals for hunger and the signals for thirst can get crossed in our brains as after sending out enough ignored thirst signals it starts sending out hunger signals instead. As such, starting the morning off by drinking at least half a liter of water is a great way to quench your body's thirst from the past seven or eight hours and should be enough to keep you feeling full for at least a few extra hours each morning.

Splurge when you want: Remember that you need to burn 3,500 calories to lose a pound a week but how you do that is up to you. If you want to have a particularly appetizing dessert or unhealthy main course that is perfectly fine as long as you make the effort to make up the difference throughout the week.

Add protein to your meals: There is nothing better at combating hunger than protein, plain and simple. It is also great for building lean muscle. If you find yourself unable to get through even 10 hours without eating, then it might be a sign that you should add more protein to your diet.

Intermittent fasting is not an excuse to eat poorly: Intermittent fasting works on the principle that eating fewer calories than you burn is a surefire way to lose weight. This theory falls apart if you use the fact that you are fasting as an excuse to eat nothing but junk food when you are eating. Self-control and self-discipline are both equally important when it comes to eating properly. Intermittent fasting has a wide variety of health benefits, why not accentuate them even more with a healthy diet to go along with it.

Break your fast the right way: The content and quality of your first meal of the day can easily set the tone for those that follow. Use this to your advantage and start your feeding window off right with something fit and healthy and you will be surprised at how much this improves your willpower for later meals.

Consider the difference between head hunger and body hunger: As you get used to the process of intermittent fasting, you will become acquainted with several different types of hunger and ultimately learn how to tell when you are truly hungry as opposed to just habitually used to eating. While it will initially be difficult to tell the difference you will come to know them both intimately in time.

Learn your body's tells: While many people consider a sudden craving for a particular type of food as an indication that they are hungry and take action to respond accordingly, this in fact is often just a craving brought on by an ancient part of the brain which equates things that are salty, sweet and high in fat as vital parts of a regular diet as once upon a time having those three qualities equated to things that were high in positive nutrients as well. This is no longer the case and tends to be the opposite these days. As such these types of urges can safely be ignored. In addition, take the time to investigate if a sudden surge of hunger could instead be related to your emotional state instead of your physical one.

Distract yourself: This is especially important as your body is adapting to your new eating habits and becomes increasingly important the farther into a fast you go. Try going out and being active when you are particularly struggling to help give you mind other things to focus on.

Don't take on too much, too fast: Even if you think you feel fine when you first begin an intermittent fast cycle it is important to always give your body the time it needs to recover and never go more than two days out of a week without eating, there is an important distinction between fasting and starving yourself.

Don't cover real issues with fasting: Those with a penchant for eating disorders or those who believe they might be should stay away for intermittent fasting as it can easily lead to more serious issues if not controlled properly. Remember, it is important to have the willpower to stop eating for a set period of time but it is also equally important to have the willpower to begin eating again once the fast is over.

CHAPTER 6

Maximize Fat Loss

Keto fasting

Up until recently, people everywhere were touting the benefits of the Keto Diet. It has helped people all over the world to shed those extra pounds and improve their health. But now, people are talking about the Keto Fast! By putting the two components together (ketogenic diet and intermittent fasting) amazing results are being reported. It makes you wonder what exactly makes the combination so powerful.

There are many benefits to intermittent fasting. Not only does it aid in faster weight loss without the need to count calories and measure every bite that goes into your mouth, but it also helps in building up muscles. When you fast, your human growth hormone increases by as much as 2,000% in men and 1,300% in women. This is the hormone that is responsible for building muscle tissue. Research studies have shown that when you have high levels of HGH, you also have lower levels of body fat! Yay! This translates into a leaner body mass and a better bone mass too. HGH is also the hormone to improve your muscle protein synthesis so your body can repair itself much more quickly. You'll notice faster recovery times from injuries than before.

In fact, there is a long list of benefits to be gained from intermittent fasting. It has been known to thicken the skin, so it is stronger and more resistant to the sagging and wrinkling of aging; it boosts your stem cell production, so your body can use them as replacements for older and damaged cells. It strengthens joints and helps to reduce instances of chronic pain.

It also improves brain function by increasing the production of the BDNF protein. Researchers have found that BDNF aids in improved learning and memory and aids the brain in building stronger neural pathways, so it can process information faster and more efficiently.

It stimulates autophagy, which is a means of self-cleaning. When you fast, you give your body time to sift through its various parts and work to eliminate anything that may be slowing it down. It gets rid of the parts that are not working and replaces them with newer, healthier parts. As a result, inflammation is less, and your overall health improves. This puts less stress on the body and allows you to become more active in everything you do.

In essence, intermittent fasting is like giving your whole body a tune-up. After you've done it for a few weeks, you'll begin to notice that your body will respond faster and get stronger in the process.

Where the keto diet comes in: But intermittent fasting is not a panacea. Even though it offers great benefits, there are still quite a few problems it can't handle. In fact, there is one major problem that intermittent fasting actually creates that could cause a major health issue for most people. It renders your blood sugar levels unstable, especially if you choose to eat a lot of carbs.

As we discussed in Chapter 1, when you are on a high-carb diet, your blood sugar will experience major rises and falls throughout the day. It'll naturally go higher after you eat, but will then start to decline as the day wears on. If, during your eating window you consume a lot of carbs, you will definitely have these unstable blood sugar readings making your fasting period that much harder.

As a result, you will lose energy faster. When your system runs dry, your blood sugar will drop too fast and too low causing you to feel drowsy. You'll have difficulty concentrating, feel lightheaded, experience extreme food cravings, and even have major mood swings. This is because when the cells run low on fuel they will start to cry out for more carbs.

On the other hand, even if you push through those cravings to the next eating window, you'll probably gorge yourself on carbs and eat far too much in an attempt to avoid those painful symptoms during the next fast. This practice will cause the opposite effect and your blood sugar will spike, going from an extreme low to an extreme high. The result will most likely cause a feeling of fatigue and an inability to focus.

This kind of yo-yo living becomes exhausting after a while. It is important to keep your blood sugar balanced so that you have a regular flow of energy throughout your body. This makes doing intermittent fasting difficult on its own; even if you have the willpower to push through. However, fasting coupled with the ketogenic diet is the secret to success.

Aids in fat loss: When you're on the Keto Diet, you drastically reduce the number of carbs you consume and substitute them with lots of fat. This may seem counterproductive since you are trying to lose fat but after you've been on the diet for a few days, depriving your body of that high glucose producing carbs, you will become more efficient at burning off those excess fat calories. Instead of burning glucose, you'll switch to a fat-burning mode and stay in it most of the time.

Since fat burning doesn't cause your blood sugar to have extreme highs or lows, your levels will remain more stable throughout the day. This diet has been so effective that many studies report that many with Type II Diabetes were able to go off of their medication within just a few short weeks. By combining the Keto Diet with fasting, you keep a balanced blood sugar level, which will eliminate cravings, that annoying sense of fatigue, and those irritable mood swings that accompany a high-carb fast.

The keto diet increases fat oxidation. When you consume a lot of carbs, your body is forced to produce more insulin. If this hormone gets too high, your body shifts into a fat-storing mode rather than fat burning. If you rely on a consistently high carb diet, your body will never have to tap into those resources so you continue to build up fat rather than lose it.

One of the by-products of metabolizing glucose is AGE (advanced glycation end-products). AGEs encourage inflammation and oxidative stress, which is an imbalance between the body's free radicals and the antioxidants. When this is off balance, they can react more easily with other molecules, which some people believe is an underlying cause for many cancers. Oxidative stress occurs when the cells rely on too much glucose for energy. This speed up the aging process and can also lead to diabetes.

When on the keto diet, the risk of accumulating too much glucose in the blood can actually work to fight against cancer. When you deprive the system of carbohydrates to feed on, any cancer cells will have a harder time to survive. They will decrease in size or they will disappear completely, replaced by healthier cells that will thrive on the fat used for fuel.

When you are in a state of ketosis, it will reduce your hunger cravings and regulate your appetite. After you have done it for a while, your body adapts to going for longer periods of time without food, so you won't have hunger pains or cravings. It is natural for the body to burn fat so putting your body in ketosis is perfectly natural, allowing it to draw energy from our own body fat to keep it in balance. The more you burn fat in ketosis, the less your body will demand of its glucose stores and your biology will become more self-reliant.

When it comes to glucose, the body is not a very efficient storing facility. The maximum amount of glucose it can hold is about 2,000 calories; around 4-500 grams in the muscles, 1-150 grams in the liver, and 15 grams in the blood. Once those stores are used up, the body secretes more fatty acids, so it can produce more glucose. When that runs out, it will turn to break down the protein in the muscles and other organs to make more. The keto diet prevents this from happening.

In ketosis, the body learns how to rely on a more reliable and bigger source of energy for its primary fuel supply. Rather than the meager 2,000 calories of glucose stored, the average person carries around 20,000 or more calories of fat at all times. Once your body has made the shift, the need to eat throughout the day will no longer be necessary. You will become a more efficient fat burning machine instead of burning through the sugar and making more every time we start to feel low. In essence, you will be carrying around your own fuel supply rather than having to top off your tank at every gas station you pass on the road.

Together they are powerful: It is obvious that on their own, both the keto diet and intermittent fasting have lots of benefits. It is perfectly okay to do them separately but if you were to combine them together, the benefits to be gained can boost your results exponentially. The overlapping results not only bring you more benefits but they also each pick up the slack where the other drops the ball.

You may have already mastered either ketosis or fasting and you may think they are almost the same, but the fact is even though they have very similar methods of generating the energy, they are both very different. But when used together, they can be extremely effective in burning fat.

We often associate ketosis with the keto diet but few realize that fasting also makes use of ketones as well. It helps to understand our primary goal here. We are trying to force the body to create ketones from our stored body fat. When we stop eating, our body is forced to tap into our fat stores to create ketones causing us to enter a state of ketosis.

With the keto diet, we are producing the same result by simply removing its go-to source of fuel, glucose or carbohydrates. Although we reach the same result using both methods, we get to a state of ketosis in a completely different way.

Transitioning to the keto diet: Once you have made the decision to adopt a ketogenic lifestyle, it is important to be aware of the fact that a state of ketosis will not be achieved after you skip a couple of low carb meals. Rather if you proceed down this path you will find that it will take as many as 7 days before you start to feel the effects of ketosis. Be warned, the interim period is likely going to be rough going as your body will be burning through all of its fuel reserves without having the benefit of ketones to pick up the slack. During this period, it is extremely important to stick to your guns as only cutting out carbohydrates slowly will only prolong your suffering. F

Forewarned is forearmed, however, and there are a few things you can to in order to encourage your body to enter ketosis as quickly and easily as possible. First things first, if you are exercising regularly make sure you are doing so on an empty stomach as this will further reduce the leftover glucose in your body. Likewise, you may find that skipping an extra meal here or there will also get you to where you need to be more quickly. Essentially, any time your stomach is growling is a period of time that is actively pushing you towards a state of ketosis. Finally, during this period you are going to want to stick to a strict limit of 20 carbohydrates per day or less to get you to where you need to be.

In order to ensure that you reach the proper state of ketosis, it is recommended that you test yourself regularly during the transition period. Essentially what you are testing for in this instances is ketones, or more accurately a substance known as acetone which is left behind after a ketone has been broken down into energy. The most common method of testing for ketosis is via a urine testing strip or a blood test. However, you can also test for ketosis naturally by being aware of the state of your breath. You will know you are in ketosis when your breath begins to smell like an apple that is slightly past its prime while also tasting slightly metallic on your tongue.

Aside from a few tricks for entering ketosis as quickly as possible, you are primarily going to want to keep in mind the types of food you are eating and the types of nutrients that are in each. This means understanding the food you eat in a way you may not have considered before which is through the lens of macronutrients. There are three different macronutrients (macros) that you are going to need to concern yourself for maximum results including proteins, fats, and carbohydrates. Balancing them effectively is a big part of not only reaching ketosis but remaining there indefinitely.

When it comes to healthy fats you will find them to be typically 90 percent ketogenic and 10 percent anti-ketogenic meaning they are a net-positive when it comes to ketosis. However, proteins are 55 percent anti-ketogenic because half of all of the protein you eat still turns into glucose. Finally, carbohydrates, obviously, are 100 percent anti-ketogenic. As your body needs protein, as well as some carbohydrates, it is recommended that you stick with a firm meal breakdown that is 70 percent made up of fat, 25 percent made up of protein and 5 percent made up of carbohydrates.

Protein: If only 25 percent of what you eat in a day can be protein then it is important to give that protein extra consideration. First and foremost, it is important to keep in mind that not all proteins are good for you, specifically those that are not of an organic nature as they are likely to contain high amounts of both bacteria and steroids. As such, you should always take special care to choose to only eat animal protein that is both grass fed and organic. The following are all acceptable protein choices, as long as you stick fast to the 25 percent per day rule.

- Fish is a great source of protein as it contains numerous healthy oils as well as healthy lean protein as long as it has not been farm raised as this is known to decrease the overall nutrients the fish contains. The best choices when it comes to fish include tuna, sole, snapper, salmon, trout, sardines, cod, mackerel, halibut, Mahi-Mahi, catfish and anchovies.

- Red meat that has been grass fed is perfectly acceptable in moderation and offers plenty of variety to choose from including beef, lamb, veal, venison and more.

- Poultry is another lean and healthy option as long as you stick with birds that are raised in an organic and free-range environment. Recommended poultry includes quail, chicken, turkey, duck, chicken, goose and pheasant.

- Pork of all types is acceptable in moderation.

- Eggs are a good source of protein and should not be ignored. It is important to always choose organic and free range variety whenever possible.

- Like fish, shellfish is a reliable source of lean proteins and you should feel free to eat shrimp, muscles, lobster, oysters, clams, and crab in moderation.

- Legumes including both soy beans and peanuts are a good source of protein but they contain higher than average amounts of carbohydrates for a protein and, therefore, need to always be consumed in moderation as it can be very easy to consume them in moderation without even realizing it.

- A special note on prepackage sausage and bacon, while these two products technically fall into the acceptable protein category, they are typically full of large amounts of sugar and other additives which means they have a much higher total carbohydrate count than they otherwise might.

Fats and oils: First and foremost, when it comes to balancing out the fats that you consume each day it is important to balance your intake of omega 3 and omega 6 as you need a balance of both to maintain a healthy lifestyle in the long term. Fish contain plenty of both types of omega fat, though if you are not a fan of fish then fish oil supplements can work just as well.

When it comes to the best monounsaturated or saturated fats the best choices are those that are the most chemically stable as this is a sign that they are good for your health as well. Great choices in this category include things like avocado oil, egg yolks, coconut oil, organic, grass-fed butter and macadamia nuts in moderation.

Carbohydrates: With only a very small percentage of your overall daily intake dedicated to carbohydrates, it is important that you make the amount you can eat as effective as possible. The best way to do this is to focus on vegetables that have the overall lowest amount of carbohydrates as possible so you can maximize the nutritional impact of that portion of your diet. The vegetables that you should avoid at all costs include peppers of all colors, carrots, tomatoes, corn, squash, and peas.

On the other hand, the vegetables that have the lowest overall number of carbs include garlic, kale, cabbage, sprouts, spinach, shallots, olives, radishes, cucumbers, leeks, mushrooms, cauliflower, broccoli, chives, asparagus, dill pickles, and bok choy. If your favorite vegetable didn't make the cut, simply ask yourself if it is starchy, sweet or not green. If you can answer no to all three, then it is probably safe to eat in moderation.

Exercise while fasting for maximum fat loss

When it comes to intermittent fasting, it is important to understand how it will affect your ability to exercise if you plan on sticking with the practice in the long-term. The biggest difference you will notice when you are exercising while fasting is that you will naturally feel weaker as less food in your stomach means less available fuel for building new muscles during an exercise routine. As such, if you do plan on exercising regularly while practicing any form of intermittent fasting it is important to take a number of extra precautions in order to ensure your new dietary habits don't end up negatively impacting the effectiveness of your average workout.

Ten muscle biopsies were taken before exercise, as well as three hours after exercise. The results showed that exercising while in a glycogen depleted state was able to increase mitochondrial biogenesis. This is the process by which new mitochondria can form inside the cells. The authors of the study believe that exercising on a low glycogen level diet may be beneficial for improving muscle oxidative capacity.

Exercise and intermittent fasting basics: Regardless if you are looking to improve your strength or your endurance, it is important to keep in mind that fats don't burn as easily as carbs do which means you are going to have less access to immediate energy. On the plus side, however, you will find that you are able to last much longer overall. This is also why you are likely to burn about 20 percent more fat when exercising without carbs in your system than you otherwise would. This is also why you should exercise immediately prior to breaking your fast as opposed to once it has been broken.

Unfortunately, the body doesn't just look for extra fat when it needs energy while exercising, it also requires available protein as well. As protein is stored in your muscles, if you exercise too strenuously then you will actually be hurting your muscles as opposed to helping them. You should be able to get through a moderate exercise routine without risk, however, as long as you don't push it too far. Thus, you should leave the heavier workouts for days when you are consuming more calories on a regular basis.

There is no consensus about when to work out while fasting, except considering when your first meal for the day will be. As we've mentioned, fasting is completely flexible. So, if you are eating breakfast in the morning and fasting for the rest of the day and overnight, then consider working out before breakfast.

However, if your meals are later in the day, consider working out about an hour before that meal, whether it's around noon or even later. With the 16/8 or Leangains Diet, you have a window of eight hours that you can eat. The idea is to work out in a fasted state, so make sure your workout before your first meal, whatever time that might be.

However, caution is also needed when looking for workout plans. You want to find someone who has is credible and knows what they are talking about. Look at their credentials, are they certified trainers or nutritionists; do they have a Ph.D.? What is the source of their information? Check out their followers and any reviews they might have. If there are no reviews, why is that? Just be careful and remember that if you start something and it doesn't feel right, STOP! You don't have to push through. Try something else until you find what works for you.

Tips for success

- Start with stretches: It is important to always take the time to warm up before any strenuous activity as getting started directly without warming first is a great way to seriously hurt yourself in the process. Warming up properly will also help to raise your overall core temperature which helps make your muscle more elastic and more willing to benefits from the exercise you are doing. Additionally, taking the time to warm up properly will ensure that the maximum amount of blood flow is getting to and from the heart which will further help you successfully push your body to the limits. Regardless of the reasons, start every workout, no matter how minimal, with a good warmup first.

- Alternate intensity: While it is natural to want to always push yourself as hard as possible, in reality, a training regimen that involves alternating intensities is actually more effective in the long run. Not only will it help you to continue exercising regularly without injury, but the variation is also better when it comes to producing reliable muscle growth. Finally, it gives your body extra time to recover from the more intense workouts while not simply sitting around doing nothing. This means that your intense days can actually be more intense because you know you will have a rest before you have to do it all again.

- Cool down: Just like it is important to always warm up before you exercise, it is equally important to take a few extra minutes at the end of your workout session to cool down properly with a little light cardio and some additional stretching. Not only will this prevent your muscles from cramping up on you later, but it will also actually help improve their growth because the cooldown ensures that they are receiving an appropriate amount of blood to maximize growth.

- Make a plan and stick with it: You will never be ready to compete in the track and field events of your choice if you don't make the decision to commit to the training process 100 percent. This means that you need to determine the right training plan for your goals and then stick with it every single time. To determine your plan, you are going to want to consider your fitness goals as well as your current state and the difference between them.

- Keep a food journal: While it might sound surprising, studies show that those who keep careful track of the foods they eat, especially those who write it down while they are eating it, are more likely to not only lose weight in the short-term but keep it off in the long-term as well. This is due to the fact that tracking your food makes you feel more accountable for what you eat, which will make you eat healthier overall. What's more, there are dozens of apps that will take care of most of the work for you, all you need to do is find the one that you like best and stick with it.

- Get more sleep: Studies show that those who are sleep deprived are more likely to pack on the extra pounds. This is the case not only because those who are up late tend to make poorer snacking decisions, but also because sleeping for less than 7 hours a day tends to slow down the metabolism which makes it more difficult to lose weight at all times because the body is more prone to holding onto every calorie it can get its hands on. This means that the slower your metabolism, the more you will need to exert yourself before you start seeing any positive results.

- While losing weight is all well and good, a more effective goal in the long term is to work on building muscle which will help you to feel better while also making you look better to boot.

- Drink more water: One pound of muscle can hold up to 3 pounds of water. Despite this fact, adequate water consumption is one of the most constantly overlooked factors when it comes to exercising with the purpose of building muscle mass. Don't forget, your body is 70 percent water and if you are dehydrated then one of the first things your body goes after is all that water sitting in your juicy muscles, shrinking them by as much as 35 percent as a result. In order to combat this, make a point of drinking a gallon of water a day, every day.

- Up your protein intake: Standard wisdom means says that you are going to want to take in between 20 and 30 grams of protein every four hours while you are awake. While intermittent fasting makes this unattainable, you're still going to want to take in between 80 and 120 grams of protein per day. If you are planning a serious strength workout then you are going to want to do so between two snacks, if not two full meals.

- Additionally, it is important to keep in mind that snacks are going to be your friend, as long as your intermittent fasting plan supports them, of course. A snack or a meal consumed between 3 and 4 hours before a workout should be enough to keep your blood sugar up through a standard workout, or between 1 and 2 hours if you are prone to low blood sugar. These meals should include blood-sugar stabilizing protein along with fast-acting carbs, for example, two pieces of toast with banana slices and peanut butter. Additionally, sometime in the two hours after your workout, you are going to want to try and consume approximately 20 grams of protein and 20 grams of carbs to ensure maximum muscle growth and to get your glycogen stores up high enough that you maintain energy until it is time to eat again.

- What to avoid: If you only have about 30 minutes before your workout, try to pick solid foods that will digest fast and limit fiber since it can be rough on your digestive process. If you do decide to work out in a fasted state, always bring some easily digested food just in case. As always, water is extremely important, so make sure you get plenty of that both before, during, and after any physical activity. Now that you're aware of all of this, you're ready to begin your first intermittent fast! Don't forget to experiment and adjust as you see fit and then continue until you find what works best.

- Wait on intense workouts until you break the fast: For the best results, the closer you can schedule your moderate or intense workout sessions to your last meal, the better. This way, the body will be able to pull from the extra glycogen to use during the workout. It also helps to reduce issues that can happen when your blood sugar levels get too low. When you are done with some more intense workouts, you can eat a snack that is full of carbs to help feed those tired muscles that need extra fuel.

Exercises to try: Mixing and matching four sets of four of the exercises outlined below is a great way to start getting in shape and burning as much fat in the shortest overall amount of time. There is a mix of opinions about the type and intensity of a workout while in a fasted state.

There are those like Martin Berkhan who support intense workouts and there are others who suggest that you take it slow as found in this article Can I Exercise While Fasting? by Nicolas J. King, Fitness Instructor, at Quora.com.

As was mentioned already, if you are just getting acquainted with fasting, take it easy; get used to fasting first, for about a week or even two. Then slowly add exercise back into your routine. Start with a brisk walk and slowly work up to running and then add in interval and weight training.

Above all else, listen to your body. If something doesn't feel right, then stop and talk to your doctor. Make sure you speak to him or her before starting any new exercise program.

- Alternating Donkey Kicks: This workout targets the lower back, and many people use fire hydrants in conjunction with alternative donkey kicks. Begin with your hands and knees in a table top position. From here, lift one knee off of the ground and pull it towards your chest. Then, send the knee back until the leg is straight, trying to keep the torso as still as possible. Continue this as well for at least fifteen reps.

- Butterflies: For this workout, you can stand. Bring your hands by your ears so that the elbows are bent, and bend over so that your back is flat.

Next, lift the elbows away from the ears, making sure that the shoulder blades are pushing towards one another. Repeat this exercise for at least thirty reps, because of the fact that you will not be using weights. If you want to experience more intensity, using weights for this exercise will certainly intensify the workout.

- Kick-ups: To begin this exercise you will want to get on your hands and knees so that your weight is supported by both your knees and your forearms. You will then alternate between legs as you lift one leg off of the ground and kick backwards so your heels face upwards. You will then return the leg to the starting position in one fluid motion. This exercise is beneficial to both the core and the legs.

- Hip Bridge: To begin this exercise you will want to lay on your back so that your knees are bent and both of your feet are planted firmly on the floor. You will then want to lift your hips as far off the ground as possible, while at the same time clenching your buttocks, with the end goal being to create a perfectly straight line between your knees as your shoulders. If you are interested in making this exercise even more difficult you can instead aim to keep one foot on the floor while at the same time lifting the other so that it points at the ceiling. This exercise is great for improving hip flexibility while at the same time stretching the spine and improving back strength.

- Burpee Jump-Ups: To perform this exercise start by standing with your feet so they are shoulder width apart with your arms above your head. Next, drop to the ground so you end up in a push-up position. Ensure that your core is tensed and you back is flat. Finally, pull your legs in towards your torso while standing and end by jumping into the air with your hands above your head. This exercise benefits the legs and the shoulders.

- Drop Squats: This exercise builds on the basic squat to enhance difficulty and results. To begin this exercise, place your feet together and jump before transitioning into a position where your feet are spread wider than your shoulders with the toes pointed away from one another. From this position drop quickly into a deep squat while ensure that your lower back remains flat while your chest stays straight. To balance properly you will need to place all of your weight on your heels. From here jump back into the standing position and begin again. Be sure to land softly to protect your knees. This exercise benefits the legs primarily though also the core.

- Walkout Push-Ups: To begin this exercise choose one foot and stand on it while keeping your arms straight at your sides. Lean forward onto the ground and then walk into a basic push-up position. While doing this it is important to ensure that your core is tensed while your back is flat. When you reach standard push-up position, do a push-up and then repeat the process in reverse, ending up in starting position once more. This exercise benefits the chest and the legs.

- Towel Pull-Ups: To do this exercise properly you need a pull-up bar and a thick towel. To begin this exercise, you wrap the towel around the pull-up bar and grip either end of the towel with both of your hands. Pull-down on the towel by forcing your elbows towards the floor. Keep your body straight while lifting. Ensure you use a thick towel to avoid accidents. This exercise benefits the shoulders, chest, and arms.

CHAPTER 7

Fasting in a Way That's Right for You

While intermittent fasting can certainly provide you with a variety of healthy lifestyle changes, it doesn't mean it is going to be the right choice for everyone. While you should be able to make it through a number of fasts without slipping, once you have done so you are going to want to consider how difficult that period of time was for you. You will also need to consider what your natural habits are like when it comes to eating and what your overall relationship with food is like in general. It is important to keep in mind that intermittent fasting is not so much a diet as it is a lifestyle which means you should focus on long term success and not think about it as a short-term solution like you would most diets.

This long-term commitment is why you are going to want to seriously ask yourself if you are going to be able to commit to fasting regularly in the long term, if not with the first type of intermittent fasting that you try then possibly the second or the third. If you have a long way to go when it comes to meeting your weight loss goals, then you may want to start with something milder than intermittent fasting and instead work up to it once you have gotten into the habit of eating healthy first. Starting off with a style of eating that has an extreme learning curve can lead to early failure that can affect you mentally and make you less likely to try again.

Tips for success

Keep a journal: Keeping a journal is a great idea; this will help you stay more motivated in the process of intermittent fasting. Write down everything that you're feeling and doing, and build off that. When you journal your thoughts and feelings, you will be able to control them a lot better as this will help you understand when you feel and how to deal with your feelings. Many successful people journal their thoughts and feelings, and it is one of the ways to ensure optimal success. Simply get a book and start writing everything from how you were feeling and how you are dealing with your issues. Whenever you start feeling similar matters on the following day, simply go back to your journal and read how you dealt with it.

Also, every month, make sure you recap how consistent you were with your diet and fasting, and try to do better the next month. These are the main reasons why I recommend carrying a journal, so go ahead and start journaling.

Stay on track for 30 days: This is perhaps one of the most important things to take home: if you can stick around for 30 days, you will see amazing results for an extended period. Here's the thing: it takes approximately 21 to 40 days to create a habit. Meaning, if you can keep fasting for at least 30 days, it will become second nature to you, and you can keep fasting and see amazing results day-by-day. This is also where the journal comes in: make sure that you are journaling every day for 30 days as this will help you stay on track. Do whatever you can to stay on track for 30 days.

Once intermittent fasting becomes a habit for you, then there is no stopping you. Journal every day; make sure you're doing everything you can to avoid breaking your fast for 30 days, like drinking more water, coffee, or tea. Once you have managed to do that, you can perhaps get into more intense fasting. As your body gets used to it, you will start being able to keep going with it. Keep that in mind when you first start your fasting.

Reevaluate and reprogram how you think: The greatest challenge you will ever face is a mental one, not a physical one. Your mindset is almost immovable, which makes taking on a new lifestyle particularly difficult. Think of fasting as a break away from eating, not as a time of food deprivation. You are giving yourself a break from worrying about your next meal, shopping, cooking, and eating dinner on time. A strong mindset will reinforce your mission of losing weight and being healthier.

Stay busy: Do your best to keep yourself busy by doing meaningful work. It is much easier to feel motivated to stay on track when you are working on something that you are passionate about! Many people get too excited to eat when they are in the middle of creating their best work. Stay on top of your hunger cravings and thoughts of food by staying busy and mentally distracting yourself.

Going along with the theme of keeping busy, try to do your most productive work in the morning, when you are still in the middle of your fasting period. It is normal to eat within a few hours of waking up. But, you are trying to break that habit with fasting. Establish a strong morning ritual and tackle your to- do list right away so you can focus on work instead of eating and fulfilling your fast.

Do not be afraid to go crazy and live it up once in a while. This lifestyle is about freedom, and rewarding yourself with an awesome cheat meal or cheat day every now and then is absolutely encouraged. There are some programs that have cheat meals/ days already incorporated into the schedule, but nevertheless, you should not feel guilty for indulging after working hard to maintain your new lifestyle.

Meal preparation: No matter which type of intermittent fast you decide to go on, you will find that meal preparation is going to be your best friend. Many people choose to use this if they go on the 5:2 diet because it helps them to get the most out of their calories when they are on a fast. But you are able to do this no matter which type of intermittent fasting you decide to go on. This is especially important if you decide to add in another diet plan, such as the ketogenic diet, for better results.

You can meal prep the way that you want. Some people simply get their snacks ready, so they have something that will help them during their eating window. Some prep so that they stay around 500 calories when they are on the 5:2 diet. Maybe you want to come up with a few good meals that will help you break a fast without going overboard? You can determine your means, as long as it helps you to get a lot of good nutrients without having to stress about eating windows.

Restarting after falling off the wagon: The first thing that you do is analyze the plan that you are going to follow. Which intermittent fast do you plan to be on? Did you have a meal plan to work with? Some of the steps you can do here include:

- Did you have a plan that was written out? If you didn't, then now is the time to get it out on paper.

- Ask yourself if this plan was just too hard for you. If you had tried to do the Warrior diet, maybe going with a different option is better. Maybe doing the Leangains plan every other day would be better. You can switch from a 24-hour fast to a 16/8 plan. Mix it up to work better for you.

- If you think that the plan you picked was too easy and you aren't getting the results that you want, then it is time to move to the second step.

- Ask yourself why you ended up falling off the plan. Be serious with yourself. Then you can take the right actions in order to solve these problems.

- If you found that the major problem you had with intermittent fasting is eating during the fasting time, then ask yourself the following questions

- Was I really hungry when I ate? If you are dealing with true hunger and that is why you broke the fast, and this happens often, then it may be time to increase the amount that you eat during your feeding window, or lengthen that time frame a bit more.

- Was I bored? Boredom can be a big reason why we feel hungry during our fasts. Find some interests or get a hobby, or just get out of the house and see if that helps.

- Was I stressed out? If you are stressed, find some way to relieve that stress. Talk to somebody, go out for a nice walk, or spend time journaling.

- Was I tired? If this is your problem, make sure that you get more sleep. You can consider taking a nap the next time you are hungry rather than eating.

Mistakes to avoid

Getting started with intermittent fasting can be a little scary. In the beginning, there are a lot of little details you have to remember. The first chapters of this book are filled with a lot of scientific information that you may not be familiar with and you may struggle to understand it all. Add to that the changes your body is about to go through and the whole process seems to be quite overwhelming.

This won't be like any other diet you ever went on, so it will require you to think differently. There are many people who have found phenomenal success with fasting and there are probably just as many who gave up long before the results had a chance to kick in. This is mainly because they didn't fully understand the basic principles behind the diet, which caused them to make mistakes.

Avoiding fats: A true keto diet is very high in fats, probably more than you would eat on any other diet.

This may sound strange considering that our goal is to lose fat. But, to be effective on the keto diet, you will have to eat a large amount of fat (at least 65-70%) in order to reach your goal. Don't be afraid of this as this is the way the body naturally works.

However, it is important that you eat the right kind of fats. Don't assume that since you have to up your fat content you can dive into a huge bag of potato chips or your favorite snack treats. There is such a thing as a healthy fat, which can be found in foods like butter, eggs, avocados, fish oils, and walnuts. One way to get these fats in your diet is through the use of fat bombs. These are made from a combination of essential fats including butter, coconut oil, nuts, and seeds.

Fat bombs can make getting your fats to count up without a lot of effort. You can think of them as your own personal energy ball and you can find recipes for them just about everywhere these days. Ingredients include essential foods like coconut, unsweetened chocolate, nut butter, avocado, nuts, eggs, cilantro, peppers, and a host of other delicious things. They have the right combination of fats and proteins so that you know you're getting the right balance of nutrients in every bite.

Overdoing the proteins: The common mistake people make is overdoing the proteins, which adds even more calories to your meals. This mistake is often the result of the old thinking that our energy comes from the proteins we eat. And since we can't have as many carbs in our diet, we will naturally gravitate towards the next best thing to be successful. It may feel strange to use healthy fats in order to get the balance you need.

But, the body can handle only so much protein and when you overdo it, you can expect to have negative side effects. When you have too much protein, the body will begin to convert it into fat, which will go against everything you're trying to do. As long as you keep your eye on your macros, you are less likely to load up on too many proteins because you'll have everything you need to succeed.

Not taking care of your gut health: When you are in ketosis, your body is changing. The gut holds your microbiome, which is a major adjustment. Most bacteria that feed on fats are high in endotoxins, this creates gram-negative bacteria. If you have too much gram-negative, you have too many bad bacteria. When these enter the bloodstream, they make us very sick causing problems like a leaky gut. Those consuming a high-fat diet have a very elevated level of positive bacteria, which will aid in improved gut health.

Not drinking enough water: For every one gram of carbs you consume, your body will retain approximately 1.3 - 4 grams of water. When you stop consuming a high amount of carbs you also stop retaining that water. When that happens, everything runs off balance and the kidneys do not work as efficiently as they should. Your body is going to try to fill that void with fat.

Staying hydrated is also a means of lubricating your organs so that they will work more efficiently. It is recommended that you consume around a gallon of water every day. That may seem like a lot, but if you make it a habit of just taking a few sips throughout the day, it won't fill you up and give you that bloated feeling. You'll be surprised at how much better you feel if you are not trying to drink it all down in large quantities at one time.

Not getting enough minerals: When you drink a lot of water, you can flush out much of the minerals you consume. Make sure you're adding food when you are in ketosis. This will make you feel good and can prevent fatigue.

Of course, these are not the only mistakes people make when starting a keto fast. Some of them are done without realizing it. That is why it is so important to not only understand what you need to do on the keto diet but why you need to do it. That scientific clarification can make it easier to understand when you have all the facts.

There are two kinds of mistakes that you might make when getting started; mental and physical. It is a lot easier to correct the physical mistakes, but we are all creatures of habit by nature. As a result, when our thinking and understanding about keto fasting is wrong, these are often the mistakes that can lead us to failure. It is best from time to time, to go back and review the science to make sure you're doing everything in the right way.

If you're not entirely sure, talk to someone who has already been doing keto for a long time. It is better to check out the facts and then proceed than to continue going along the wrong path and end up with lackluster results because of it. If you find you are not getting the results you want, stop and review everything again and then backtrack to see where you went wrong, readjust and start again.

Abusing stimulants: It is not uncommon for women to take too much coffee. This is wrong because you can end up with a caffeinated euphoria. It is okay to have one or two cups to kick-start your fast day. What you need to avoid is becoming over-reliant on coffee to get through the day. If you have to, drink a cup or two and leave it at that. Try not to consume more coffee after your lunch break.

You start off way too ambitious: All too often, people start a diet program or a healthy lifestyle like intermittent fasting with high expectations. It takes most people a long time to get used to hunger and coping with it. You should not be too hard on yourself and do not be way too ambitious. Going from regular eating to a single meal per day can come as quite a shock to most people. Go easy on yourself and cut yourself some slack. You should not try to achieve everything all at once but instead, try and take one step at a time.

You think that more is better: Sometimes people tend to think that fasting for longer means better outcomes and better results. This is not necessarily the case. While intermittent fasting for 16 hours per day is recommended, you should not fast beyond 20 to 24 hours. You will do more harm than good if you increase your fasting hours unnecessarily. In fact, according to a recent study, most fasting benefits begin to dwindle past the 20-hour mark.

Being obsessed with time: Some people are obsessed with time and cannot be flexible. You need to embrace a relaxed lifestyle without undue concern about hours, seconds, and minutes. Basically, an obsessed person stares at the clock and thinks that a single minute past time will ruin their entire fast experience. Many experienced people will eat anytime within their eating window without worrying about the minutes or seconds. If you freed yourself from the 6-meals-a-day program, then you should free yourself from the clock.

Conclusion

Thanks for making it through to the end of *Intermittent Fasting A Beginners Guide To Weight Loss And A Healthier Lifestyle: Everything you need to know to incorporate Intermittent fasting as a weight loss and health rejuvenation tool*, let's hope it was informative and able to provide you with all of the tools you need to achieve your goals, whatever it is that they may be. Just because you've finished this book doesn't mean there is nothing left to learn on the topic, and expanding your horizons is the only way to find the mastery you seek.

Now that you have made it to the end of this book, you hopefully have an understanding of how to get started with intermittent fasting, as well as a strategy or two, or three, that you are anxious to try for the first time. Before you go ahead and start giving it your all, however, it is important that you have realistic expectations as to the level of success you should expect in the near future.

While it is perfectly true that some people experience serious success right out of the gate, it is an unfortunate fact of life that they are the exception rather than the rule. What this means is that you should expect to experience something of a learning curve, especially when you are first figuring out what works for you. This is perfectly normal, however, and if you persevere you will come out the other side better because of it. Instead of getting your hopes up to an unrealistic degree, you should think of your time spent improving your eating habits as a marathon rather than a sprint which means that slow and steady will win the race every single time.

Finally, if you found this book useful in anyway, a review on Amazon is always appreciated!

Description

If despite your best efforts to eat healthily and live a semi-active lifestyle, you just can't seem to shake that extra weight, then it might not be what you are eating but when you are eating that's the problem. If this sounds like you, then *Intermittent Fasting A Beginners Guide To Weight Loss And A Healthier Lifestyle: Everything you need to know to incorporate Intermittent fasting as a weight loss and health rejuvenation tool* is the book you have been waiting for.

Inside you will find everything you need to know about intermittent fasting in order to ensure you have what you need to get started on the right foot, starting with an overview of basics of intermittent fasting and how it can lead you to look and feel better than you have in years. While intermittent fasting has many proven benefits, it's not for everyone which is why the next chapter will discuss who should and who shouldn't consider intermittent fasting as a new long-term lifestyle. With the basics out of the way, you will then learn all about the different types of intermittent fasting that are at your disposal.

From there you will learn about why you would want to do all this hard work in the first place with a breakdown of intermittent fasting's many benefits. Next, you will find a variety of tips to help you eat properly while fasting as well as the things you can do to maximize your weight loss once and for all and additional tools to help you ensure that you are able to turn intermittent fasting into a new lifestyle.

So, what are you waiting for? Take control of your waistline like never before and buy this book today!

Printed in Great Britain
by Amazon